Land of Hope and Glory

The NORTHWAY Series

Tom Northway

My Father's Hands

Land of Hope and Glory

Also by Marshall Terry

Old Liberty

Dallas Stories

Ringer

Land of Hope and Glory

A True Account of the Life and Times of Gen. Marcus Northway, Ret., and of the Character of His Eminent Friends

Marshall Terry

University of North Texas Press ✤ Denton, Texas

First edition 1996

10 9 8 7 6 5 4 3 2 1

Requests for permission to reproduce material from this work
should be sent to

Permissions
University of North Texas Press
Post Office Box 13856
Denton, Texas 76203

The paper used in this book meets the minimum requirements of the
American National Standard for Permanence of Paper for
Printed Library materials, Z39.48.1984.
Binding materials have been chosen for durability.

Library of Congress Cataloging-in-Publication Data

Terry, Marshall, 1931–
   Land of hope and glory : a true account of the life and times of
Gen. Marcus Northway, Ret. andof the character of his eminent friends /
   by Marshall Terry.
      p.   cm.   — (The Northway series)
   ISBN 1-57441-006-7
I. Title. II. Series: Terry, Marshall, 1931–   Northway series.
       PS3570.E699L36   1996
  813′ .54—dc20   95-46719
                                                          CIP

Cover design by Amy Layton
Cover photograph courtesy Marshall Terry

Preface

It has been more than twenty-five years since I wrote *Tom Northway*, a story based on the life of my grandfather, and a number of years since I thought of developing the chronicle of the Northways into a series. The present volume is the third in the series.

The chronicle is an old form that from the beginning has changed along the way from annal to interpretation. I call this whole a "chronicle" because it has to do with the moral history of my time, not that my fictional characters are meant to be *exempla* in the old sense of a race or nation. They are, as creations, people I do know in some form or other, studies in the American character in various eras, while being also, I hope, real human individuals on the page. They are not great or noble in any way, but they seek to love and understand, and their lives seem to me to point to something proud and painful in the real lives of those I have been close to in this nation in my time. The characters in this chronicle belong to a time past, though some operate in present time; but that quickly becomes past. The genealogical and chronological record of a family here is as much a fiction—one the author relishes— as it is a look at the labyrinth of meshed families and characters within them that has been my lot to observe.

The parts of this work, as the present one, are akin to novels. They have much the same shape and dynamic as the novel, yet they also are like the old "whitened board" or "album" of the chronicler: each an impressionistic album in which the characters come and go and may or may not appear again and in which the character telling is also telling in course his own human history.

Our America, the United States, growing so excitingly diverse now, has always been an overtly idealistic nation which honors the ideal in its subversion. We have believed that the impossible and improbable are possible, and sometimes have been able to prove it as individuals, or together. More often, as small figures in the mosaic, we stumble individually over paradoxes in the national "character" that would have tripped a mythical hero. So with my Mark and Marcus, Tom and Ida, Louise and Clara and Remember, and "Bo" who tries to tell it.

And so again I quote Robert Lowell's "Epilogue," which comes so close to my intention in the Northway chronicle.

> *Yet why not say what happened?*
> *Pray the grace of accuracy*
> *Vermeer gave to the sun's illumination*
> *stealing like the tide across a map*
> *to his girl solid with yearning.*
> *We are poor passing facts,*
> *warned by that to give*
> *each figure in the photograph*
> *his living name.*

My appreciation to Dean James F. Jones, Jr., Dedman College, Southern Methodist University, for his encouragement of the Northway chronicle, and to Jill Bagwell of the SMU English Department for her keen editorial eye.

This novel is dedicated to the memories of
Wallace Stegner and A. Kenneth Pye,
each tough-minded and of rare faith,
wit, grace and courage.

ONE

Dr. Marcus Northway, Maj. Gen., Ret., sat at his desk in his study in the suite he kept in the Waldorf-Astoria Hotel, his pen in one hand, cigar in the other, onion-skin sheets before him, looking out the window at a day whose grayness was only slightly alleviated by the hope of sunshine struggling through the clouds over the city.

"Jehoshaphat," he said half-aloud, shaking his head, his thoughts as scattered as the clouds. It was a cold May, this May of 1919, the coldest, they said, in forty-five years.

He looked in from the gray day to a vision that came to him of his mother Sally Ann, arthritic and worn, stooping in the garden to pick some truck in their plot behind the brick house in their village there in Whiskeyville. His father Sam— Samuel Cincinnatus—would be farther out in the hops field, and he himself, the boy named Marcus Aurelius, would be, hoe in hand, with him there. Sam Northway, whose father had also toiled in the hops field there and in making gin and wine and beer, had named the next nearest village "Marcus" for his son, as Sam's father Philo Northway had named the nine square acres of hops and swamp land all the Northways together owned "Northwaytown" and had cut down the girl Molly Leary from the hanging tree and married her. They, all the Northways, had been content to be there, in that benighted village of Whiskeyville, since 1796. It was a backward place! He, young Marcus, had been the only Northway capable and with vision enough to leave, to get out and get educated, to raise the family name. Now he family name. Now he found himself in his seventieth year, yea three score and ten, sitting at his desk, where Ida had posed him, pretending to be working on his damn'd Memoir.

"Jehoshaphat!" he said again, aloud, as he threw down the pen and reached for the tumbler of good whiskey.

At that moment Ida, his second wife, whom he had married shortly after the death of his first wife Lutie Krause, whose nurse she'd been, loomed in the doorway to the study, filling it.

He saw a smile beaming from her large Irish face with its lustrous blue eyes—girlish, hoydenish at times. They must have company, as company always made her happy. Seven blissful years ago he'd married her for her naturalness and her adoration of him. Yet now, in her fifty-third year, she yearned to be a Great Lady married to a Great Man with a memoir.

"It's the Colorado Kid come to call. He says you sent word you wanted to see him."

"Ah, yes. Thank you, Ida dear. Show the Kid in. Come join us if you wish. It is regarding Billy."

"No, thank you just the same, Marcus. I have many things to do. The morning has gotten away. Have you been writing? You haven't been into the whiskey already, have you, dearie?"

He stood and gave her an imperious look. He had not, but only by the grace of the god who pulls these handles of fate and circumstance. Whiskey had been his lifelong companion, stimulant, his chief prescription in practice. Whiskey, oil and bromine were his trademarks. She need not worry, bustling, emotional woman, that he could not handle it now. It was just this damn'd writing. He, who had written out by hand in this same black ink on these flimsy pages with this same fine pen through the years so many speeches, articles and treatises, still had to battle to do it, the damn'd writing. Always he had preferred taking action—rising to speak, daring to try remedies and solutions the Regulars would not, bluffing the gods of Power and Politics—to this scribbling; though always too he'd been a devout believer in the power of the Word.

Ida shrugged. "Here's the Kid," she said and unblocked the doorway.

Marcus Northway stood and adjusted his pince-nez and the folds of the dark double-breasted suit upon his firm, trim body. He had elegantly silky white hair, full, sensuous lips, a Roman nose and very dark brown eyes that could be kind or stern in turn. The strange slant of his eyes gave him an Oriental look. He smiled at the Colorado Kid and waved him into the second leather chair.

Legend had it they had called the fellow that during the war they'd shared, but Marcus Northway had not beheld him until they met in this city of New York a few years ago. The Kid having been a private never out of Manila, and himself doing his research and medical duty always there in Porto Rico during the Spanish War.

He did not offer to shake hands with the dapper little journalist, who wore a checked suit and a renegade hat he had not removed and who was lighting up a fag as he sat. The fellow wrote yellow prose on the subject of ballplayers and prize-fighters and consorted with them and with prostitutes and gangsters. Marcus Northway's hands were strong, soft and kept immaculately clean and free from casual contact with other human beings. Recently he had published an article on the pernicious dangers of hand-shaking and kissing in greeting, between male and female, male and male, and female and female. The germs of pneumonia, la grippe, pleurisy, flu and the dread phthisis were all around, carried to and by everyone on the street.

"Howdy, General," said the Kid, smiling from the depth of the leather chair. "You are looking fine. You are the embodiment of the physician who heals himself."

"Thank you, Al. You are looking spiffy yourself. You must be a few bets to the good. May I interest you in a spot of the Brown Ruin?"

"No, General. Thank you, I'm sure. It is a bit early, and I am in the midst of doing a lot of this and a lot of that around and about the town this morning. I thought I would drop by since I was in this part of town, as your man Albert found me last night and communicated your desire to see me. He also is looking fine. About your age, isn't he? Looks just the same as he did back then, as blacks tend to do. Damn tough old Rough Rider. He scared hell out of three of the toughest Irish guys around on his way to me last night."

Albert LeMaistre had been given to Marcus Northway by Colonel Roosevelt as a bodyguard when he was doing his medical research in the camps and villages in Porto Rico. Now he served him still, as did his son Dennis, just back, decorated, from service in France. Like Al Runyon, called the Colorado Kid by those who knew the connection, Albert and Dennis LeMaistre were from Colorado, where Albert had been a renowned black cowboy before joining TR's blue-polka-dotted Harum Scarums for the romp up Kettle Hill.

"I have been to the Knickerbocker just now," the Kid went on, "to visit with the great Caruso, who said to express his greetings to you, as he knows you are a supporter of the Opera. He and I have some plans afoot, but unfortunately he is suffering from a throat, quite worrisome in his line of work. Do you happen, General, to have a special remedy for a sore and aching throat?"

The General smiled and poured himself a glass of the whiskey. He knew quite well that Runyon was a teetotaler, while sharing with himself a horror of the tyranny of Prohibition over a free people. The Kid knew he understood this and that it might adversely affect the writer's reputation if generally known.

"Whiskey and peppermint candy is the best remedy I know. Whiskey without the candy would be better."

"Alas, the great Caruso does not drink."

Doctor Northway reached for a prescription pad on his mahogany desk, uncapped his pen and carefully wrote out: *Flour of sulphur and glycerin triturated into an emulsion, ounces six; tripsin one drachm and peroxide of hydrogen 2 drachms. Use clean swab each time and burn when used.*

The Kid seemed appreciative. He mentioned that his plans included naming a car and a horse for the great Caruso. Marcus Northway nodded. The magnificent voice of the Great Caruso, in his opinion, resided in the mind and body of an oaf.

"Have you seen my brother William?"

This was the reason he had summoned the denizen of Broadway. He had not seen or heard from his younger brother William Northway, known fondly to those he scrounged a living from as Billy, since last his junior by fifteen years had conned a C note off him. Billy was loose, with no particular profession, on the streets of the city, dapperly dressed, a smile his umbrella, a potential terrible embarrassment as always he had been to the Northway name and a constant worry to his brother since he'd quit his fairly steady job bartending at the Hoffman House. Marcus had been thinking he must put some real salt on Billy's tail. His plan was to exile him to the small Sea Point Inn he'd bought there on the beach at Amagansett. Billy could loaf around there and drink up his brother's whiskey and smoke his cigars and mismanage the little inn beautifully.

"Why no, General. I do not believe I have seen your brother and my good friend Billy Northway, oh, neither here nor there, for—a while." The Kid smiled, brilliantly, lighting up another fag, evading him. Then his expression changed, as he sat up straight from lounging in the large black leather chair. "My God!" he cried. "What's that?"

Through the wall from the living room came a loud cacophonous sound, or combination of unmeshed sounds: dear Ida banging away at her beloved white Baby Grand piano, accompanying herself by singing, emitting one of her favorite hymns, causing the hotel to shake.

"Why, Al, my Goodness, don't you recognize it? It's one of my wife's favorites, 'In the Garden.'"

"Oh sure," Runyon yipped, laughing, "mine too," and began to hum along.

Marcus rose, thanked the Kid for nothing and saw him out, then by a deep breathing motion signaled to Ida that he was going out for a breath of air. She nodded. She would play her hymns for hours, or at least for the hour until the lavish lunch she had ordered up for them arrived. He donned his velvet-lapeled coat and rakish hat and took from the stand the lion-headed walking stick with slender sword sheathed inside, his old companion while walking in the streets of the city. He softly closed the door to this suite he had kept here since the hotel opened in 1894—for most of the years since he first met his dear friend Al Edison in this city in the later Eighties and invested in the California project with him. He went down the hall and took the elevator down.

Someday Ida wanted a house of her own, in California, land of her birth, about as big as this hotel and with an elevator just like this one.

"When can we go there, Marcus?" she said just lately, "to California? To Los Angeles or San Diego? Oh, that is the land of the future, the true America!" It always had been, for her. Ida Bailey's father was a foreman on the railroad there. She was born at Pacific Junction, just a work station at a crossing in California. Right now, strong as a buffalo, she could probably drive more spikes than her father's Irish crew. She had made herself a nurse, and had come East, and then nursed his wife Lutie in her frailty. She had such passion. He had married her for her strength, her admirable unremitting damn'd strength . . .

"And, oh, Marcus, I hate this city, and this apartment, so! And Willowstone . . ." Willowstone was the gloomy pile he'd bought for her in Greenwich when first they'd married, a place which he also had come to dislike. This Waldorf suite was his nest; he loved it dearly. "Oh, will you live long enough, Marcus, for us to go there, and have our own real house and live there in California? Oh, why can't we up and go, Lovie? What is it that's holding us?" she had entreated him.

"I have some things—some affairs by nature political, Ida—you know this—that hold me here for now. But I assure you that, as do Edison and Ford and the wondrous Burbank, I plan to live a hundred years. At least to a hundred, and vigorously, my dear. We have time, and I will consider it. We have all the time in the world."

"And she of course is here, or mostly here. I know that is part of it," she said, referring to La Pajarita.

"She has her life, Ida. Dear Lord, you know that. She flies here and there over the world, bringing happiness where'er she goes, but always back to me. That is as it should and must be and always has been, Ida dear. It has nothing to do with you and me."

Now he felt a warmth radiate through him, thinking of being with her soon, sending her a Thought Wave, his lovely bird, his Pajarita.

He walked over to 34th Street towards where the old Fifth Avenue Hotel had been the pride of the Eighties, at Fifth and 23rd. It was there, he recalled with pleasure, that he was called before General Dodge's Committee of the Government to give his reason for the spread of Typhoid Fever in the Army camps of this country. Following his research in Porto Rico, Dr. Marcus Northway had been the first to state the Fly as cause. He remembered it was a fine clear day, unlike this present chill grayness, here in the city, and he was the subject of much praise, having been at first criticized by those of Slow Mental Gait for a sensational report. And it struck him now how significant had been his lifelong medical achievement and how grudging overall had been the damn'd Regulars to give the Homeopath his due.

It was the indomitable Ida who had encouraged—yea, ordered— him to attempt to write out some sort of Memoir, the idea being subsequently to publish it and so make his claims to fame as other great men had done. Well, he would try. He would damn well try, and do it, as he always had. Perseverance was his motto and the motto he would carve out for the Northways, whether the rest of 'em wanted it or not. But right now, as he strode along, breathing correctly and walking vigorously, he felt unvindicated in all he'd done, and—what?—heirless. It was not Ida's fault, or God knows, Lutie's, or his own. It had just played out that way. And now, he also felt, with some sort of a dread like germs or the beginning of the terrible Itch deep within himself, that he had played a wrong card in this political pickle he was in, and would pay for it, or at least his conscience would. Ida had called his hand on that, told him he was wrong, and he had clouded his brow and bluffed it by her. But it was eating at him badly. And now they wanted him to . . . Ah . . .

Yes. Well.

General Marcus Northway walked back to the Waldorf, his primary residence at present. He whacked at a cur and shook his swordcane at an urchin who wished to pick his pocket as he walked along.

He and Ida lunched at her little Pembroke table on broiled fish and potatoes escalloped and tomato aspic salad and pie and ice cream.

"Did he know of Billy's whereabouts?"

"Oh, he's out there. The Kid just wouldn't say. Thieves' honor, you know."

"Are you having just one piece of the pie? I think it's very good. I think it's dandy."

"I think I will save it for breakfast, my dear. Pie makes a fine breakfast, almost as good as fruit and bread. It's what all the country Northways ate for breakfast, what I'm sure they still eat for breakfast there in Whiskeyville, you know. Apple pie."

"And beer for lunch, and whiskey for dinner," she said. "Fine, have it for breakfast then, that piece there. This little piece right here I think I will take out of its misery now, if you don't mind."

"Of course not, my dear. I am delighted to see you on your feed."

He did not tell her he was thinking really of a cleansing, soothing enema. She should pay more attention to her bowels. She slept flat out on her back, not as she should on one side then the other so that the colon could do its work. If she would pay more attention to regularity, she would not be so nervous, so emotional.

2

For breakfast he ate a delicious Burbank plum. For lunch, escaping Ida, he had a Burbank pear. For dinner he would try a Spineless Cactus. Ha ha. Ho. In fact, he'd received a Thought message from the luminous Burbank, the genius he adored, inquiring of him. Was he well? When was he coming to see him, there in California? His own Thought message, in return, assured Luther that Marcus would soon be there, perhaps in June, around the time of his day of birth. Luther replied he was content and would be glad to be with him.

"I'll tell you how they write 'em, the Memoirs, if you're stuck and want to know," Ida said to him that morning. He stared back at her from the redoubt of his desk like an old caged lion.

"I do not know how you are trying to begin it. The proper way—I have studied this in the library because I know it is your fault, but also your genius, that you never like to do it like the other fellow does it, Marcus, medicine or whatever. The way to begin is with a proper notice and introduction of yourself. That is how they write 'em—the memoirs. Here is Ford's, that is what he does. Maybe we should hire you a hack to help at it, like this person that writes for Henry Ford."

"No. I am perfectly capable of forming it. I have composed many articles and—I mean, Ida, your help is all in the world I could possibly need or desire." He unwrapped the cigar and cut its end with his gold clipper.

"All right. I will leave you to it, if you are going to smoke," she said, trundling out. "Marcus," she called back, "I want to hear that introduction when you've done it." What a force she was for ordering his existence. He must soon as he could get her at least for a vacation there to California where she could walk on the golden beach and exercise. She was getting to fifteen Stone avoirdupois.

Well, how was he to begin? He had to scratch something out, if only to satisfy the relentless tyrant Ida.

Ida had brought in Ford's Memoir. Dear God! Odious little power-hungry popinjay! Think of having to write for Ford, to try to make sense of his utter foolishness and illiteracy! "Thank God I am not quite that vainglorious," Marcus Northway thought.

Ford, the fool, thought he was some Egyptian god come back to lead us all down the road to Putt Putt Town. He was an obsessed and childlike man who would tell a tree how his first memory was of four eggs in a song sparrow nest. "I believe," chuckled Marcus Northway, "Ford was ten at the time." His own first memory was of being, about three years old, very sick in Whiskeyville, and an old man gave him some bitter tea, and he drank it and felt better . . . .

Ah, light this fine colorado and grasp pen firmly, for Ida was right. He had something more of the world to tell than Henry, who did not even invent his car but simply got the hang of making it, putting all the parts together, who still could barely read and had all his simple ideas from his schoolboy Eclectic Reader. Why, compared to Edison, dear and true friend for whom Ford had become a Judas goat, Ford invented nothing, yet now paraded himself as genius and as seer, loving that stiff cod, that fool for Peace Woodrow Wilson. Ford floated a boat for Peace yet in his heart hated Jews and did not truly love mankind nor ought but himself. Ignorant man: testified, he did, that this nation once had a Revolution, in 1812! Jehoshaphat!

And taking pen in hand he began to write.

I am Dr. Marcus Aurelius Northway. I am at present seventy years of age. At the moment I reside with my beloved wife Ida Burke Bailey Northway here in our suite in the Waldorf-Astoria Hotel and in the mansion Willowstone in Greenwich, Connecticut, and own properties in New York State and Florida. I grew up as a boy on an extended Hops farm; left to pursue my Education on my own; never, like Edison sold newspapers off a train or worked as a mechanic, but managed to obtain higher education in Medicine and to attain some Fame, though little Fortune, as a well-known Physician in this State and Nation. I married Fortune.

I am first son of Samuel Cincinnatus Northway, landowner in New York, grandson of Philo Northway, early settler of Whiskeyville, N.Y. and great-grandson of Benjamin Northway of Freetown, Mass. who married Lany Bee, and descendant of Thomas Northway, who landed on Block Island R.I. in 1630. I am of English (it is said, alas, Black English) extraction (accounting for occasional moods and temper). Many Northways, including three of my father's brothers, Elmer, Elijah and Edward, moved to the Western Reserve to take up farmland there in the early 1800s.

I passed my boyhood days in the rural setting of Whiskeyville, where I attended the Academy. Made my way to Cleveland with some slight help of relations and began Medical education there. Was graduated at the Cleveland Homeopathic College in 1872 at age twenty-four, taking the second prize for scholarship and studying with Prof. S. A. Boynton, cousin of President Garfield.

I began practice there, but desirous of an environment offering greater professional opportunities I removed to New York State in 1873, settling in Utica to engage in the practice of medicine and surgery. Never a straight Hahnemannian in practice, over the years I have become respected as an Eclectic Homeopathic Physician.

During the winters of 1879–1881 I studied at the New York Ophthalmic and Aural Institute under Dr. Herman Knapp, and attended the lectures of Drs. Roosa and Noyes on the eye and ear, those of Dr. Janeway on physical diagnosis, and of Dr. Bryant on operative surgery. The next winter I spent studying histology, pathology and microscopy and visited regularly with classes of a clinical character in this City at Manhattan Eye and Ear Hospital and the Bellevue Dispensary. Also I studied abroad, visiting clinics in London, Paris and Germany. In 1895 Governor Martin appointed me Surgeon-General with the rank of Brigadier-General of the State of New York. My patents include the now famous Northway Stretcher and the Northway Field Case, both tested during active service, including War.

At the beginning of the Spanish-American War, President McKinley, a wise and good man, saw the stupidity of barring Homeopaths from service. Immediately, as my family had connections in Ohio and I had known and served him before, the President placed me on active duty although I was a Major General in entire charge of the Medical Department, including the Hospital Corps. I was at that time forty-eight years of age.

During the War I was in Porto Rico, going down there on the Hospital Ship *Relief* with Col. Nicholas Senn, Chief of the Regular Medical Service. Before his death and upon the publication of "The Soldier's Medical Friend," my contribution to our effort in the Great War just concluded, Col. Senn penned me this endorsement: "My dear General, I have always regarded you as one of the most progressive men in the profession and esteem you the more because you belong to another class of practitioners. I often mention your name and accomplishments to my influential friends."

We set out to obtain the facts on the development of Typhoid Fever and made careful examination of more than 200 cases of the fever as they presented themselves. In this work I noted the principal symptoms of each and tabulated the Whole. I wrote up these cases; and on my return, was sent by Gov. Black to ascertain if possible the causes of the great spread of Typhoid Fever in the Army camps in this country. I was the first to state the Fly as the cause of the spread of the awful Typhoid of those days. This report, severely criticized and considered sensational by some, went to New York and Gov. Black and from there to Washington. Its truth was verified by Gen. Breckinridge in charge of Camp Chickamauga. My grilling before the Committee of the Government chaired by Gen. Dodge in this city was a triumph for my assertion. Before my revelation that Flies were to a large extent the cause of Typhoid Fever, the belief was that the fever was spread through the medium of water and of milk. Now the Government and all former disbelievers acknowledge the truth of my assertion.

Throughout my long practice I have been a steady writer, and many of the measures urged in my scores of papers and addresses have been generally adopted by the profession and by Boards of Health. To my own mind the most important are:

Ammonia chloride in prostatic diseases; the Oil treatment of appendicitis; bromine as an antidote for septic wounds of all sorts, such as dissecting, dog bites, gunshot and gangrene; carbolic acid and glycerine treatment of carbuncles by hypodermic through crucial incision, and peripheral painting with collodion; the specific action of drugs; cure of insanity through operative procedures; sanitation in the Army; manual Rotary Dilatation in particular with free use of vaseline to hasten labor and largely relieve pain; and most of all, surgical necessity avoided by Preventive measures.

I have found most efficacious the medicinal use of oil and whiskey. In fact, I have founded my reputation and practice on the use of Oil and Whiskey. I am as well an expert on diet, and proper elimination, and have long been a friend of Luther Burbank, that saintly man who is improving the Dietary of the Race through his amazing New Creations.

From youth I am Episcopalian and as early as 1887 did criticize the method of administering Communion, leading an effort toward the more sanitary method of the Single Cup.

I retired from active Medical practice in 1905, at the age of fifty-seven. I am a member of the Association of Military Surgeons of the United States; the Association of Medical Officers of the National Guard of the State of New York; the American Institute of Homeopathy and the Homeopathic Medical Society of New York (ex-president); and member of the American Yacht Club and the Automobile Club of America. In politics I am a firm Republican—did not endorse that fool Wilson in 1916, as did my friends Ford, Edison and Burbank—Genius can be deluded, but Sound Sense can not—and have been twice married. In 1905 I married Mrs. August

T. (Lutie Morrison) Krause, of Cleveland, Ohio, widow of the president of the Ohio and Trans-Western Railroad and major stockholder in Standard Oil. (Then I truly did believe in the efficacy of Oil!) Upon her tragic death I married Ida B. Bailey, R.N.

In features I am fair though dark of eye, some say my features of an Oriental cast peculiar to the Black English of my ancestry. In height I am exactly of the stature of Thomas A. Edison and Henry Ford (though I believe Ford to be shorter) and a shade taller than Luther Burbank, though in real stature miles below him. I am Sexually active in this my seventy-first year.

When he had finished, he called for Ida and read it to her.

"Well, it's terribly factual," she said. "But then right away you can put in some wonderful thing that happened in your youth or a great adventure that you had."

"Yes."

"I know you want to make your claim, but I'm not sure about the references to Ford and Burbank, and Edison. And how you married fortune. Do you want to say that flat out? And that about the oil and whiskey? You always do let your imp come out just when you should keep it in the bottle. I don't know whether I like the reference to your sexual prowess or not."

"I thought you liked it quite a lot—" He uncoiled from the leather chair and began to make towards her, circling. She squealed with pleasure and held out the mail to him.

"I'm sure it will be fine, and establish you as you should be for all time. Here, you goat! Dear God, didn't Lutie Krause tell me she was dying mainly of your excessive sexual demands? Hah? Oh ho— Let go of me— Here's a letter from the Cleveland Northways, about the boy, young Marcus. I have already opened and read it; I am sure they meant it to the both of us. I hope you do not mind my assisting you with your mail. I do not believe you receive as much as you used to."

"What we receive is your endless, inconceivable stream of bills.

What does the letter say? How is the boy?"

He retreated back to his desk, seeing she had firm hold on and wished to communicate the content of the letter from the Tom Northways in Cleveland. The letter was doubtless written by Mattie Northway, his younger cousin Tom being a slipshod and lazy sort and a correspondent sloppy in both logic and syntax. They lived practically rent-free in the large house on Euclid Avenue where he and Lutie had lived before leaving Cleveland. A year ago he had visited them, gone there in some haste responding to their deep concern that their son whom they had named for him "Marcus Northway" had contracted the dread Influenza that swept the country during that fearsome year of 1918. He had made out a medical program for the lad, then sixteen years of age, and prayed that the boy would have no further effect of the Flu, though some physicians already thought that the disease might affect the nerves and vital system later in life.

"He is well, Mattie says. He seems quite well, fully recovered. A vigorous boy, handsome and strong. Of course she is his mother and would say so. He sings, you know, she's told me before, like his silly father. This says he is now a senior in high school and is learning tennis. I think, Marcus, that you should charge them more rent, if they are turning frivolous. Tennis! Mattie says the daughter, Lellie, is considered a beauty, at fourteen. Mattie would think so, as she also considers herself a beauty . . . "

"As do I."

"Hah! Young Marcus, she reports—They seem to call him 'Mark'—"

"Yes. I think from the first. This is a debased age, Ida."

"He has a good record in school and so is considering colleges, not that they are sure they can afford it. Ah, do you think that is why they're writing us this little billet-doux? They think he will probably go to Ohio State."

He jumped up from where he sat. "Ohio State! Good God! Jehoshaphat! Ohio State! Read it again, surely it can't say that! Why, any moron can go to Ohio State! He is a Northway—He is Marcus

Northway the Second! He . . ."

"When did you get so interested in him, dearie? You let him be another pumpkin ripening on the vine for fifteen years . . ."

"I sent him a bond when he was born, and often talked to his feckless father about his future, damn it! Why, young Marcus—My namesake—Holy hell, woman, he should be going to Harvard or to Yale—considering a career—a real career—a great career . . ."

"Like 'Doctor' maybe, eh, Marcus, is that what you suddenly have in mind? He should follow in your footsteps?"

"The boy should go to Yale—I could get him into Yale . . ."

"Oh, Marcus, my love, be careful! He is the apple of their eye, poor Tom and Mattie. He is what they have. He is not your boy, whatever they named him. He is not your son."

She stood in the room, all in gray silk, like a gunboat, clutching the letter. He clenched the desktop fiercely with the strong lean hands that had saved lives and lost some too. His pince-nez had come off his nose and dangled down. He straightened and sat back, his operating hand still clenched as if holding a lancet. Their eyes, hers brightest blue, his dark, blazed at each other so that the intensity in the room was like the blaze of one of Jules Verne's ray guns.

"Yes," he said. "Is there anything else in it, the letter?"

"Not much. They wish you Happy Birthday in advance. And sent the rent."

"Other mail?"

"Oh—you know. Something from your bank. My bills, as you say."

She looked sad and as if a long way away from him and he was summoning up something witty and ebullient to say when the telephone rang. The Colorado Kid came on the line saying he had just gathered the intelligence that William Northway—Billy—had been arrested in a roundup of known Communists and was in the central jail.

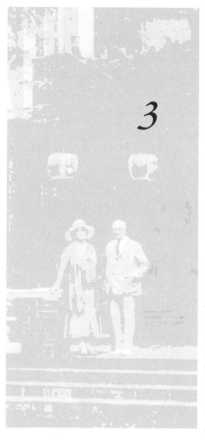

3

"The Kid says he will call back, when he finds out what exactly happened," Ida said. She looked at Marcus, who was cursing his brother Billy in his mind. For years Billy had lived along the Rue Regret, using whiskey not for medicinal purposes, a charmer, a Prodigal, which parable his elder brother detested most. Could do a fine soft shoe, borrow your cigar, sing you "Smiles" at a drop of his ratty derby. Ah Jesus, Billy! Maybe jail was the perfect place for him, the solution to the problem, Marcus thought, maybe they should just leave him there, in that gray fortress in the city. But a Communist! No one had ever accused a Northway of charity, let alone socialism. Why, back there in Whiskeyville they fought their neighbors for every inch of hops land and hanged their enemies or drowned 'em in the swamp!

"Well, you know William," Ida said, after the Kid called again, making her report. "He was trying to help a friend, to right a wrong, it seems. Has some friend named Gustave or something who has a bookstore and is a suspected Communist, spreads ideas I suppose, so Billy goes to bail him out and for some reason they throw him in too. You know they have been cracking down on subversives and such, all over the place. Well, we must get him out, the damn fool. He is a Northway. Do you wish me to come along?"

"No, Ida. I do not. It would be unfair to the police."

He rang for Albert LeMaistre, the old Rough Rider, and told him to bring his son Dennis. Instructed them to wear their livery. He put the ribbon of his highest decoration in his buttonhole, took hat and cane, and they repaired to the hoosegow to fetch Billy, driving in the Franklin. A year ago he had asked Henry Ford, with some malice, what was the finest car made in America. Henry said Franklin and he bought one. Now his mouth had begun to water for a Rolls Royce. There was a quality car, as far as possible from your mass-produced Model this and Model that!

At the desk in the great gray and maroon cavern of the jailhouse he said, "I am General Northway. You have detained my brother William Northway by mistake."

"Oh yeah?" said the beefy Irish desk sergeant. He looked at his record book. "Northway. He's in league, see, with a known Communist, one Gustave Klinck. We're pullin' them in, and their sympathizers, I don't mind tellin' you. This thing is just beginnin', this round-up. You'd better watch it, fella, or we'll lock you up too, just like we did your brother."

"I beg your pardon?" Marcus Northway said, rapping smartly on the desk with his cane.

"You heard me, Dad. Oh yeah, General. I'm sure. And that goes for your tan monkeys, too."

This exchange produced a moment of tension around the desk. Albert and Dennis considered the sergeant's remark discourteous, but Marcus murmured to them they must proceed by diplomacy. He had more than once, for the sake of the nation, exercised such diplomacy in China, where he went for dear old McKinley, and in Japan and Mexico and Porto Rico. The stupid fellow at the desk was quite Irish, therefore obtuse, and obviously doing his duty as 'twas given him.

"May I make a call?" he asked, producing a bill with the picture of U.S. Grant etched upon it. The cretin of the law had no trouble accepting it. Marcus placed a call to a hotel in the city and by luck reached his man, in his room, who whispered, yes, he was of course willing to do his friend this favor, as several were owed both ways, but he did not wish it known that he was here in this moment and not where he should be in Washington, D.C.

"Tell him you are at home," Marcus suggested. "He won't know the difference."

He handed the instrument to the policeman, who stared at him in growing wonder as he listened to the voice coming at him, stared as if he feared the old general was a sorcerer, then said, "Yes, sir, I understand. Thank you, sir," and put the instrument in its cradle.

"Yes?" Marcus said to the astounded fellow.

"Guy said, 'This is Warren G. Harding in Marion, Ohio. You are in the presence of a great American patriot. Do as he says.' Jesus."

"Your Jesus, and raise you a Jehoshaphat! I will trouble you for my brother."

When they produced William Northway, he wanted Gustave released as well. His brother asked was Gustave a citizen? Billy claimed he was. Was he a Communist? Billy laughed merrily. "Oh hell, brother Marcus, there ain't a Communist in the whole place!"

"Release him too then," Marcus demanded of the sergeant, producing more bills for bail and whatnot, "How is it a crime to read a book?"

"Gustave don't read 'em, he just sells 'em, actually," Billy said.

Gustave sent out word that he would stay in and fight this ridiculous charge in court, and they cleared out of there.

On the sidewalk Billy held out his hand to his brother, who stood trying to decide whether to whack him on the head with his cane. Despite the probability of germs, he took the hand. Ida was right. The idiot was a Northway. What *do* we have if not family and its honor?

"I know it's yer own Pooh-Bah reputation yer worried about, but thanks fer springin' me, anyway," Billy said with a smile that would be touching were he on the stage.

"You may take him out and shoot him," Marcus said to Albert standing by.

"Really?" Albert seemed pleased with the idea.

"Well, it might be better to drown him, since he is my brother."

"Yer a card, old Brother Marcus, a real card," Billy said. "But thanks, I mean it."

"And?"

"What?"

"I was thinking of your future. You are fifty-five years old and still acting like a boy. You should have finished trade school, way back then, with my support. You could have been a fine carpenter, a plumber, or on the edge of things, an electrician, had a nice little family."

"Never," Billy says. "Speakin' of the future, I find myself a little short of funds just now . . . "

"William," his brother said, in the tone their father used to use to them. "I am going to hire you. Put you to work. There is a little hotel at the end of Long Island, at Amagansett, do you remember that I bought it? It needs looking after. The sea breezes are salubrious and you will, I am sure, find the pace there restful. Albert is going to drive you there and you will have the pick of rooms for yourself. I am sure you will find life easy there, and I will visit often. It is one of my favorite places to set up my easel and to paint."

His brother, shorter and with red-rimmed dark eyes, the derby on his head, in a shabby suit, with his boy's face looked at him.

"The alternative?" he said.

"There isn't one, Billy, if you wish to keep my love and my support."

"All right then, Marcus. I'll go there. Hell, will I have to learn to spell it? I'm . . . I'm pretty tired, anyway. So, thank you, I suppose."

"You are welcome. The time to help someone, you remember old Sam, our father, saying, is when he needs it. Not that he ever did it, that I recall."

"No," Billy said. "He never."

A day or so later Marcus Northway read in the Hearst newspaper, the *Journal*, that a police sergeant and three friends on the force were interrupted in their evening revels in a bar in their Irish neighborhood and thrashed, sending the sergeant to the hospital with contusions and a concussion. The Negro men—monkeys?—disappeared without a trace. Albert and Dennis were now in Amagansett, taking a little time off from the wear and tear of the city, helping Billy get settled in the Sea Point Inn. Well, Marcus reflected, life has its ups and downs and is full of some of this and a lot of that, as the Colorado Kid was wont to philosophize in and out of the columns that he wrote.

But he wished he had not had the stupid idea of calling Warren Harding in his love nest in the hotel, where he doubtless was with his "girlie," N—. Now it put the balance back on his owing one to Warren. Gentle frightening Warren, ambitious senator from the great state that had produced so many statesmen, presidents and morons, handsome bumbler whom he'd known since Warren was a boy and whose father's reputation he'd once saved to Warren's ever-lasting gratitude—or chagrin. Yes, thoughtlessly in the moment of helping Billy he'd fallen deeper in the trap. Now it would be harder than ever not to let himself be part of the plot that Warren and the Ohio gang were weaving.

4

La Pajarita, his lovely bird, flew, or steamed, back into the city from a time abroad. She had a present for him. Ida appeared at the study door, entreating him to be careful, walking out in the evening on the city streets. Wouldn't he have Albert go with him? Albert was away, upstate, he reminded her. She edged back out, sadly, like Aida being hoisted from the stage.

He reached into the bottom drawer of the mahogany desk fashioned for him by Altman's and took a jewel from his Oriental collection that he thought would surprise and please La Pajarita.

As he walked over he thought of Woodrow Wilson and his idealistic Fourteen points. Wilson was now traveling for thousands of miles across the country in a railroad car named *Mayflower* and giving endless sermons along the way. He felt sorry for the Professor, the fool, but would never—just as the nation would never—forgive him for his treatment of T. R. and of General Leonard Wood. Not allowing him to raise a regiment in the past War killed Theodore, Marcus Northway believed, that and his son Quentin's death so near the end there. Wilson's talk of making this capricious world Safe for Democracy had been and was nonsense. Now the true Party must be restored to the nation, and such folly cease—and he must play his part, sticky or not.

He met her at the Ritz Hotel. All the other hotels had a ban on smoking by women. Pajarita would smoke simply because there was a ban. She was lovely. She appeared to him so youthful! Short hair, rouge, dark and flashing eyes, crescent curve of scarlet mouth! They sat and smoked, his Cuban cigar and her cigarette in long ivory holder, a new touch for her. The night before she had been to see Pickford in "Daddy Longlegs" and adored it—and him!

He gave her the small ruby. All evening she grasped it in her soft brown hand, from time to time holding it up to the light. She gave him his birthday present. Laughing he put it on: a Basque beret from Santander. She had been to Germany and Spain, dancing. On the continent and in Mexico she was Madame Esmeralda, her dances famous, *sin* fans *o con* fans; her following devoted. On this trip she heard some Black Americans playing something beyond, deeper than, ragtime—their own jazz music from the soul. She must make a dance to it. As he gazed upon her, whose life he saved for the benefit of the undeserving world, she made him think of a brilliant red-headed woodpecker that would peck at an old ash tree outside the rooming house where he stayed and studied night and day when he was in college there in Cleveland. How lonely he was, all those years, and later too, for all the first fifty years of his life, as he made his arduous way towards accomplishment and fortune.

Looking at her holding the ruby to the light, she equally as lovely in shape and color as the unflawed ruby, he felt his goatish glands stir, a feeling more like lust than protective paternalism welled up in his vital parts, in his heart. But he put the reins to it, the whip to this inner striving. They must keep the relationship they had. She must always fly free, and free of him. He had saved her life. He was her noble, kind and generous friend. What irony! And yet how rare and beautiful this relationship, as well.

"And were you well received?" he asked.

She laughed, in her usual soft and graceful manner.

"Oh, yes. Mostly. *Sí.* Except you see in Germany the *alemanes*, the German men, they are so mean-looking, and thick and serious. No? I dance and they sit and look at me like they are seeing sausages, no expression on the face. I think maybe I am terrible, I should run off the stage, I have lay what you call it, *quiere decir*, a big bird's egg, no? But then at the end they stand and clap and stamp the foot and yell for more."

"They were hypnotized by the fans, my dear. Or are still in a state of stupefaction. They've been through a hell of a lot, those fellows over there. Well, are you glad to be back?"

"Yes, but I don't understand about some things. My wise friend must tell me. What about this Suffering Amendment? What is it? Will it pass? And the Prohibition? Surely you will not let them do that?"

Settling back, becoming the wise friend and mentor, he told her there were two Amendments up, one good, the other bad. He thought the Suffrage Amendment was good and should pass. Women have sense, probably more than men, he had noticed. As for the damnable Eighteenth Amendment, it would take effect in July, making Prohibition permanent, and was sure to be the ruin of the nation.

"So I will be able to vote?" She arose, stretching, unable to be at rest for long, so much still the girl he first beheld.

"Well now, we would have to get your citizenship straightened out for you first, as I wanted to do before. You would have to study, and take the test . . ."

"Oh," she said, flipping her shawl, holding the ruby up to the light, smiling at the prisms it made, like old and golden port, "let others vote."

She was a citizen of the world, La Pajarita, flying between continents, over oceans, free, almost always away from him but always, as they agreed, in touch with him by thought.

They danced, a little. Before they parted she said she was going to California for a while, to live on a hill in a place called Hollywoodland and make a try for motion pictures. She was wild to dance in films. He told her he was going soon back to Ohio on a political fact-finding trip for the Party, on behalf of Warren Harding. She made a face at him and said she had never heard of such a person, but if it gave him pleasure to do so he must go. She would see him the next time in California. He said it gave him little pleasure. She laughed and said men did strange things, and he agreed.

Walking back he swung his shoulders and cracked his stick upon the sidewalk so that no one would take him for an older man, then gave in and hailed a taxi. Walking and riding and going up the smooth elevator to his abode he let his thoughts dwell on politics, and on the card he'd played that implicated him now, when he could be retired and finally free from all of it. Sadly, he let his thoughts play upon his last experiences with Theodore, the leader whom he had truly loved.

It was late, or early in the morning. Ida had long retired to her room. Instead of going into his own bedroom he let himself into his study and turned on the small desk lamp, Al Edison's magic incandescent bulb, and took the tumbler and poured a glass of whiskey—he'd had none all evening with La Pajarita. Then he took the box of special Havanas that Al himself had sent to him and clipped and lit one and took a nice mouthwash and swallow of the good whiskey, and then another.

"I know you love her more than me," Ida had said late in their first year of marriage, soon after she had learned of Pajarita.

"Oh my dear," he had replied, "there is no comparison, there cannot be. It's not like that, not at all. I could not love you more, as wife. She is simply—Pajarita. She came into my life—I have told you that I saved her life. And, for the years since, has been God's special gift and trust to me. You must try to think of her, as I do, as a daughter."

"Hah! What I can't help wonder, Marcus Northway, you—you goat—is do you . . ."

"Sex, you mean? No. Of course not. That could not be. That is in no way possible, Ida. Neither of us has ever or would ever consider it!" True, in the sense of it in which he must persevere, though his feelings had made a lie of "no consideration" tonight.

"I would like to meet her some time then. I wonder, did Lutie Krause know of her, or ever meet this creature?"

"Yes. Perhaps you will one day too."

"You know, Marcus, my dear and darling man, I doubt it. For some reason I doubt it. I have to wonder, I must tell you that I wonder, isn't she some figment of your man's imagination, an un-real Bird of Paradise that you have created in your head?"

He shrugged and smiled back at her. What could he say to that? If he had reached out for her last night, his soft and lovely little bird, he would have found her real enough. Since then, bless her good heart, Ida had adjusted to it, though Pajarita's coming or his going to her always made his wife seem sad and made her withdraw, for a while.

So.

Last fall he had paid his final respects to New York's Mayor Mitchell, who had died in an accident in Louisiana. Marcus chose not to attend the funeral but did greet the attending party at City Hall and then spoke with Whalen and with Colonel Roosevelt. Theodore had looked even more frail and unwell than the last time he had seen him. He was only sixty years old. So frail-seeming now who had always been pure bone and muscle. Marcus had believed that T. R. could never stop exuding his rare vitality. Theodore shook his hand softly, as would a boy, and smiled but not radiantly as of yore. He carried a small black hat in his free hand that, as he was wearing a mourning suit, helped make him seem small, formal and Eastern, a pro forma figure of the former man and President the nation knew and loved. Marcus had wished he'd carried his old daredevil Western hat, that image of him that we keep even now. In a few days, then, his son Quentin was to perish, and the *elan* go out of him altogether.

General Northway was with several other officers of the Reserve and Regular Medical Corps, and they proceeded to a point from which to view the parade, including the gun carriage of the deceased Mayor Mitchell. Theodore Roosevelt walked the whole mournful route, five long miles it was, from City Hall to St. Patrick's Cathedral in the muggy heat of that fall day, and that was the last time that his devoted servant Marcus Northway saw him breathing.

Now he realized that on the noble Theodore's countenance that day was etched the strain of his terrible Brazilian adventure— discovering the damnable River of Doubt, and the sadness of his incomprehensible rebuff by that pacifist fool Wilson.

Now his thoughts went back farther, but still less than a year ago to when Warren Harding had astounded him by asking him— yea, begging him—to set up a meeting of reconciliation between himself and the former president. Or, for God's sake, there, Doctor, just see if you can't grease the wheel, propound the proposition to him.

"Don't do it, Marcus," Ida said. "You've done your bit, oh, back ever so far, haven't you? How many times did President McKinley receive you in the White House?"

"I went to China for the Major, and met him twice in his office in the White House, dining with him and Mrs. McKinley. Her name was also Ida. She had convulsions during which intervals the President would look away, or cover her with a cloth. I visited Theodore in the President's office three times, once presenting to him my young cousin Tom Northway."

"Yes. So you have told me. Warren Harding is a weakling, Marcus. Everyone knows that. You know him and his background. My God, can you begin to think he'd be a proper president of this poor tired country? No, I would say, Marcus, leave it alone, do not dip your stick in it."

But Marcus, in his pride and in his desire to be with T. R. again, went by one morning on Oyster Bay and spoke with Theodore about this and that, real estate thereabouts—Lutie when married to old Krause had kept a house at Mamaroneck—and the weather and that Warren Harding would like to come by and shake his hand. Theodore bristled. He kept big chips on his shoulder and he had one there in regard to Harding, who had helped stop him at the 1912 Convention when he had so unctuously nominated the Fat Boy Taft. Marcus left Sagamore Hill, thinking he had finessed the hand. Then in a week a letter came. Theodore wrote—he had the letter right here in this drawer—that his prayer now, his own political trail leading nowhere, was to help bring the Republican Party back together. He was willing to see young Harding, but he wanted Marcus to tell him if he thought the fellow was sincere.

"Tell him 'No,'" Ida said.

"He is, though. That is not his problem. He is sincere and has a genuinely good heart."

"Ah," Ida said.

In his reply Marcus wrote that he had known Warren and his father, a Homeopath, in Ohio from the time that Harding was quite young and that as a man he was unfortunately less Bright than Alliterative and was smooth as glass and pleasing to one and all by his genuine nature. He, Marcus Northway, had always taken the fellow to be sincere and to have a heart, a big heart if a soft one. "Oh well, Christ for breakfast, Marcus, bring the fellow on!" So he did and they met there at Oyster Bay.

"How are you, Colonel?" Marcus said.

"Mr. President," said Harding, handsome and perfumed.

"Fine, Doctor," Theodore replied to Marcus, his old companion. He did not say "Bully" or "Splendid." His high voice was hoarse. He had years before injured one eye boxing; now the good eye looked popped. Marcus' medical eye discerned that T. R. had a slight fever, perhaps remaining from his terrible adventure in Brazil. Marcus surmised from the attitude of Theodore's body that he was suffering pain.

Theodore noticed his scrutiny and looked at him scowling, sternly, then sweetly, for he always was an agreeable and thoughtful man; but he wanted from Northway no physician's prattle now, but just to get down to the business at hand as best he could and seem as much himself as possible to Harding.

Yet it was hard for him to treat Warren as an equal. Even after shaking the Ohio boy's hand he quickly turned back to Northway and said, "General, I know of your interest in purchasing a property here on Long Island. They tell me there is a picturesque little inn for sale that just might suit you in the village of Amagansett."

"Thank you, Colonel," Marcus replied. "It is thoughtful of you to mention it." And the next day Albert drove him there and he bought it.

Warren *bloviated*—the lad's own term—at the former president about the future of the Party and its destiny, and T. R. seemed to accept it well enough. There was a reconciliation, though in no way did Theodore endorse Harding as his heir. Marcus knew that the tough little man kept it in his craw that W. G. Harding, good-natured soaper from Ohio, had, after all, never done anything. But it was both their aims, as it should be now of all good Americans, to restore the Republican Party to power and to try to repair the damage Wilson—whom Theodore among other names called "the Logothete"—had done.

Then on January 9 at 4 A.M., a bitter beginning to this year, our great Leader-Hero-President passed on. Theodore died peacefully, as Marcus ascertained, from a blood clot going from a vein to the lungs in his sleep, thus taking from the nation—friend and foe—the most dynamic spirit of the age.

After his death Warren *bloviated* that now if alive T. R. would certainly be supporting him, as he was coming into the center where Warren always had been. That might or might not be a brand of Ohio horseshit, but Marcus did not blame Warren for contending so. Politics is a circus, one that Theodore loved, T. R. himself being not always mild or correct in his contentions.

What Warren really wanted now God only knew. Maybe just to sit and *bloviate* in the Senate. He loved the Senate racket. What was dreadfully clear was that he himself was the best of them, that Ohio Gang. What bums, dullards, incompetents, corrupt idiots were the rest of them, Daugherty and the bunch! Yea, dumb like wolves, like foxes, ravening wolves, so that actually he feared for Warren, the foolish feckless fellow, soft sweet sincere Warren, with his sweet bird, the foolish N—, too often in his hand.

Well, it was nearly morning now. He would take a bath, do some Yoga, massage his limbs and greet Ida as miraculously fresh in a few hours. She was not happy about his proposed trip, but that was a while off yet. She would be less happy, he was sure, about the other junket he had in mind.

He had conceived the idea of going on a birthday jaunt, for inclusion in his Memoir, back to Whiskeyville. Going back to roots. Oh yes, to Roots—and Hops—Ha. Ha. Oh ho.

5

He awoke feeling young to the first clear, bright day in a month. He rolled his colon and did his limbering exercises with growing desire to return to the place of his birth and rediscover the boy he was there.

"You can't be serious!"

His wife was in a state of agitation. The Armenian linen drummers were coming to the suite, and she was not sure just what to buy. (But buy, he knew, she would. Already they had in storage vases, lamps and Oriental rugs that would not fit here or at Willowstone from their trips to Asia, Asia Minor, and Florence, Rome and Paris.)

"Come here," he said, and sat with her on the loveseat, luckily the sedan model, and put his arm around her as she put her head upon his shoulder. It pinched a nerve but would not be for long.

"I will be back for my birthday."

"I thought you were going to work on your Memoir. You've made little progress on it."

"I have a notebook and will take notes, and work on it in Whiskeyville."

"But where will you stay?"

"With someone in the village."

"Is he a Northway?"

"No. I don't think there are any Northways left. I'll stay with a childhood friend."

"But, what in the world am I to do here all by myself?"

"Now, surely, Ida. I thought you had an Evening, a Poetry

Evening, planned?"

"Well, yes. Would you go off and miss it?"

"I am sure I would enjoy it were I here. Who have you engaged for the Evening?"

"Miss Teasdale has consented to return."

"How nice. If it were Miss Millay I'd be here for sure. I thought she was a peach. I like her 'little Sorrow born of a little Sin.'"

"You scalawag! You didn't even listen to her poetry, but just ogled her!"

"Quite right! Quite right!"

Actually he had enjoyed Ida's spring Evenings in the past few years. He got along famously with the vagabond poet Vachel Lindsay who came in and blasted them with "Boomlay! Boomlay!" from the Congo. The fellow had walked all over the country. "Aren't you from Ohio?" he asked him.

"No, Illinois. But I went to school in Ohio. I was turned down by the love of my life, oh such a sweet, small lass, 'Remember' was her poetic name, there at Hiram, which misfortune sent me on the road . . . " A tear formed in the slouchy fellow's eye. They got on fine until Marcus offered him a snort. Fellow walked away. "Dear God, you didn't!" Ida roared. "He gives talks and readings to the Anti-Saloon League!" But they'd gone to the concert hall to see and hear dancers dancing to the music of Lindsay's spoken poems. It was damn good, real American stuff. Teasdale was terribly boring, but her husband, Filsinger, was fairly interesting on the subject of economics. It was good for Ida to do these Evenings, but she never could pull in the big boys. Such snobs as John Hall Wheelock would not darken their door any more than New York Society as a whole would deign to let them in.

"Is Albert driving you?"

"No, I thought that I would drive myself. I am going on my own. That is the point of it."

"Oh Marcus! You haven't driven yourself in years! You don't know the road anymore! I am afraid you will be lost! What would I do?" A real tear formed in her lustrous blue eye. He embraced her.

"And you will return, so we can celebrate your birthday next week?"

"Yes. I will return in four days. And I will wire Albert if I need him. And we will celebrate the birthday. How would you like to celebrate it in . . ."

"Oh, Lovie? California?" She sat up and clapped her hands so quickly he almost fell off the loveseat.

"Yes," he said. "Of course." Thinking quickly. He could book reservations before he left, then come back and make it over to Ohio in the fall. That would be all right. He'd had Amagansett in mind, see about Billy there, but now discarded that and played his California aces. "We'll go to California, to Los Angeles, on the Chief and then how about going to our favorite place, go to San Diego and stay in Coronado at the dear old Del?"

"Oh, Lovie, that will be so fine! That will be dandy!"

The next day he departed, with his Medical Bag and notebook, pen and ink. Actually he cheated, having Albert drive him out from New York and all the way up to Utica.

There he had engaged what he thought would be the right car for the country roads, Henry's buggy, the inimitable Model T. It was of course a famous car, though he himself had never had one. A few years ago Ford had given one to John Burroughs, the upstate naturalist, who was proclaiming that the motorcar would pollute the countryside. Now Burroughs was a maniac to drive all around since Henry—nothing if not shrewd—gave him one. And Ford also gave Al—"Mr. Edison" he always called him—a T, "made by hand" in his back yard. Edison, who was a terrible old wag when you knew him, remarked to close friends that he'd rather have had one off the famous assembly line than "made by hand"—especially by Henry.

Ford also took trips armed with notebooks. His were small pocket notebooks, just suitable for him. He only thought of one word at a time, and then could not spell it. Ha.

"You sure you can ride her, General?" Albert said, shaking his grizzled head at the ungainly buggy.

"Think so," he said. "Thank God Henry Ford didn't give me

this. If he had I'm sure I'd have to set the spark and throttle lever on
the wheel and crank her. Have you heard the saw, Albert, 'If you are
a self-starter, your boss won't have to be a crank'?"

"No, sir. White man's wisdom, sounds like to me."

Marcus Northway laughed and climbed in by the right hand
door as you did on a Model T. He was well bundled and had the
finest rectified preventative and restorative in his Bag and the sun
was hidden by clouds and it was chilly, but he hoped for clear
weather along the way as the going would be open. He started her
up and chugged off, waving back to Albert. He felt pretty boyish,
really.

It was nicer, fresher, more Spring-like out here than in the city. It
was not very far out from Utica, much less far than he had
remembered, for very soon shapes and scenes and contours that he
seemed to recall unrolled before him. It was a lonely road—no one
else at all on it this early afternoon.

It had been, he figured, forty-five years since he had come back
here. Even when practicing in Utica he had not come out this way,
towards Whiskeyville. Why would he have?

Yet now something snapped in him like a watch with precision
parts being set to correct time that told him, where what was left of
his romantic heart was, that he truly loved this country, this valley
of his beginning.

He putt-putted by rolling hills, shallow valleys within the larger
valley, lovely stands of trees. Now in late spring fresh new corn came
up from this rich soil, the purest pure brown color of any earth, surely,
in God's world. Ah, the freshness and joy of Spring in the Valley, in
the hills and valleys and trees of the fresh-plowed ground of the
dear country outside Utica where he, an Ignorant farm boy, had
grown up . . .

He passed by mailboxes painted red and old barns not painted
red as in Ohio but unpainted, weathered to deep shades of gray. His
painter's eye began to turn on, and he chided himself for not taking
up brush and easel and painting more. He'd had classes before he

married, to vary the tedium of medicine. He was a terrible, too earnest impressionist dauber but not bad at your representational scenes. Over this hill the clouds flattened, lying like rafts up in the sky, it a pewtery blue color—a panorama of clouds and sky, like the pale green of the Valley mirroring the blue-gray of the Sky.

Now, he thought, he must be down the road from the tiny village of "Marcus," founded by Northways after his birth and named by his father for him, and the town of Rome; then would come the hamlet of Cincinnatus, and on to dear old Whiskeyville.

No, he was wrong. The village of Rome came before Marcus. He had dis-remembered. Here the valley was magnificent, gray and azure; off to the right, the plowed earth like a rippled bowl patiently waited for its crops—of spuds!

They surely grew the best potatoes in the world here along Rome Hill—though Burbank, he knew, would hold differently.

Nobody, he told himself, the stately seventy-year-old speaking to some one else uncorked within him, but a bucolic boy could so love and appreciate such utterly simple country, and its simple crops of hops and barley, spuds and corn . . . .

And . . . Ta-da, ta-da . . . The "Village of Whiskeyville" . . .

At this approach to town, he recalled, old Philander Beck always kept a herd of milk cows in his pasture of nutritious grass bestrewn with dandelions and yellow wildflowers. If so, it was nothing but ragged grass now, looking rank, but there were dandelions enough.

He had time before dusk and he thought that before presenting himself to Miss Cora Bartlett, with whom he had arranged to stay, he would proceed to the old house, the Samuel Northway abode, where he grew up. He drove through town and on to the corner just before the highway took up again, the junction of Whiskey Road and Northway Place.

Well, here it was. He stopped the shaking car and climbed down, took off his goggles and gloves and duster and took his notebook in hand. At about 4:30 the day was warm as it would be. He did not easily perspire but began to. His heart was in his throat. He stopped on the walk to the gate, to breathe: five deep breaths in and out, expelling stale air, reinvigorating. And looked up.

As remembered. Three magnificent trees in front, going up now five hundred feet. The front yard full of fir trees and fir trees along the walk to the front door of the house. A great oak guarding each side of the door, each trunk twice as wide as a man. The solid old Georgian brick house. It was bigger than he had remembered. Memory had shrunk the house. Deep red brick. He stepped back.

Memory was capricious, eh? He'd had the need to reduce the house. Hell, they had not been poor. The house was not that grim, but one of the best in Whiskeyville. Yet he'd carried it poor, grim and shrunken in his memory. Myth had it also that Edison was poor, yet his real background was substantial if less so than Marcus Northway's. And Ford's as substantial, or more, than this, let their myths say what they might—or what the men themselves fed into them. For truly it was so that the smaller you can make the boy, the larger you may fashion the man . . . .

He stood by a flowering Judas bush off back in the yard and looked at the house. It was a brick box of a house, plain but solid, four windows on each side of the front, the whole rectangular upstairs and down. A narrow chimney. The back porch, gazing around the corner, he remembered, built from round stones from the local Northway quarry. He stood back and took a mental picture. Those very tall trees behind him, he thought, might be Norway pines. He really didn't know what they were. They sure weren't half that tall fifty years ago!

Taking another deep breath, he went up and knocked at the door.

After his visit to the house and grounds he sat in the Model T by the edge of the yard's grass, by the old hitching post in front, and put on another sweater as the day was cooling down. Slowly, he took out pen and notebook and wrote:

Nothing in there. Jesus. *Nada.* No emotion in there or in myself. Man invites me in; we sit at ratty table in disgraceful kitchen. House a-clutter. Fellow rolls and smokes a cig., down on his luck, apparent victim of Paranoia, dull of eye, has Brain Fag. Bought house from man who bought it from Northways, don't know who last was, could look at record. Parks Northway, I think. Moron hopes I want to buy it back, is having trouble keeping it up. All Whiskeyville a slum, he says. I have enough places, I tell him. "In that case, can you loan me a few bucks?" "For your gracious hospitality," I tell him—never moves from kitchen table, smokes and swats at flies—and give him from my wallet a Ben Franklin. He can tell I am a Swell. Am I sure I do not want to buy the house?

Some memories in the house. Mother. Father. Billy as a baby. It was a good house, they good people. What did they ever do? Did they ever dance? I do not remember music being played, but Mother had the narrow room she called Ballroom with hardwood floor, the piano that still sits there covered in dust, keys cracked. Father's little room the Pool room. Smoke house out back, carriage house, dirt cellar, silo, all the usual.

Upstairs is blocked off by the moron. He sleeps in a cot in the living room. If I went upstairs to the room where the boy lived—fretted away his youth—I do not think I would find him there. I leave the ape sitting in his kitchen. Walk out to the back. There is the round pond well-remembered from boyhood—'twas always full of bullheads near the surface waiting to be fed. Choked with sedge, none there now. But there are still blueberry bushes on the hill beyond.

I have waited too long. Scoured and scrubbed my mind, like hands for an operation, free of all of it. Nothing. Am glad.

But Whiskeyville itself . . . Whiskeyville, the idea of it and all the Northways who helped make it—now gone—seems more alive to my mind and spirit, more Emblem to me, than this dead house or I myself as some former inept impotent Self here . . . .

So here I go to meet, dear God!, after all these years, Cora Bartlett, Guardian of all that.

6

Miss Cora Bartlett lived in a Victorian house on Town Street in the center of Whiskeyville. Her house stood on the street, with decaying abodes all around it, like a prim reminder of a better time.

She greeted him and let him in. All the light wood of railings, facings, floors and furniture gleamed under Edison's miraculous light. Her hallway was filled with Bartlett portraits, men and women who looked like her, Revolutionary officers and squires and ladies, and she was the last of all of them.

Her hair still black at his own age, Cora seemed vital, young and happy. He would have in a chance encounter recognized her as the girl who ran beside him in the fields and sat by him in church sixty years ago. Her figure was trim and her face still unmade-up and pretty. He had known a number of women who did not, by choice, marry and had marked their spirit and happiness.

"Marcus Northway, you are a handsome, distinguished-looking dog. Here, put your things right there. It doesn't hurt to marry well, does it? How old were you when you first got hitched, over fifty? I thought maybe you were planning to come back here, for me."

"Why do you think I'm here?"

"Does your wife—your second wife so far, is she?—know you're staying over night with me?"

"She thinks it is an inn. The Bartlett Arms."

She hooted, like a girl.

She had a roasted chicken and a cobbler and a downstairs

bedroom for him and offered him the use of her study with its high windows and pretty cherrywood desk. In the morning she said, "Here are some records, Marcus, an old history written by Deloss Northway years ago and, oh, photographs and stuff, if you want to look at them. Where would you want to go? Do you want me to fix you sandwiches? Do you like cucumber sandwiches?"

"I adore them."

"I suppose you'll want to see again the old village. Remember, down along Whiskeyville Creek was where they first came and settled, 'huddled,' around the water there? 'Whiskeyville Huddle' they called it, as you know."

It came to Marcus that Cora had for many years been a teacher.

"China Northway was one of them. Where do you think he got that name of 'China'? Same place you Northways got those slanted eyes, at the getting place, I reckon. You will want to go to the old cemetery, that's where they all are now, your kin, and mine. Why, Marcus, this is so strange, isn't it? Except there aren't any male Bartletts left either—just fifteen, twenty years ago there were more than a dozen Northway surnames still here in Whiskeyville.

"Of course," she said, "most of them were by then widows, or spinsters like myself. Miss Alice Northway, the librarian, has gone into Utica and is, I believe, still fairly active, if you wish to visit her. Kate Northway was the last here, lived on down Town Street a ways. Now her father was Jacko Northway. Oh my! I can tell you I remember Jacko. He was a redheaded fellow, dancing the Square dances! His son was called 'Court' Northway because he made a lawyer and went in to New York City. I suppose you would know 'Court'?"

"Yes. Judge Horace Northway. He has retired from the State Supreme Court. He and I—Well, modesty allows me to say we were the ones from here who went out and got higher educations."

"Oh, I don't know. How about Fred Northway? He became a dentist."

"On sunny days I might count dentists."

"You are an arrogant man! *General* Marcus Northway, indeed!

And then," she said, "you will want to go back out to the Swamp—the 'Northway swamp.' Nine square miles of swamp and hops land they owned there, your Northways, and the saying was they grew the hops and drowned their enemies in the Swamp! Remember, you follow this street out along to the last white farm house, that is Skunk Hollow Farm, and turn on Gilead, to the cemetery. And then on the farm road to the Swamp. Perhaps you'd like me to escort and direct you?"

"Please do come along. I might end up lost. May I help you make the sandwiches?"

"You are domestic?"

"Well, I can slice cucumbers. And I like a slice of onion."

"In the garden, Marcus. My favorite pastime, being in the garden. Sweet white onions. Keep you regular."

"Exactly," said the Homeopath.

In 1783 Captain Earnshaw built the first sawmill on the site of Whiskeyville, and the second settler, Judge Black, built a second mill and a grist mill in 1796. He proposed the name "Watermill" for the town in 1808, but it was thought too common a name, and China Northway proposed "Whiskeyville" as reflecting what they did here best. It won out over "Black's Mills" and "Mason's Tavern" by China's own vote.

The first stone house was built at the edge of the village in 1799. They were distilling all along, and it is of record that the early Northways bought their land for the price of nine gallons of gin per acre. Later a paint factory and other industries came and by 1857 a newspaper and extensive farming. The soil at Rome in the valley was a sand calcareous loam, the surrounding timber maple, beech, elm, hemlock and butternut, and all the land around, as he read in Deloss Northway's account, "Rich, Hilly and well watered" by two strongly flowing streams. By 1840 came the Episcopal Church and its first rector, Canvass Smart. All Northways there were always in faith and practicing Episcopalians.

"I must admit this buggy does go places where you'd think only a horse could go," he said, driving them along in Henry's limber contraption.

They stopped at the old cemetery. There Cora communed with passed Bartletts, and he visited with hundreds of passed Northways, dear God, fields of them, all laid beneath crumbling stones: the Lodemis, Alices, Maggies, Jameses, Williams, Amelias, Freds, Elicos, Berzillias, Isaacs, Antoinettes, Philos, Sallies, Samuels, Johns, Horaces, Orins, Prudences, and Mollys of their day.

"Now," Cora said, riding along, loudly into the wind, "of Northways, Fred, Elico, Edward and your father Sam—for a while— were later on in the distillery end of things . . . "

He stopped the car to hear her better. His hearing was quite fine, but he was all goggled, wrapped and muffled, his Basque beret down over one ear.

"I have read that old Edward Northway ran six hundred bushels of grain per day and distilled twelve to fifteen quarts, of high wines, then whiskey, from each bushel. But it all ended—'folded' I believe they say—in 1857, when the weather set back the hops so badly. A disaster, Marcus. Do you recall it, the consternation of our fathers then?"

"Your father had a banker's consternation, eh?"

"Quite right. We were nine years old, you should recall it. Well, then, as I have since read, they tried desperately to use our abundant potatoes to make pure rectified brandy and whiskey and gin—Oh, it all led to quite a bit of *Mania a Potu* . . ."

"I remember that they recovered and did well again. That my father Sam was president of the Village after I had gone off to study in Ohio."

"That was 1870. You were twenty-two. You had said you would keep in contact with your friends here in Whiskeyville, but you did not. But you did become a doctor, didn't you, if not a Regular one?"

"At that time, I will remind you, Cora, Homeopathy was dominant in America, as to medical training and practice. The centers of medical learning were homeopathic. And the Cleveland Homeopathic College was the oldest and best of them."

"Yes, Marcus. Splendid. Yes, they did recover. They were

pluggers, whatever else you'd want to say of them. The Northways were like a pack of hunting dogs, they never quit and never stopped howling along the trail, howling at the moon!"

Yes, he thought. Quite right. The plugger Northways. Perseverance was his own true motto. He must help Ida, so often lost in her genealogical digging attempting to glorify the family, to find a proper family motto reflecting that glory—in Latin.

Seven sets of Northways, as Cora had recalled, lived some miles out of Whiskeyville in seven Federal houses on the edge of the nine mile Swamp and owned all that swamp and contiguous fertile land. They passed by where several of the old houses stood, decaying and crumbling, their eagles fallen. Cora did not know who owned any of them now. He didn't care. Obviously the land was worthless, the hops barely surviving. They proceeded along the fair but narrow road to Rome Valley, passing by the purling stream there, and then up an even lesser road on the way to hilly upland, the hills before them riding hundreds of feet above the valley.

"Now let me drive," Cora shouted at him, thumping him on the shoulder. "I'll show you something!"

And Jehoshaphat! She took off driving like a demon!

After the road petered out, she yelled, "Hold on to your hat!"

She drove across the highland fields and on up the main hill, or small mountain, to a spot high over the valley. Now the going was rough, the area thick with trees. Below you could see plowed ground with its beginnings of rows of green. She zipped them into a clearing at the top rimmed with a stern phalanx of tall old beech and elm trees. The buggy chugged to a stop, and she dismounted, pointing with her duster arm, hat askew, to the line of trees.

"This little meadow so far up here," she said, "was called the 'secret pasture' of the Leary Gang. As you have doubtless heard, they were a large Irish family of what you might call brigands, oh, some years before the War of the Rebellion, in the early 1840s, as I recall. The Learys could look down from here. They had some shanty houses, a little settlement, I believe. They could look as we are now over the whole valley and see who was coming.

"They raided everyone but especially the Northways down there in the Swamp, also known as 'Northwaytown.' The Learys would from time to time relieve them of their sheep and what they considered only a neighborly portion of horses and cattle. But the Northways were not known for their charity or kindliness . . ."

He could hear the relish in Cora's voice.

". . . in fact, they were themselves a rather fierce clan or tribe, with their scowling faces and black eyes and impatient tempers. And so, Marcus, my dear old friend, one fine day . . . Have you heard this?"

Lying to her, he said, "Never."

"One fine day the Northways got together, villagers and Swampers, and marched up here and took the Learys, every one of 'em, and hanged them along this line of trees. Hanged the men and boys by the neck until they jerked to death and hanged the women and girls just for half an hour plumb by the thumbs until, you know, they'd got the point, then cut 'em down and took 'em home, along with their sheep and cattle and whatever else the poor unsuspecting Learys had, and married and adopted 'em! Now doesn't that make you proud to be a Northway?"

"Oh my yes. An inspiring heritage, indeed!"

And one of those cut down, dear Cora, now so flushed and happy with your story, was Molly Leary, who became the second wife of my grandfather Philo Northway, his first wife Clara having passed in 1835. Clara was mother of my father Sam and his brother Elmer while Molly then gave birth to Elijah and to Edward, who moved to Ohio on the farmland out from Cleveland there. And Elijah was the fat and lazy father of my feckless younger cousin Tom Northway, who would have happily stayed there on the farm if I had not taken him in hand and set him on his course of being a dentist, which profession he has never loved but at least he is a second Northway of all of us to have become a professional.

My grandmother, Marcus mused, was a solid Dutch woman, Clara Weatherwax, and my mother Sally Ann a Humphrey, of old English stock. I, he thought, looking at the beech trees he imagined young Molly Leary had hanged from by her poor bruised thumbs, escaped the taint of Irish blood, and thus by such chances are our lives and fate formed—or the form given to us to forge by force of character!

"Marcus?"

"Yes? Oh yes—Clara. Would you like to picnic here, under these memorial trees?"

"In the Northway arbor with a Northway? Why not, Marcus, why in the world not?"

They ate their sandwiches and drank lemonade on a blanket in the meadow by the grove of Hanging Trees, and then he drove them through the terrain back down the hill and to the road and by the Swamp and on along the valley home.

There, Cora said, "I am making a pork roast for you tonight, with some *pommes* from the good brown earth here and a salad of my young peppers, radishes and the sweet onions, my tomatoes of course are not ready. Do you take wine? I have continued the Whiskeyville tradition and have several kinds of homemade high wines."

"Yes. For medical use there is no substitute for whiskey, but for table use I do take wine. Wine is a study in itself. From the early Romans on . . ."

"Yes," she said, and went into the kitchen.

Late at night, Cora retired He sat in her light-wood study at her cherrywood table with his pen uncapped and the notebook before him thinking what, if anything, of this hegira he might record.

He was in need of a smoke, but the lady had mentioned she preferred not to have fumes invade her house. There was an odor of roses, heather and lavender in the house, in this room, some sort of potpourri, he supposed. It made him want to sneeze. But it was a lovely room. He did not think that anyone had sat in it at this desk for many years. If he were of the persuasion of Al Edison or Warren Harding, he might cut a plug and chew a bit, not that he would deign to cultivate so nasty and plebeian a habit, and surely Miss

Cora would not any more appreciate his spitting than smoking.

The events of the day, and the day before, had made him feel an uncharacteristic nervousness. He had felt, strolling with her after dinner up and down Town Street, that he would like to jump in the T buggy and take off driving, not *into* but *away from* the Past.

For the first time since being here the images of his parents had come to him. He saw his father Sam's furrowed face, his sometimes terrible frown. And again the image of his slim mother as she bends then straightens in the truck garden, wincing, as the arthritic pain shoots through her back and limbs—God, he was never able to come back and help her! And what might he have done if he had come back, to here, to this burg, this lovely, lonely backward place? Rage . . . rage . . . at them . . . the poor plodding fools . .

He must remember that Sam loved Sally and she him and that they were happy here and did not have and did not wish any other sense of things. And when Billy came along, and he himself was leaving, how they loved and coddled and spoiled the boy! Billy was the gift of their older age—and was still just a boy when they both died and he roamed around and only later came into the city like a boy-man drunk on the lights, or anyway, for the most part then, drunk.

He hoped he'd rescued, finally, Billy. He had formed young Tom Northway, by God made him into something more at least than he might have been. And now the fool, Tom Northway, would send the fine boy Marcus, his namesake young Marcus Northway II, to Ohio State where they educated dullards, and so put two strikes against him in this dog-eat-dog Darwinian society and world! Not if he could help it! We'll see about that . . . We will see.

Why was his heart beating so? Was he having palpitations? Was there a Thought message coming to him? Was it Pajarita? Where was she—at sea—in some foreign port—? Oh yes: California. There in Hollywoodland. No, it was not she. He must shock his system, calm his nerves.

Ah. Reach down into the Medical Bag. The initialed cup, the pint of whiskey. So. A swallow or two of whiskey for medicinal purpose here late tonight in Whiskeyville, place of my birth, my beginning, as my day of birth approaches, forgotten village by history and by me. A swallow or two more, to invite and induce sleep.

Last year when he had visited him once again in Florida, at Fort Myers there, his friend Al Edison, the most natural and easy companion in the world, had shaken his lion's head and smiled wryly and said to him, "Who—in the holy hell—old Marco, old Polo—is this great 'Thomas A. Edison' they all write and talk about? Sometimes, hell, often, Marco, I wish that I knew the genius fellow!"

And who—after all these years—three damn score and ten, and another to be quickly added—in the holy hell—was he?

All the dead Northways in their graves out in the cemetery . . .

All is flux and illusion, says Heraclitus, the river as a permanent thing only constant in its changing flow. All smoke, as the Stoics taught. How are we to be remembered, our name go on?

Not by some damn scrawled-out "Memoir" . . .

As he capped his pen, he saw, startled, someone in the doorway. It was Cora, with a candle. Dear God, she looked, in her white gown, like a ghost.

"Are you all right?" she said.

"Yes. I am sorry to be up so late. I am just finishing a—passage. I am writing a Memoir. And today, this visit—Cora—has been very—useful."

"It isn't the pork, or the peppers, then?"

"Oh no," he said. It was not the pork.

7

In the fall he went on his mission to Ohio for the Party. He left Dennis, who liked the city duty more than his father did, to squire Ida from shop to shop in New York and had Albert meet him with the Franklin at the train depot in Columbus and drive him. He did not want to run into Harding's henchman Harry Daugherty or any of his lackeys and so avoided the Deshler Hotel in Columbus and set out for the Ohio burgs and hamlets.

There were remarkable old courthouses around town squares full of giant elms. The colors of the leaves on the trees in Ohio were memorable. They drove and enjoyed leisurely visits with folks through Bowling Green, Washington Court House, Burton and the hamlets, Bloomfield and the rest, around the location of the Northway farms. Only old Edward and Aunt Alvinia, called "Gussie" because of her love of getting "gussied up" and going to church or into town, still occupied and farmed the Northway land. They spun down south to Cincinnati and then back to Ashtabula, resting place of so many Ohio Northways.

He found Warren Harding's father Dr. Harding lazing around in Marion. They drove together to Blooming Grove and had a visit. A dark, wiry fellow, Dr. Harding was indeed a Homeopathic physician but hardly a credit to the profession or their camp. He was scarcely trained, kept old books, was always careless as to the histories of individual patients' cases, and had meager equipment in Bag or office. Years before Marcus Northway had rescued him from a pretty bad jam when he got in over his head trying to treat a patient. By now he hardly practiced medicine, thank God, but as far as Marcus could determine just idled around and about.

Marcus did not mention his son's Affinity, Warren's affair with N—, to the poor soul. As far as he could tell, the bumbling old blackamoor was in the dark as to the affair. Nor did Dr. Northway discern through casual conversation with a multitude who savored gossip and would have loved to tell him of it any knowledge of the secret in the Ohio towns. (The foolhardy business of N— was of course known full well, and relished, in the circle of the Ohio Gang.)

In Cleveland he went up several flights in the city's Rose Building and let himself into the anteroom of the dentist's office of his younger cousin Tom Northway, whose fate Marcus had decreed was to be this.

The room was a bit dusty. Beyond he could hear Tom, who considered himself a crooner of note, humming as he bent over someone's mouth. On a table in the anteroom were two ledger books. One was of appointments ahead and of services rendered, with fees. "Mrs. Ben Osters, cleaning, $2.00." "Ruth Marble, filling, $3.00." "Mr. Pike, x ray, $6.00." My God, no wonder Tom Northway hardly made a living! The other book seemed to be a former appointments and record book now pasted over with pictures and text from various journals and magazines, dental and other-wise, mostly on the side of the exotic, picturing romantic scenes and far places and homely bits of wisdom. On the first page was written in Tom's large cavalier hand: "This book is planned to receive ideas that may be of great value. Anything on any subject welcome as long as the Idea conveyed seems reasonable and helpful."

He sat quietly in one of the waiting room chairs and thumbed through his cousin's book of stuff. He was becoming absorbed in Captain John B. Trevor's record of how many Americans were British, North Irish, German, Jewish, Oriental and so on as of 1918 as he heard Tom say, "There! That should fix it so it won't hurt until we can put in your b-bridge. I am glad we did not have to use g-gas, Mrs. B-Billington . . . Oh, that's all right, you c-can just wait to pay until next time, until we f-finish . . . "

In a moment Mrs. Billington, a large woman wearing a muskrat around her neck and holding a handkerchief to her mouth, passed by without seeing him and went out the door, fleeing home to her husband and all the little Billingtons. Marcus rose and went to Tom's office door, quietly, for some reason wanting to behold the fellow in his habitat before revealing himself.

Born in the centennial year of our nation, Tom Northway was now forty-three years of age. In his white dental coat he sat in his dental chair with the Praying Mantis-like instrument bank and arms in front of him, a serene look on his fleshy, handsome face, his fair hair awry, his spectacles pushed up on his pink forehead, his bright blue eyes slightly protruding as was the wont with those of thyroid disposition, looking at an X ray. On a stool beside him sat a round fishbowl with a shell configuration within the water, and through the shell world swam tiny goldfish. Tom always did need a creature by him, fish or bird or dog. His handsome wife Mattie, Marcus believed, kept a singing bird in the solarium of the house they rented from him, old Krause's musty pile, on Euclid Avenue.

He had thought of ringing them, giving them fair warning, and calling on the family in the rambling old house where—it seemed aeons ago—he and Lutie once had lived. The girl, Lellie she was called, would be there, the daughter, though of course young Marcus was away, down at Columbus, at Ohio State. (He had curbed a strong, almost demonic, urge to go by and see—surprise—the lad in his dormitory on campus there.) But he knew that to go back to the old house of Lutie's lugubrious first mate August T. Krause would be rash, or would cause him one. Usually he and Ida, for invariably she had been with him when coming here (except for the emergency trip two years ago to be physician to the flu-struck boy) would arrive and summon the Tom Northways to a suite they took in the Statler Hotel here in Cleveland. So he had come, like Sandburg's Fog, "on little cat feet," relishing the chance to surprise his younger cousin in his office here.

"A-hem," he said, not wishing to upset him by his sudden

appearance, knowing he would be upsetting him enough in the course of conversation.

"A-hem."

"Eh, Mrs. B-Bill— Eh? Oh— Dear G-God, M-Marcus N-Northway! General! Uncle M-Marcus! My God, I thought I was dreaming, looking at this picture of a j-jaw and then seeing you appearing in the d-door—How n-nice to see you, Uncle Marcus . . ."

The portly dentist managed to heave up out of the dental chair, hit his head on the operating apparatus, come towards Marcus with outstretched hand and a mighty attempt at a smile on his face.

"H-here," he said. "S-sit down, Marcus." He pointed to one of the two leather chairs in the waiting room. Marcus sat again where he had sat. Tom Northway checked the appointments book, saw he had none, and sat. "What brings you so un-ex-pected-ly to this n-neck of the w-woods?" he said.

"Well, Tom. Thriving, I take it? I am here in Ohio on a trip I did not anticipate, so I did not alert you to it, checking on a—ah—future investment. I see that, when excited, you yet stammer. Are you still doing your breathing and speech exercises?"

"Yes. No. Not m-much. It is just simply a—surprise—to see you like this. I do not believe that you have ever g-graced my office before."

"Are you still experimenting with the use of gas? I believe a few years ago you would demonstrate its effect on young Marcus, using him as part of your demonstration?"

Ida claimed that Mattie, Tom's wife, furious, had told her that her husband had embarrassed the boy badly once by putting him under, and he had involuntarily voided, staining for all to see his new white ice-cream suit. Tom had laughed and said it was very effective in teaching the lesson that the patient should go to the bathroom before having the gas administered.

"We perfected it, Uncle Marcus. My colleague and I. We have a pa-patent. I have high hopes for it." He glared at his older cousin whom he had long called "Uncle."

Marcus smiled. "That is admirable, Tom. I have a patent or two myself, you know."

"Yes. You invented a s-s-stretcher!"

Tom Northway laughed. Marcus Northway had heard people laugh at that before. He saw no joke or humor in it. What was so damned funny about benefiting humankind, those sick and injured, maimed and wounded, by devising a lighter, stronger, more comfortable carrying device for them? But he knew that Tom, his fat cousin here, had once, after a dram of something, told his brother Billy, "Any m-moron could invent a s-s-stretcher!"

"You seem to be having trouble with the sibilants," he said.

"Sometimes," Tom said, very carefully, visibly controlling his breathing.

They sat and regarded each other, Marcus Northway with his strong, soft, clean physician's hands clasped over the head of his stick, Tom Northway with his strong, soft, clean dentist's hands clasped over his stomach. Dark brown almost black eyes now meeting eyes a deep stern blue.

"Well?" Tom said. He was not stupid.

"Well," said Marcus, smiling. "I have," he said, "a proposition for you, Tom, dear cuz. I think it will profit you and your family— our family—to listen to it."

"Y-yes?"

"I want you to come, oh, let's say in late spring or early summer, all of you, to California. Ida and I plan to stay on Coronado, you know, the peninsula off San Diego, for the spring and summer. Come visit us. I will pay your ways of course. I don't believe that you or Mattie, let alone the children, have ever been to sunny California, have you? You could come out on the Chief, a famous train, as you doubtless know."

"That is your proposition?"

"The step to it. So that we can—relax—and visit. Have a good visit. We never really have, have we, all of us? Just our infrequent stops here. And talk about the future. The boy's. All our futures. Eh? I don't suppose you'd want me smoking a cigar in here? It's been a long time since we smoked a cigar together, you and me, hasn't it,

Tom?"

Tom Northway nodded. It had been forever. He nodded, remembering when.

"I will t-tell Mattie. We will think about it."

Marcus Northway nodded in reply. They would damn well do it, or he'd know why—if ever they wanted his help again!

"How is the dear boy doing, there at State? What classes is he taking?"

"J-just what, you know, they all take, G-Goddamn it, Marcus! Passably, I guess. He is doing all right. Says he's happy, if that means anything, and I for one think it means a lot! Trying for the tennis team. We are p-proud of him. He's just barely got there yet, you know . . ."

"Ah. Splendid. Yes. Well, Tom. Let's see . . . I visited Ashtabula, scene as you know of the Great Train Wreck of 1886, when you were ten, scene also of Northway graves outnumbered only by those in Whiskeyville itself. I sat once again rocking on the porch of the Robinson House Hotel. Had a vision of your father, old Lige, sitting, rocking, smoking his cigar there after he retired from the farm, so many years ago, after you'd gone off and your mother finally passed away out of her Melancholia and misery. Eh? Yes. Met an oddball there, a character by the name of Jake —Jake Northway, that is—just back from service, no one seems to know just what branch of the family he's of, who his father was . . ."

Tom Northway was giving him a look that he had seen before, the look that let him know he hated him for all he'd done for him. Marcus stopped his monologue and stood. Tom rose, met him halfway and shook his hand. The fellow was not weak, but strong as a bull physically.

"I will expect you then, Tom—all of you—in Coronado in May or June. 'Won't we have a jolly time, eating cakes and drinking wine . . .'" He quoted the old song they knew, one of Tom Northway's favorites, but it did not seem to cheer him.

Marcus returned and reported to Simon Cameron and the other Eastern bosses of the Party that as far as he could tell nothing was generally known of the Affinity business in Warren Harding's home state. In his opinion there would be, as of now, no basis for embarrassment or spread of rumor. In his own mind, he excused himself by rationalizing that surely Warren would be utterly discreet should a miracle occur and he claim the White House. Does not the office enlarge the man?

Ida did not like it. He tried to distract her from probing into the business with his new story on this Jake Northway character he had encountered in Ashtabula. Even as a Northway Jake was not considered too bright, so it was of some interest when in the recent conflict he had gained the high rank of corporal and the trust of training carrier pigeons to carry their messages. Marcus offered Jake, judging from his appearance and conversational ability pretty much a moron, a cigar and asked him how he did it, train the pigeons? "Oh," Jake replied modestly, "you just have to know a little more than the pigeons."

Ida curled her lip. "I believe he is a moron," she said. She did not like any story that depreciated the vast intellectual or other worth of the Northways.

A month later, after a chilly and dismal Christmas in New York, she brought him in a letter from his friend Botkin in Oxford announcing the death of the great physician Osler.

"Oh my . . . How could I have missed it?"

"Why, Marcus, are you crying? Your eyes are wet . . ."

"He was a great man, Ida. Teacher and healer. Always kind to me. We served on two cases together in this country and attended a service together, I his guest, in Christ Church Cathedral. You have been there, Ida. He . . . "

"Yes, dearie? Oh, I am sorry, I should not have sprung it on you."

"He was so young!"

"Your age, Marcus, exactly, I think. It says here—Dr. Botkin writes—Yes, he was just that. He quotes a phrase, Marcus: 'The days of our age are three score years and ten . . . So soon passeth it away, and we are gone.'"

"No! It was the Pneumonia got him, wasn't it, there in England? Of course. Bitter, raw and cold, in Oxford. Three-score and ten should be the average age! Unless surprised, in foul clime or with some hereditary reason, a man can now control the pattern of his life and the length of his life. Why . . ."

"Sit down, Love. Here. Would you like a sip of whiskey? Let me get it for you . . ."

"Ah? No . . ."

He went to her and embraced her, feeling her great heart beating in her strong frame. She hugged him back with strength and passion, and, coquettishly, whispered in his ear: "California, Marcus! Sunshine! You can live forever there!"

"Minx," he whispered back, feeling strong again, the shock of Osler's death fading away. He felt like dancing, holding her, and slowly, like a large boat pulling off from shore, they began to rock together, and then to take some steps in union on the ornate Chinese rug with the pattern of an elephant's foot . And in his heart he agreed. He owed her, dear Ida, California, and he would give it to her.

TWO

8

In June, then, of the year 1920 Dr. Marcus Northway found himself in his usual comfortable suite in the Coronado Hotel looking to the ocean across the bay from the pleasant town of San Diego.

It was a Grand Hotel and one of his favorite haunts. It had been electrified by Edison, his first great project outside the East, at the time of construction, in 1888, shortly after Marcus had met Edison in New York City and made an investment in the venture. Through all the years Marcus had stayed many times in the airy ocean front rooms that they kept for him in this red-domed rococo gingerbread extravaganza, standing where once was nought but sand, briar patch and rabbits, on the calm Pacific.

Ida was off up the coast for several days visiting her cousin Patsy Rourke in Los Angeles. She was happy to be back in California. Ida was so miserable in Greenwich and off-base in New York City, where in truth only the medical-political circles, with a few vagrant artists, poets and nuts thrown in, were open to them despite their wealth. She had been no happier in Cleveland, Lutie's birthplace and old Krause's home base. Cleveland had its own airs, had its own Blue Book in which were listed no Burkes or Baileys, or Northways either for that matter. Marcus Northway cared not a fig for society or social pretense, but Ida was crazy to elevate the Northway name, his reputation and her Place.

Well, everything was newly minted, in creation, still in process here in California. The state was a circus (taking form) with the tent still going up. Maybe they could be stars out here, he and girthful, graceful Ida, high wire stars . . . Ha. Ho ho.

California had proved fertile ground for Burbank's wonders, his wizardry, his "new creations." Marcus thought he must go see the dear man, dear friend; perhaps, if things went well here, take Marcus II along with him. They had exchanged Thought messages and Luther had indicated, why, yes, Marcus, that would be fine, bring the boy, I am busy but will find time for you. I would like to meet this young man who is your namesake and will perhaps carry on your work as well as your name.

He had bought a new Packard runabout which he could drive himself to keep here in California. Albert and Dennis had driven the other cars across country for this special visit of the Tom Northways here. He and young Marcus could drive up in the Packard to see Luther at Santa Rosa. It might be just the stimulus the boy needed, to behold the wondrous Burbank at work. Yes: ambition is often fired by contact with Greatness.

Ida would be back day after next. Meanwhile he was free to noodle around, think his thoughts, write a bit, and be at leisure. Soon it would be his birthday again, and life was fine, fine as high wine in the summer time as old Sam liked to say when work was done and hops picked and sold or transformed into their next stage of usefulness. And, ah yes, entertaining in the old hotel tonight was the celebrated Madame Esmeralda, singer, dancer, mime extraordinaire, acclaimed by audiences in Paris, Rome and Tijuana, whose fans of rich hue were known throughout Europe, South America and Mexico. In truth he was just idling now, anticipating her arrival, his heart as always in such anticipation singing like a boy's.

He lit a cigar and strolled through the corridors and grounds of this Hotel Del Coronado built in the style of Queen Anne, if she had been just a little bit drunk. Built fast and hardly with a plan, the Hotel reigned, all higgledy piggledy, all uneven and with capricious symmetry from materials used to the various kinds and shapes of windows up and down and across, the whole to his eye a glorious hodgepodge.

Used to be, when he would stay here, the guests would come over on the old ferryboat named *Ramona*, thence by bus to the side door of the Del. They advertised the hotel heavily from the start, claiming it to be "the Acme of Perfection." And indeed it was, and was still. Flowered chairs and couches, dainty lamps and sprays of lilies sat in the large lobby—used to be as well a private Ladies' lobby. The story of his time might well be how women had gained access to everything and everywhere, had got the vote—and then, by God had voted in Prohibition!

The ballroom with its brilliant lights would be stage and auditorium for La Esmeralda this evening. Now he stopped in the Writing Room and sat at one of the desks there. No one else was in here to write. Marcus puffed his cigar and took out his Waterman and regarded it. He must get back to the damn'd Memoir . . .

He'd had in mind for months, on the other hand, to write a piece against Prohibition, from the medical standpoint. Bennett, he thought, at the *Herald* might use it . . .

A man with a beaky nose who looked like a large bird that might have flown in off the ocean popped his head in and nodded at him several times and popped his head back out.

The fellow made him think of another odd bird he had encountered here in the hotel. It was around 1905, 1906, when he had retired and was very angry with the pompous fool Dr. Wellknecht who had left him entirely out of his definitive medical tome as an act of spite to himself and Homeopaths. Marcus was staying in the suite here with Lutie. The strange fellow's name was Baum, the German word for "tree." Kept lurking around the hotel with a crazy look in his eye. Approached Marcus and claimed he was writing a children's book, staying in the hotel and writing it right in here, in the Writing Room and up in his own room. Marcus thought at the time he was glad it was a children's book, for surely no adult would read it. He had seen no evidence that the fellow ever accomplished this task, though he could not claim to keep up with ephemera. He recalled the fellow Baum said the work had something to do with a mythopoeic view of Al Edison as mechanical wizard, and that had interested him. Poor Al, everyone making a myth of him, and now Henry Ford, the moron, had bought Al lock and stock and barrel too.

Marcus passed by the famous Crown Room, for dining. It had polished wood floors and a remarkable ceiling, vaulted, all inlaid, no nails in it. Evenings the room was a symphony of light, glass and linens. Now they were preparing it, and the whole place, to receive the young Prince of Wales. He would like to be here for his reception, to salute the lad. The General was sure he was a charming rascal, the Fop of Wales. Many with fame and fortune had passed along these halls in the old hotel. President Harrison came here early on.

Marcus stopped in the long downstairs gallery where photographs festooned the walls to see that he himself, General Northway, had come here in 1915. Here he was in a photograph with Albert and Theodore and a bunch of other fellows in blue polka-dotted neckerchiefs when T. R. had come for a reunion of his Rough Riders. And here was the Fat Boy Taft who had come in 1913 to meet the Mexican Diaz. This gallery was interesting. He was in several other pictures along its length.

Yes, he came in 1904 when Edison returned to light the giant Christmas Tree he had electrified. Ford came with him, for Henry had latched on to him by then, and they brought along young Harvey Firestone, whom Marcus thought of alternately as young "Firewood" or "Fireplug." That was just before the lugubrious August Krause died, and here were old Krause and the fair Lutie in a pose outside the hotel here. He had declared his love for Lutie and had tracked her here and in Fort Myers and New York City as well as in Cleveland. They were standing in the picture with Al and himself and Ford and Fireplug.

And down the line here another of just Marcus Northway and T. A. Edison at that same time standing by the blazing Tree arm in arm, two pals. Making the incandescent system here was a big deal for Al and got him out of a temporary slump in his career if you want to know. He was happy then to come back in '04 and do the

Christmas tree. Got a lot of publicity for that, too. Al never minded publicity, I'll tell you.

Marcus repaired to the terrace to enjoy a lazy day with hanging clouds and sky shifting from blue to gray and back again but no rain in the air. He got a newspaper, lit another cigar and feigned interest in the news of the day, though in his heart he considered he had by now done his part. Marcus knew also, as all old stoic men knew, that events were not controllable by human beings. By now he kept the coil of well-regulated skill and fear and carefulness he had achieved deep within and only let it show in flashes in certain moments, revealing it as immense dignity or as sudden (and to others, inexplicable) mirth.

He saw in the morning's Los Angeles *Times* that the Jap grip was tight on China, the Tokio militarists at a weak China's throat. Peace in the Orient—he had been on missions there for his nation twice—remained a fool's dream. The rebels in Mexico, just south here, were after Carranza, a weakling. They would need to get Black Jack down there to protect our citizens and interests. It made him think of Wilson. The Logothete, on his last legs, spoke to a crowd in San Diego in Balboa Park last year and then came sadly over here to the Del and sat on a wicker chair just where he sat now on the terrace and gazed out upon the Pacific. Suddenly relenting, in the beatitude of his mood as he awaited Pajarita, Marcus hoped—for the fellow had needed solace badly then and after all had done his best for his doomed cause of peace, which had got all balled up with hypocrisy, greed and war—that the vast, calm Pacific had been a peaceful symbol for him, for Woodrow Wilson.

He thought that such idealists as Wilson must live by symbols so large that somehow they transformed into wonderful abstract language untroubled by the concreteness of the real experience of their lives.

Ah well! Hey la-loddy loddy li, hey la-loddy loddy li!

He ordered up on the terrace looking to the water a lunch of shirred eggs à la Espagnola and Fard dates in anticipation of her, then rose and rubbed a cramp in his left thigh and resumed his stroll.

Good-looking women all around, dear God! Saucy hats. Enticing strides. Ladies in pink and pastel summer dresses playing Bridge at tables on the veranda. Inside he stopped by the desk in the lobby and idly checked the ledger for names of people who had stayed here through the year: from Rochester and Tacoma, Boston and Portland, Milwaukee and Worcester, Mass. "F. Dings and Daughter" were here from St. Louis. Ah, how deep his sorrow that he did not get to meet them!

He walked on out and down by the giant Bathhouse and to the dock. The ferryboat was approaching. Now it was named *Virginia*. There was a large boat house for sloops and motor sailers. J. J. Spreckels, the "Sugar Prince," who had taken over this hotel, had his yacht tied there, a vessel larger than Marcus Northway's boat, which was kept off Nantucket on the Atlantic and rarely used. Marcus liked belonging to the Yacht Club but did not adore being on the water. In fact, sailing frightened him. Now Ida, she would not even approach the damn boat, wanting quite a bit of good solid earth under her size nines. It was Pajarita, of course, who spent half her time aboard ship, sailing o'er the world.

The ferry docked. These days there was a train from the ferry slip to the hotel. He walked back over to the siding to wait to greet the train.

The last off of course but she is here. She emerges. She adjusts her brilliant parasol and smiles coming out. Stands beautifully in the sun. Smiles again, at him. Looks so young and jaunty!

He doffs his hat, steps forward. Addresses her: "Madame de Forestier, I believe?"

She gives him her hand, light as a feather, brown as leather, soft as silk. "Qué nombre, señor?" she says.

"El Duque de Coronado," he says, bowing over her hand.

"Charmed," she says in Spanish, and laughs like a girl.

They bathe, she in a costume with candy-striped legs and polka dot cap. She insists on doing the Outdoor Plunge into the salty brine. He confines himself to the indoor plunge in the mammoth pool where there are benches and steps to jump from and the safety of life preservers on the walls. Latterly, in terms of physical escapades, he has found himself going even beyond Falstaff: Discretion is all his valor!

After bathing they repair to the Tea Garden, by the small rock-walled pagoda. In the evening they dine on black bass and broiled barracuda, hers with anchovy sauce, and Spanish Pudding, sauce au cognac. He does not go to her performance, for he has seen it all before, but afterwards they talk for hours before she gets sleepy. He kisses her once, this child, this daughter he never had but through a gracious act of fate does indeed have, and leaves her, no lust and much love in his heart. In the morning she will go back to Hollywood to her little house with spiraled roof on Beachwood in the quaint section called Hollywoodland, where still she is all a-flame to dance, be an actress, on the flick'ring film.

At least she will be safely off the water for a while, on solid land, though he thinks in a place where all, even the hills and streets and crazyquilt houses, are part of some strange illusion.

She will go and Ida will come, and he will resume his larger role.

9

All the next day before Ida returned he sat at the desk in the suite and, drinking nothing but chilled water, wrote, in his large fine hand in black ink on the flimsy sheets, stacking each one carefully as he finished and blotted it:

I wish to make in this journal, or Memoir as the case may be, my claim to some Medical Firsts that in their own way should qualify M. A. Northway to rank with T. A. Edison, Luther Burbank and Henry Ford as they, through similar method, delivered to the nation and mankind Firsts in their particular fields— Electricity, Horticulture and Mechanized Industry. All important firsts, granted, but none more vital or significant than the very Health of human beings, the physical and often spiritual well-being of men and women. And none of the above mentioned as experimenter has come close to dealing as extensively as I with Women!

What follows is, I believe, Original.

I wish to elucidate on the following. I. Can Women Escape Normal Labor Pain at Parturition? II. Has a Law Been Evolved through the Research of Dr. M. A. Northway Which Shall Do Away with the Agonizing Features of Child Birth? III. Oil in its Relation to Relaxation of Muscular Fibers. IV. Manual Rotary Dilatation.

It is now more than forty years since I began my Observations on the value of oleaginous material as a Relaxant and as an assistant to the elasticity of muscular fibers. My first thought on this subject, in the early eighties, was the result of an experiment in consultation with a physician in a case of so-called Dry Labor. The doctor called me for the purpose of securing my services for instrumental delivery. My examination revealed a condition not uncommon, in which the muscular fibers resist and become irritated under the normal process of labor, as a result of which there exists exaggeration of temperature and, at times, an oedematous state of the parts supervenes.

I had slipped a pound of Vaseline into my pocket, and now required the doctor to allow me to use it freely and defer instrumental delivery for a short period. The method pursued on this occasion was the introduction of Vaseline in as large quantities as was possible, the same being passed into the neck of the uterus, during the cessation of pains, by a Rotary Manipulation. This being done, we took a stroll for half an hour, and on our return arrived none-too-soon to greet the new-born babe, whose advent occurred without instrumental assistance.

I have in the time since not been able to dislodge from my mind the importance of that experience, which has since proved the basis of a Philosophic Fact bearing upon other conditions of a surgical nature.

A case quite similar to the one just cited occurred within a few years later: that of a surgeon's wife. The surgeon was very apprehensive, fearing laceration, but would allow nothing to be done, preferring Nature to take her course, and simply desiring my presence for its moral effect. After a period of the usual severe pains incident to primipara, the doctor accepted my suggestions and allowed me to use a Lubricant, which speedily led to a relaxation of the parts, and the woman was delivered with instruments without rupture. In this case I simply pushed back the tissues between pains and used about a quart of Sweet Oil, insinuating the same by the method described in the preceding case, namely Rotary Dilatation.

Before describing the main case I have in mind I wish to illustrate the Principle of Relaxation of Tissues in other surgical emergencies.

My first citation is that of an older gentleman, eighty-five years of age, who had worn a Truss for many years for the purpose of retaining a Right Scrotal Hernia. On this occasion I was called in consultation, the hernia having been out three days, and the patient not being able to reduce the same as he had on previous occasions. I found the parts so intensely swollen, red and inflamed that it gave one the impression of a marked case of Hydrocele. I immediately suggested Herniotomy, but this was refused by the patient and his wife. They stated that he was too old and could not live through a surgical operation, but felt confident at the same time that I might suggest some measures which if carried out could relieve him. (Patient was a fine old fellow, had been a Major in the War of the Rebellion, 34th New York Brigade.)

The parts, then, were thoroughly lubricated with Oil, which was absorbed by using a heated shovel as near the parts as could be tolerated, after which flaxseed poultices kept hot were applied and continued for two days. An ounce of sweet oil was given every twelve hours—no food being allowed. On the morning of the third day, the same treatment being continued, the entire area showed such a marked decrease of inflammatory action that I determined on a reduction, and under the use of chloroform the hernia was returned with scarcely a manipulation.

One more case to illustrate the relaxation of tissues under Oil, before showing the adaptation of this principle in cases of Child Birth. The aim being to carry a Parturient Woman through successfully without laceration or the usual pains, Nature's labor being supplanted by Lubrication and Rotary Dilatation.

I was called about midnight some five years thence, to see a young man of about twenty-five years of age, who had an acute strangulated Right Scrotal Hernia. I found the patient suffering excruciating pain, and Taxis was immediately instituted for the reduction of it. Failing in this, and the hour being late, and the surroundings unpropitious for an operation of so much moment, I concluded that I was justified, in view of my experience in the methods heretofore explained, in placing the patient under Relaxation Treatment until the morning, giving at the same time Aconite, for the temperature, which had risen to 103.

The next day the patient was much more comfortable, temperature reduced to 101, and he continued to improve, the symptoms of strangulation lessening for four days, at which time he was free from inflammatory action and pain. Having proven to my own satisfaction that the danger incident to the strangulation of a Gut could be thwarted by the method described, and failing to reduce the hernia, I conveyed the patient to the hospital (this was in Ashtabula, Ohio) and performed the operation of Herniotomy. I wish to remark that the intestine showed no sign of destructive inflammation. The patient made a happy recovery but was, I have learned, subsequently killed when struck by a trolley car in that same town.

It will be noted by the judicious reader that I have outlined the development of the philosophy of the relaxation of Tissues under Oil by illustrative cases.

It now remains for me to explain what I have mainly in mind— the Manipulatory method, by which women at child-birth may be relieved of the child without the painful efforts of Nature. One case, it may be said, hardly furnishes sufficient evidence to warrant one in establishing a Theory which claims to accomplish so much. For this reason I have illustrated the growth of this general principle of relaxation of tissues under lubricants, as it in fact developed in my experience. It is to be hoped that I am not mistaken in believing this to be a comparatively Universal Law, and that most cases of Parturition can be carried through as the one which I shall now present for your consideration, or to such an extent as may be desired by the Mother.

This principle is to my mind and experience at least as universal as: Similar Cars come off the end of the line; a certain Grafting produces always the same or similar Apple or Potato, or given the Process and Electricity the Bulb, all bulbs, will produce light for x hours or years.

I received a telephone message, then, two or three years later, requesting me to be at the hospital in Cleveland at a certain hour, as a patient was on her way, some ten miles out, having Uremic

Convulsions.

I arrived at the hospital soon after the patient was received and found her physician administering chloroform in order to control the convulsions. He stated that her term of gestation was considered to be complete within three days. She had had no pains. I asked the doctor what he desired me to do, and he replied, "Anything to save the life of the woman, and the child also, if possible." The ordinary procedures published and accepted as legitimate, when the induction of labor seemed indicated and was made necessary by existing circumstances, were discussed between us, but did not seem adequate to the occasion. The doctor was quite positive in his conviction that ordinary methods would be of no avail and begged me to institute any measures which, in my opinion, would speedily deliver the woman.

Taking my position in front of the patient—she was turned crosswise on the bed, with legs flexed, as in the position for instrumental delivery—with fully a Pound of Vaseline at my side, I began the process of insinuating the same into the vaginal outlet.

The cervix was not at all dilated and presented no indication of labor. I was soon able to introduce my finger into the same, after using a sound, and then began what I have denominated as a rotary manipulatory dilatation.

The parts yielded comparatively rapidly. The interior of the os being thoroughly lubricated, and under a similar process of manipulation the vagina and os began to show marked signs of relaxation, but no contractions were at any time present in this case. I became exceedingly interested in what I was doing, even under the trying circumstances presented at that moment. I could soon enter my hand, and arm, for that matter, into the vagina, and as soon as the os was sufficiently dilated the forceps were placed in the high position and the child delivered alive and in full vigor. There was no laceration.

From the beginning, when I took my position in front of the patient until the completion of the entire operation, was just one hour and twenty minutes. She was unconscious for two days after delivery, but left the hospital four weeks from the day of entrance in excellent condition and nursing her baby. A chemical analysis and micro-scopical examination of the urine showed it to be normal, although as might have been expected, early examination showed marked Albuminuria.

I believe that the assumption herein maintained is correct and that a Law has been established, and that I have made no mistake in estimating the value of this Method here explained in its relation to Parturition. I hope that this procedure may in future be published and recognized in such Medical Encyclopedias as that of Dr. P. B. Wellknecht so that it may bring ceaseless benefit to Mothers and the Accoucheur alike along the humanitarian lines of this advanced thought.

(I may add a footnote of a further case. While serving in Porto Rico in 1898, I was called, while investigating the conditions in a native village, to an emergency situation involving a beautiful young woman twenty years of age who had conceived not in wedlock and was in a terrible state of excruciating Dry Labor, she crying for Help from God or any other agency. Having had the experiences herein described previous to my military service, I, now a General, decided it was not beneath my rank to act and that an American could and should act to save the life of a poor Porto Rican in horrible distress. I decided to employ the method of Rotary Dilatation. I had no surgical implements, nor forceps, in that moment in my Bag, not much else but the useful pound of Vaseline and pint of whiskey. I applied the whiskey to myself and the Vaseline to the woman. The baby was born dead, but the young woman survived. I have been able to further assist her through the years and am pleased that by her vitality and talent she has been able to make some mark of her own upon the world.)

He paused, pondering whether to let the passage stand, then blotted it, deciding to let it be for now part of whatever it was that he was writing, and wrote below the last paragraph with a flourish:

*Inscribed by Dr. Marcus A. Northway, Major Gen'l, Ret., June 18, 1920,
Hotel Del Coronado, California.*

Ida came in that afternoon, as Pajarita had, by the ferry-boat
Virginia. He walked to meet her at the train stop, and they strolled
arm in arm back to the old hotel.

"And did you have a good time visiting with your cousin Patsy
Rourke, my dear?"

"Oh yes. I do adore Los Angeles! They live in a nice new part
called Beverly. Harold does well, selling life insurance. Patsy gave
me the recipe for our old Aunt Huldah's Salve! You take and mix it
up with beeswax and . . ."

"What in the world would you use Huldah's Salve for?"

"Oh—My, I have forgotten. But it's been in the family for ages,
as a Bailey remedy. For anything, Marcus. Do not be so picky. For
anything that's bothering you, you know, externally."

"My dear Ida, you are a nurse. You know we are not of the school
of Folk Medicine. Nothing is used indiscriminately but each thing a
specific to . . ."

"Oh pooh. Huldah's Salve is like the sauce I make for Sailor Duff,
the steamed pudding you adore. You say it would be delicious on
an old rubber boot."

"Quite right. But, as Jim says to Huck out there on the raft, is a
pudding sauce a medical ointment, Ida dear?"

"Piffle! I won't be dragged into the likes of that, arguing with
the great Marcus Northway!"

"All right. We must make up some of Aunt Huldah's wondrous
salve, so that I can carry it at all times with me in my Medical Bag."

"I know what you carry in your Bag!"

"And are you hungry, dearest?"

"Ah God! Marcus, I have to confess, after that train ride I could
eat a horse."

"Well, let's look at the Menu, and see what they are offering in
the Crown Room. Let's have a lovely evening, Ida dearest, before
the Cleveland Northways arrive tomorrow, eh? Yes, here it is: Roast

of Horse, Mint Sauce."

"Ha. You are a mischief, Marcus. A terrible mischief. And what have you been doing in my absence?"

"Today I have been writing a critical passage, making a Medical Claim, in the Memoir."

"Ah? Good. I'm glad to know you have got back to it. And glad to see you and to find you in a good mood. Sometimes lately you are so—pontifical. Is that a word?"

"I believe it is."

She gave him such a stout hug it cracked at least two ribs.

They dined in the Crown Room all a-glow with light and sparkling crystal, and had a proper meal: Ribs of Prime Beef. Ham Glacé with Champagne Sauce. Mashed Potatoes. Baked Apples. Sweet Pickled Figs.

"Have you tried the Spanish Pudding?"

"Yes," he said. "It is delicious."

Afterward they went dancing in the Ballroom, bouncing about to the music of Gutbucket McKinney and His Gutbucketeers, who had replaced Madame Esmeralda on the stage. It was lively, Rag and Jazz, much enjoyed by Ida who loved dancing, hopping all around. She found herself other partners when he quickly tired of it. But when he rose to retire she came right with him, and they retired gently to their bed.

In the morning he was up as dawn first cracked o'er the Pacific, the light so clear and pink and wonderful coming up, and had a satisfactory bowel movement without aid of enema and was ready for the several days with the Ohio Northways, ready to help direct young Marcus to his destiny.

10

The LeMaistres, Albert and Dennis, in two cars met the Ohio Northways in the afternoon at the train station in San Diego and fetched them to Coronado and the Hotel Del Coronado, crossing the bay by ferry. He had arranged for them to occupy rooms on the top floor from which to have a view of the ocean.

They arrived and refreshed before presenting themselves to the elder Northways. Marcus and Ida greeted them in a warm spirit of reunion in a private pavilion of the hotel, where they all dined on a meal ordered by Ida: Sweet Figs, Rib Roast, Roast Duck, Sea Bass, Baked Apples à la Montagnard, American cheese and ice cream for the darling girl and handsome boy.

Tom Northway was dressed fairly well, at least he was in a suit, though with cigarette ashes on his cuff, as Ida noted. His wife Matilda, or Mattie, who had been an Elton in the northern Ohio farm country there, was just a bit younger than her mate, full of figure, with (Marcus Northway thought) a darkly beautiful face and lustrous locks. She had won his heart years ago. Marcus could not conceive why she would consent to take the blunt hand of his younger cousin whom he had rescued from the farm, but there was no accounting in this life for the oddities of the unions of men and women, women and men, Vide, if you will, Marcus Northway's own unions—take Lutie or take Ida! But they—Tom and Mattie Northway—were good human beings, and stout hearts, both! Yes, he thought, in the vigor and beauty and excitement of the day, they were that!

The daughter Lellie, all dressed up in a blue dress with sash which Ida had had made for her in Paris, seemed to be a Flirt. Her saucy eyes and laughing mouth in her girlishness almost seeming to mock a certain relative, an old (as she might suppose) Prig of a general. Ha! They would have to watch her.

His namesake, whose hand he shook, then embraced as two men together, finally whaled upon the shoulder a time or two, was a well-made lad of handsome though still boyish mien. He had a sportsman's build of body and was half a head taller than his father Tom, and so a head already above the original Marcus Northway. He had, Marcus thought, the look of a true Northway, which is to say he looked much like himself: his skin fair but faintly almond, the slightly Oriental cast of facial bone and eye, the Roman nose, the generous mouth and firm chin. Pleased at beholding the youth, his namesake, he once more embraced the boy.

After dinner he proposed a brandy and cigar for the Northway men.

"Yes, fine," Ida said. "Come, Lellie, let's walk around the grounds, settle all that food! The sunset is lovely over the water. Mattie, are you coming?"

Mattie seemed to hesitate. She looked at the General and at her Tom and her son the general's namesake almost with apprehension, as if she did not really want to walk off and leave them seated together at table on the pavilion. She had been a school teacher at seventeen in the Ohio country and was terribly keen and awfully sensitive, verging, he thought, on a nervous condition. Ida, dear God, was wearing part of her collection of Chinese snakes, silver snakes all inlaid with jade and onyx for eyes and tongues. She looked like Nefertiti with all that stuff around her neck and arms—or maybe two Nefertitis—and Lellie seemed to shy away from her as if uncertain of the snakes. But Ida grabbed her and Mattie, one in each fist, and propelled them to the View.

The lad smoked his cigar well, as if he enjoyed it, but rapidly, puffing at it like an engine coming down the track.

"There are many jokes about cigars," Marcus Northway

observed, "but a cigar is no joke. It is one of life's great pleasures. I have these from Cuba. They are finest leaf and wrapper. Remember always to smoke a good cigar just half-way down. It is the mark of one who appreciates what he has, of a gentleman. Anyway, even the best get tougher after that."

"Yes, sir."

Tom Northway had let his cigar die out. Now he reached in his pocket—his suit was too light in color and material for the evening— and brought out a crumpled pack and lit a fag.

"And your health has been good all this year, since the Flu?"

"Yes, sir. Tip top."

Marcus poured the lad's father and himself a dollop each more of the Courvoisier. Young Marcus had scarcely touched his, as was appropriate in a youth. He could tell the lad was bright, sociable, politic, unlike his feckless father. He might go far.

"I hope we'll have a splendid time here. I am so glad you've come. Your first visit here, isn't it, to California? And this is just the prettiest part. And yours too, eh, Tom? Yes. And along the way I trust that we can talk—speak of the future."

"Yes, sir."

"Look here, Uncle Marcus . . ." Tom Northway broke in.

"I'm your cousin, Tom."

"I kn-know that, God-d-d-damn it . . . What you are . . . Mark here is on a pretty good course now as it is, his mother and I think . . ."

"Of course! I know he is. But all paths do not lead to Rome, Tom, as you and I decided years ago, and some, why, they hardly lead to London! Ha. Ha ha! And so . . . Shall we also stir our stumps, as Ida wisely suggested, assist digestion? It is rare to ingest fish and fowl and meat (which I did not) in one sitting. Shall we join the ladies in viewing the gold and purple of the sun sinking into the sea? Marcus? Mark?"

"Yes, sir. Okay, General Marcus . . ."

"Oh, call me Marcus, that is, Uncle Marcus. I am your Uncle Marcus."

He took the boy's arm. They went off together stride by stride, the boy's father shambling along behind.

"Yes, call me 'Uncle,' dear boy! What friends we'll be now! Ah yes—two hearts that beat as one!"

He was pleased the lad did not say "Yes, sir" to him but just walked vigorously by his side to the beach where they joined the ladies.

The next morning he arose again early and dressed, Ida yet snoring the mighty Bailey snore, and took a walk along the beach in the cool dawn, selecting first a light Malacca cane with sharpened point for lancing jellyfish.

The houses beyond the avenue on this island of Coronado were in various styles, most grand. It was increasingly in his thoughts to purchase one and bring Ida permanently here to California. He would have to keep the Waldorf suite as retreat and for continuing political, financial and personal business—the Memoir, his vowed opposition to Prohibition, etc. Surely they—she—could "make the grade" in San Diego!

A too large, really huge, house seemed to be made all of orange stucco. Gauche. But he liked the orange trees set beside the olive trees along the avenue and very much liked the oddly Spanish vista of the giant fir trees (as of his early home) set beside the palm trees, as if the northern and southern realities had blended. The yellow sand and the somber depth of green and blue of the Pacific Ocean completed the picture.

He had been in his time to China, Japan, India, the Philippines, Cuba and Porto Rico, Morocco—Ida did not wish to, as he did, go to Africa—Spain, France, Italy, Germany, Austria, England and the Rock of Malta, not to say the nations of America to the south. Yet he knew full well that a man need not travel off this vast and beautiful God-given continent to view and participate in the most incredible beauty and diversity. "Land of hope and glory, Mother of the free," he hummed walking along, whacking a sea oat with his cane.

Returning after an invigorating walk to the premises of the hotel, having yet an hour before the special breakfast Ida had ordered for them in the Crown Room, he went strolling through the lobby. There he encountered the darling girl, Lellie, or spied her peering down over him from the lobby's upper deck. He caught her eye with a motion of his stick, waved to her and ascended the striped-carpeted stairs to her.

"What are you up to, young lady?"

She half-curtsied to him and blinked and smiled. "Just lookin'," she said. "This is a neat place. How old is it?"

"Why, 'twas built in 1888 I believe, and my friend Thomas A. Edison electrified it that same year."

"Who's he?"

"Dear God, child, are you joking?"

"Sure. Everyone knows who old Edison is. He invented electricity."

"Oh, he did, did he? Here, sit down a moment with your Uncle Marcus, Lellie. That's a pretty name, alliterative and full of liquid sounds, eh? You sit there and I'll sit here, side by side, and we will get acquainted."

He pointed to twin chairs, each carved with a ferocious bearded face and claw feet, upholstered in some jimjammy colors. They sat, she gingerly.

"What do you think, my dear?"

"These are hideous chairs."

"Yes. They most certainly are. I really do think that Lellie is a pretty name."

"My real name is Melissa. They call me Lellie. Didn't you know that? What are those?"

"They are called Pince-Nez. Because they pinch your nose, you see."

"Why do you have a cane? Are you lame?"

"Certainly not! I was walking on the beach. It was for spearing jellyfish."

"Neat! Can we go spear some?"

"Later. Now, tell me, if you will, Miss Melissa Northway, is that another Paris gown sent by your Aunt Ida?"

"Oh no. I got this in Cleveland. But I love the things she sends. I still keep the blue velvet coat with the fur collar and fur cuffs she sent me years ago. She sends stuff with lace and satin and chiffon. Oh, I can't wear it much, and a lot of times it's not the right size. But . . ."

"What?"

"I hate the snakes. They scare me. I wouldn't want to wear bracelets that look like old snakes!"

"Your Aunt Ida, who adores you, dear, is Irish. The Irish like snakes. Snakes are symbols, you see, to them."

"Cymbals like you clang?"

"Exactly, if you are Irish. Like Ida clangs her snakes. You are a bright child. How do you like living in that big house there, in Cleveland?"

"Oh, Uncle Marcus, it's just a marvelous place to live! I feel like I'm the Little Rich Girl, though we aren't rich at all, because we live in that big house, and I know you are the one who lets us live there. Of course Papa is always talking about moving out of it. He and Mama want their own house, they say we'll be moving soon, they hope, to a swell street in Shaker Heights!"

"I'm pleased you're happy there."

The imp smiled. She was of a funny cast of mind and spirit, a devil in her eye.

"We're happy except when you or Aunt Ida call or come by," she laughed, "especially the Mrs. General, I mean Aunt Ida . . . Oh, I shouldn't say that . . ."

He laughed. "Tell me. I'd like to know. Really."

"Well, the telephone rings and Bridget, our maid, answers it and she comes in running, yelling to Papa, 'Oh, Doctor! Doctor! It's the Jineral! The Jineral's on the telephone for you!' So that's sometimes how I think of you, as the 'Jineral.'"

She giggled. He laughed and winked at her. He had not talked and flirted with such a young girl in years! She was a Corker—maybe worth bringing to New York to put for Finishing with Miss Finch.

"And then Mrs. Jineral—your wife—Aunt Ida—she gets on the

phone . . ."

"Yes?"

"And she tells Papa he hasn't done this and he must do that . . . And we all have to get dressed up, like this now, and we always have to come down to the hotel to meet you. Papa always says you should come to us at our house . . ."

"He has a point."

"Why don't you, 'Jineral?'"

"Why, Lellie, dear, I do not mean, nor does Ida, harm, or arrogance, by it. That house, you see, belonged to the husband of my first wife . . ." He did not say that said husband died there, in her parents' very bedroom. ". . . and I remember her there, my first wife, poor soul, who also then expired—died, I mean to say— untimely, and I have sad memories of the place. But it is a fine old rambling house, that is for sure, and I am glad there can be life and happiness in it now."

"Oh, I see. I guess."

"Yes. It is pleasant visiting with you. You are a good and open girl. I will not let Ida wear the snakes. They scare me too. We still have a little time before breakfast . . ."

"Oh, I've eaten."

"Then you will eat again, I fear. What were you on the way to do?"

"Going to watch Mark. He's on the courts. He's a tennis player! He's on the team, at State!"

"Do you miss your brother at home?"

"We all do! He's the best brother in the world!"

"I am sure he is. And what has he been doing there at Ohio State, besides playing the Sport of Kings?"

"Oh, he plays the ukelele too! He sings all the college songs, and all the songs Papa has made up, like 'Robinson House Hotel' and 'Duck Foot Sue,' and he's made up one himself, about a saloon . . ."

"How splendid. Shall we leave these hideous chairs and go watch him for a moment, then?"

The lad looked all right at tennis, though Marcus thought his backhand stroke labored and not natural. Both young Marcus and Tom Northway then appeared at breakfast without coats and with sleeves rolled up and wearing bow ties. It upset Ida.

"Eat your Philadelphia Scrapple, dear, it is delicious," Ida said to Lellie.

"Ugh. It's horrible. I hate it," the dear girl said.

"I had it specially prepared for you and your brother," Ida said. "Eat it."

"P-pig-f-fat fried in deep f-fat . . ." said Tom Northway. "I do not notice your hu-hus-band eating it . . ."

"Eat some of the nice melon, Lellie, and a piece of toast, that will be fine," Mattie Northway said, giving Ida a keen mother's look.

Ida beamed back at her as if that was the fairest proposition she had ever heard.

11

They proceeded in two cars, Dennis driving behind in the Franklin presided over by Ida with Mattie and Melissa Northway aboard and Albert driving Marcus and Tom Northway and the Namesake in the silver Rolls Royce which had been purchased a month earlier. Marcus had capitulated to his belief that Royce was the world's best car maker, putting up quality against quantity—of course you could buy a fleet of Henry's cars for what Sir Henry soaked him for this palace on wheels!

They toured through the city of San Diego, in part an old and historic town in regard to the early Spanish settlers, seeing the original "huddle" and the mission but not stopping at the dusty old place. In the main town Marcus pointed out to Tom and young Mark the house which Marcus had engaged for Burbank four years before when the horticultural sage had "honeymooned" with his new young wife. They proceeded to the Mexican border, with Tijuana across, and stopped there for Ida to arrange them for a group photograph. Ida took it and Marcus felt a tremble of laughter go through him: when developed the picture would show Tom Northway standing by his "uncle" and his son holding, as instructed, Ida's purse!

At last they proceeded to Marcus' favorite point in San Diego, the Sunset Cliffs. He thought he might choose to build a house, to live here, if not on Coronado, for it was as quiet and lovely as the latter.

Stopping the cars they disembarked at a Lookout over the Sunset

Cliffs—sheer, unstable, dangerous cliffs eroding out over a small and peaceful bay. This spot, again, put him in mind of Spain. A house like a fort with small high windows and a red tile roof sat up in the hills just behind them, on a hill high over the cliffs and bay. Gentle wavelets broke right at the foot of the sheer cliffs.

Marcus and young Mark stood side by side there, becoming in this moment, truly Pals, feeling the closeness each to the other, or so it seemed to the older man, looking out together at three sailboats spaced like a triangle out beyond the reddish-purple bar, one in the middle with a red sail, the others with sails white. Ah, I will paint this scene from memory one fine future day, Marcus thought.

Looking out at the scene together, Marcus puts his arm over his namesake's shoulder. Mark looks at him and smiles. He feels the life, blood and vigor coursing through the lad's body. Ah! What could be more hopeful, more thrilling, for a lad of nineteen years than to have Power, Prestige, Wealth and Possibility standing by your side, supporting and directing you. It had not been so for himself, for young Marcus Northway of Whiskeyville . . .

Beyond the bay itself, as his painter's eye must remember, the water went green, blue, purple, tan and deeper green—the basic colors of hope and faith.

"Turn around here, you two, and let me get your picture, and the little boats beyond," Ida says.

In the evening they dined together in the Crown Room, except for Tom Northway; the querulous dentist complained of catching cold in the wind at the d-damn'd cliffs and stayed in his room to snuff some hydrogen peroxide and water up his nose.

The next morning was the time set for the two Marcuses to have their outing together—to have their talk—and it had been arranged for all the others to be otherwise engaged. When Marcus II appeared before him again in the short sleeves and bow tie of the day before, the General sent him back to his room to don the proper clothes which he had sent him just for this occasion. The lad did so naturally and with no embarrassment. Now they were in tune with the law of Similars, each in Navy blue jacket and four-in-hand and white flannel trousers. Marcus Northway wore a handkerchief of gold and blue Chinese silk in his breast pocket, the boy one of pure white linen. Marcus wore a jaunty straw hat with wide brim and navy band, the lad none as was the wont of youth.

On the ferry over to San Diego they stood together by the gleaming silver Rolls sheening and sparkling in the sun of the bay, and Mark spoke of his feats of derring do at the university in Columbus. He was proud that he had been on the freshman tennis team. He had studied but one language, Spanish. Marcus told him he was fluent in it.

"Did you study it in college?"

"No, for, you see, Mark, I took only technical courses related to medicine in my training all that time ago. It was another age, you understand, and few who were not going to be ministers or teachers took the so-called liberal studies."

"So how'd you learn it?"

"By travel. On duty there in Porto Rico, on diplomatic missions later, just as I learned a bit of French and Chinese also, and—ah yes, the Spanish I learned also through affinity with one who spoke it." Marcus felt, again, close to the lad in the moment, telling him that.

"That would be okay with me, learning it that way. I wouldn't mind learning French or Spanish either one that way."

He admitted it was a pleasant way to learn. He regretted that Mark's course at Ohio State did not force him to face Latin, which was the one language strictly required in his medical training. It had been of immense benefit to him as physician and as writer.

"Now Yale College, my boy, has a very strong course of classical learning. You could learn Latin, and Greek too, at Yale."

"I couldn't get admitted to Yale—oh boy—on a bet!" the handsome boy said, his eyes flashing and his Northway lip curling. How much he reminded Marcus of himself when young!

"I have already paid off the bet," Marcus said, but not aloud. He did not wish to tell Mark, at this fragile beginning point in their true relationship, that he had seen Mexican generals less corrupt and on the make than college presidents. Such lessons would come later.

Albert drove them through Balboa Park, a spacious, pleasant area. Marcus thought that if ever they settled here he would like to have some sort of memorial to himself located here in Balboa Park.

They came to the zoo and released Albert and the car. Strolling they shared thoughts, mostly the older man's, on the state of the American nation, the coming election, and the horror of atheistic Bolshevism. In the zoo they admired the colorfully plumed birds in their trees, the great snakes in their houses, the African and Indian elephants in their environs. They looked with admiration and awe at the arrogant Sacred Baboons with their great red butts and balls.

Then stopped at the cage of an old but mighty lion.

He lay staring straight ahead as if he were an Egyptian carved figure and they not there, though he seemed sad and somewhat withered by the growing heat of the day in the cage Marcus considered to be outrageously too small and narrow for his greatness, for his majesty.

"It is a shame," he said, standing there, "to keep this fellow here like this. He is worth far more than most who come to stare at him."

He prepared and lit a cigar, colorado, and pulling on it said, as entry to the maze, "Yet, despite their incarceration of wildness, I have always liked zoos. I have visited them all over the world. They have in zoos done much to find and relieve diseases that afflict animals and to preserve certain species from extinction. That is always sad, young Marcus—Mark—when a whole category of birds or beasts with which God the Great Spirit also populated the earth dies out. I hope that man, in his mad and endless rush for material progress will take care not to let it happen.

"I have been," he continued, "all my life concerned with life and death, the preservation of life, and I agree with my friend Burbank, whom I hope you will meet while here in California, that there is an inviolable rhythm to life, a rightness in the order of all fauna and flora that is essential. But we are not very wise about it. Man's pride, Mark, can only be related to the health and well-being of the smallest creature that has an equal right to live, to the blooming of the smallest plant or flower, to our brother the spider and our sister the crocus."

He cut his eyes from the lion and saw that young Marcus was listening to him raptly, nodding his head, and so continued: "The whole of our Father's Creation, as we know, should serve as a symbol, and a model to us, in the rightness of its symmetry. That we, as men with short times here, should each find his useful, proper place in life, the purpose and meaning that are rightly his. That is the faith I have had to believe through all my years, in success or failure, and the faith I have tried to live, a Transcendent faith, as Homeopath, as healer . . . And to find such true and useful function in your own life is my prayer now for you."

He puffed the cigar down to half and discarded it, looking to see the effect of this Knight's gambit on his namesake.

He seemed quite moved by the peroration, in fact as if he might be nearly moved to tears, but rather like a fish with its mouth open, at a loss for words. The lad seemed rather inarticulat—Dear God, Marco, old Polo, you old fool, why don't you lay it on a little thicker? Jesus and Jehoshaphat! When you were his age, you hardly knew the meaning of the shortest word just spoken! Marcus saw that he must more lightly tread.

"Did you know," he said, in a moment, "that the last passenger pigeon died in the Cincinnati Zoo just two years ago? My God, the passenger pigeon, once among the most common and numerous of creatures!"

"Oh yes. Dad told me. He believes all this, as much as you. Do you know that? My dad knows a lot. The passenger pigeon didn't adapt, you know? Its tail got to be larger than its wings."

"It did adapt then, eh, to waddling around? But yes. That can happen. You don't want to get to be a Dodo. *Rafus cucullatus.*"

"Look here, Uncle Marcus . . . What is it that you want me to do?"

Ah, the young buck comes up to the saltlog. He replied with all the warmth and sincerity within him, eyes glowing, fully facing the boy, the lion in the cage now just a backdrop to his passionate desire to help, to guide, to be a true father to the boy.

"I have, young Marcus Northway, conceived a great interest and faith in you. You are my namesake. I have no son of my own. I have the hope that you might become a wise, intelligent and forceful man and make a contribution to the life of our nation and this poor deluded world. Your Aunt Ida and I would like to help you achieve this goal.

"I do not think you can do so by playing tennis and studying a general course at Ohio State. With Marcus Aurelius and the stoic Epictetus I believe that if you want to become a wrestler you must learn to wrestle. It was . . . arduously . . . so for me. You must aim for a profession. Medicine, or maybe law, are my ideas of professions—unless you have genius hidden in you that makes you sui generis, like Edison or Burbank."

"Not me, Uncle Marcus!"

"No. Ohio State does not, and you must simply let me tell you this and believe me, afford the opportunities for meeting the sort of people necessary to propelling achievement—no more than did the Cleveland Homeopathic College in its day! I made my mark at a fairly late age through medical achievement in the military service, and before and after that had come to know and to serve Presidents, and at the turn of the century found myself in a rich social circle spanning New York and Ohio, and before long married, you see, a wealthy widow. Which, my boy, you might call the Slow Path. Ha. Ho. Yes. Slow and not too damn sure either . . . Ha. Ha ha."

He found his grand nephew beholding him as if he might be, after all, a bit off, odd, and so gave him a jovial clap upon his blue-jacketed shoulder.

"Because of the faith I have in you, Mark, I have made arrangements for your entrance into Yale College. Eh? I am prepared, and happy, to pay your way through to graduation, and then on to a superior school of Medicine or of Law, if that should be your choice, if the scientific studies prove not to be your meat. What is your chief interest, if I may ask, professionally speaking, now?"

"Why," said the lad, making a strange face, shaking his head. "I guess I haven't really thought. I sure never did want to be a doctor, and God knows not a dentist, or a lawyer either, no offense, sir. I just

. . . I have an apprentice job this summer, when I go back home, in Cleveland, in an advertising agency."

He brightened and smiled at Marcus. He was a beautiful lad when lit up. "It seems to me that advertising—as I understand it, moving and selling all the new products that are coming out since the war—is the hottest and most exciting thing going in America, now!"

Marcus frowned. "Yes. Advertising. I do not think that we will find a professional school for that, for advertising. Oh, it is important, I understand your feeling for it, of course. A kind of . . . ah . . . dynamo to the operation of business in our society. The thing is, though, if Business is your interest, you should be in position to run the damn business, not get stuck in the mere promotion of the product."

"Soon they'll be doing it, Uncle Marcus, over radio!"

"Yes. And we will become a nation of morons then. Well, what do you say to my proposal?"

He thought that it had become awfully warm standing here. The odor of the lion wafted to him.

"Gosh, I never thought . . . I thought I'd go along at State, stay in Ohio. I've never lived anywheres else. I mean, it's great here in California, you know, but not like where real people live?"

"'Anywhere,' my boy."

"Huh?"

"We do not say 'anywheres.'"

"Anyhow. Gosh. I would have to be a Freshman all over again? I'd hate that, being a Frosh all over again."

"Yes. Quite right. To enter the Classical course. You would read history, literature and philosophy, and do some science, the experimental method, dear God, what could be more valuable—to see if you have the knack for that."

"I don't! I already flunked Chemistry in high school!"

Marcus raised his eyes to the burnished sky.

"That was then," he said. "I mastered many subjects I thought at first I could not riddle. It is—life is—all a matter of perseverance, Mark. Well. I am sure this is the right path for you, and I am pleased to be able to offer you this help. Talk this over with your parents, and then let me know your decision in the morning. Right? All right! Meanwhile, how would you like to go with me to visit a famous and wonderful man, the genius Luther Burbank, at Santa Rosa up the road here after your family departs? We can re-arrange your travel plans for something so significant, I'm sure."

"Oh . . . Why, sure. That would be okay, I guess."

Marcus turned to salute the sad, hot lion in his cage. Man's power, because he can create his own world, is immense. He put his finger inside his collar where there was sweat, the beginning of an itch. "Here," he said, "let's take these damn coats off, Mark. That's right. Sling it over your shoulder. Why in the holy hell do you imagine we came out today in flannel trousers? Jehoshaphat! Where do you think Albert is hiding? Having a cool beer, I'll bet."

They walked back through the zoo, arm in arm again. Ah yes: chums. And as they walked along and Marcus moved his arm firmly around the boy's body and to his shoulder he could feel from the rhythm of his Systolic function that he would accept, and do it.

12

The next morning, after a breakfast of figs and cream and poached eggs, Tom Northway took him aside to say: "I can see what you are trying to do, and I appreciate it. I r-really do. It is generous, and all. But I must tell you, this has to be the boy's own decision. It's up to him."

"Yes, Tom. All right. Of course it is." Marcus knew he could not count on a push from undisciplined Tom. "If your son does not have the will, Tom, it would not work out anyway, would it? No. But I trust he does and that you will not impede him. Where is the lad?"

"Gone off down the beach walking, to think on it."

"Ah! I should have thought . . ."

"And listen here, Uncle . . . I mean, Marcus. I w-want you to k-know . . ."

"Yes?"

"That we—Mattie and I have decided—We'll be getting out of that house, that b-barn—before long. Move in to a house of our own. I figure in about a y-ye-year . . ."

"Fine, Tom. I am, as my old friend Theodore would say, dee-lighted. It is time, surely, for you to do so. I never imposed that house on you, did I? No. I am no tyrant, Tom. I only mean to help people, as you of all of 'em know, when they need it."

Tom Northway gave a cough, and sneezed and blew his nose, and went off to have a smoke and dribble ashes over his light suit, which seemed to be the only one he had, or at any rate had brought to California.

When young Mark came to him, properly attired, he said, in a boyish yet manly way, "I would like to do it, Uncle Marcus, give it a go, take you up on the deal. I appreciate what you are trying to do for me, and I'll go to Yale. And I will try to live up to your faith in me—and to the name I bear."

The older Marcus Northway embraced the younger one, then arm in arm again they strolled through the gallery of the hotel, the General pointing out his image with Edison and others in the various photographs along the wall.

Later, as he sat smoking and reading the newspaper in the hotel's Writing Room, Mattie—Matilda Northway—suddenly appeared. She was flushed, as if in some stage of parturition. He looked up and smiled at her, so flushed that she looked rather beautiful and when he did so to his immense surprise, nay amazement, of all things she shook her finger at him. He sat back, surprised, so that the wicker chair squeaked.

"Now . . ." she hissed at him. "Now! Now Ida has been after me—the gall of you two! To let Lellie come to Finishing School, for God's sake, in New York! Dear Lord in Heaven! Well, you won't get Lellie—She's too smart and slippery for you—for either or both of you . . ."

"My dear, I did not . . ."

"Hah! You old goat! You insufferable arrogant old quack! How dare you! My son!"

"Yes?"

"You had best remember that he is my—and his father's—son! Not yours!"

"Dear Mattie, we have always been friends, you and I. I am trying to help him, don't you see? Set a course for him superior to the one he is on, using what assets I have . . ."

"I know what you are doing!"

She was, indeed, now beautiful. Her dark eyes gleamed at him, as darkly brown as the eyes of a ferret, full of fire and passion. Her rich hair coiled on her proud head. A handsome, fearful, wounded mother . . . He smiled at her. When he did so he thought that she was going to scream, go into a rage at him.

She glared at him for a moment and turned away and left.

Marcus liked to think of himself as a gentle person, a gentle and restrained man. But in that moment measuring the space where she had been he was filled with the wish that she were his patient back in the Heroic age of medicine and was suffering from such fever and emotion so that he might, as common practice had dictated then, take a lancet and bleed and bleed and bleed her . . .

Instead he relit and puffed at his cigar.

He insisted upon, or ordered, the new arrangement, which Tom and Mattie accepted with little seeming reluctance, Tom himself being a great fan of the genius Burbank and declaring himself jealous that his boy was going to get to meet him.

They took off, then, on a fine June California day, Albert driving them in the Rolls, up the coast road past Los Angeles the first day, then on north through San Francisco and to Santa Rosa.

Burbank greeted them at his home there, where he had but a small plot for his experimentation, and had constant guests and gawkers, such was his incredible fame among all Americans, and immediately had them drive on to his "proving ground" at Sebastopol. There he had six acres of all the wondrous stuff—plums, prunes, potatoes, nuts, the Shasta daisies, all in rows and clumps, all his "new creations." He had a great bonfire going there, the gentle genius burning thousands and hundreds of thousands of rejected trees, shrubs, plants—berry bushes, cherry plants, cacti, flower bulbs, apple and peach trees—that had not yielded the one result he sought, which had not improved themselves.

"Gee, no wonder they call him Wizard," young Mark whispered, rubbernecking, surveying it all, in awe.

"Some say he creates unnatural things, monstrosities. That is not true. Often he does shortcut God's own work, progressing plants naturally but skipping some of their very processes. He does it for the benefit of man, as the millions who love and respect him over the world understand. He is not out of tune but in tune with Nature, helping her, unlocking her, as when you find a new—but always old—natural medicine or way of healing that restores the flesh or the natural function of the body, that gets at the cause not the symptom. He has improved as no other human being in history the Dietary of the Race, and made the world, to boot, more beautiful."

As they go along through the proving ground, Luther smiles at Mark, who smiles back. He is a frail-seeming, sunny-eyed man tieless in shirt and vest and rusty coat, wearing a floppy hat. He is now seventy-one years of age, just one year younger than Marcus Northway. In a way he is friends also with Edison but is not a member of that crowd. He does not know John Burroughs, the naturalist who tramps about with Ford and Al Edison. In Marcus' opinion, Burroughs is merely a writer, one who goes about in Nature, thinks thoughts about her, while Luther holds her keys. Al and Henry Ford came here by train to visit Burbank several years ago, from a convention in San Francisco. Luther met them at the station and showed them around. He loves Al, and Edison averred that visit was the best day of his life. Luther said that Henry stood around like a bewildered dunce and hardly spoke and that Harvey Firestone managed to step on a Quince bush that was just coming into bloom but did not damage it since he was so light of weight. Marcus considered it the best fortune Luther could have that he was here in California across the continent from Henry Ford, who could not so easily appropriate him as he had appropriated, bought out, Edison.

Sunny, calm of eye is Burbank, carrying pruning shears and scalpel, little grafts of things in various pockets. How does he do it? It is like a Homeopath keeping track of the minute record of illness and reaction to medicine of ten thousand people all at once, bouncing here to one and there to another, with hardly a note noted in his Notebook.

He stops to talk to them at a bed of his famous Spineless Cactus that once was thought might reclaim the desert by providing food there for beast and man. In mid-sentence—he is kindly asking Mark his interests, reaffirming in the lad's mind the serious necessity for same—he pauses, cocks his head at a linnet's note. He is keen of ear, and does not smoke or drink. He must, he says, be able to taste and smell like a precision scientific instrument.

"The redwing blackbird is very late in appearing this year," he says, as if that might be the secret, the clue to it all. Gently he inquires if Mark might have some interest in this line of work. He has little help, looks always for strong, intelligent, selfless help.

"It's fascinating," Mark replies. "But I have no training for it."

Luther turns his happy eyes to Marcus. "Ah," he says, as if they shared a rich joke, "who does?"

He gives them four hours of his time, which is extraordinary.

"I received your Thought message, as you did mine," he says to Marcus at parting, back in Santa Rosa. "It was a good time for you to come. I am glad you did. You are fortunate to have such a fine lad for a namesake. He has a good mind and a good heart, I sense. Keep him pruned of folly, Marcus, and rooted in the world, for his spirit seems to lead him to seek upwards, the Ideal, the Cloud lands, eh? If you do, why, maybe—how can we ever know or say?—you'll not be disappointed."

"What did he say about me?" Mark inquired.

"To keep your eye upon the doughnut and not upon the hole."

They laughed.

Luther's mystical strain, Marcus mused on the trip back, his attunement to the waves that are all around us but invisible to and unsensed by most clodhoppers of this universe, came from his mother and was shared, he knew, by his sister, who cared for him before the young wife, who was his secretary prior to conjugality, came. Marcus' own mystic sense waxed and waned but was always strong between Burbank and himself.

Sally Ann, his mother, had it. She knew when old Sam, his father, had died in the field, and went slowly walking out there from the house, by the blueberry bushes, saying goodbye to him as she approached his remains.

Pajarita and he shared this deeply, continually communicating by thought through distances. Marcus was always interested in this phenomenon as it occurred in individuals and was on the lookout for spirits so akin. He had found none of it in the other members of the Northway family now surviving. Looking over at the lad beside him, snoozing as they rolled along, or pretending to, he sensed not an ounce of it in him, in Marcus II.

"Well, it cost an arm and a leg, a fortune, Marcus, to get 'em out here and put 'em up and all, but I thought it was a pleasant enough visit, and of course you got your way with the boy, didn't you?

"I still really do not know why we could not have done the same in Cleveland, but as for myself I was glad to be here, and Mattie seemed to like this old Del as much as I do, though she turned a little bit sour, I thought, right at the end there.

"Oh, but you had to go and see the great Luther Burbank, didn't you? And how is his child wife, so many years younger? That is a scandal. I'm glad the boy came around, and without too much fuss from Tom. I like Tom Northway, after all, the man has a touch of the Irish in him underneath it all. His grandmother was the girl Molly Leary that old Philo cut down from the tree there, my genealogy says, and so Irish and different from your own grandmother Clara. An old, stern German, she was.

"And the girl, Melissa, or Lellie, I believe there is also hope for her.

"Well. The Sea Bass is back on the menu again tonight. I thought it went all right, didn't you? I thought they did not appreciate the breakfasts as they should, I went to a lot of trouble about them, rare fruit and stewed prunes and all. They really did not like the Scrapple, did they? Well, that is an acquired taste. You have to be a pretty good eater, for the Scrapple."

"It all went fine. The breakfasts maybe were a bit late and large for them, as for myself. But don't you worry about it, Ida dear. Let's not bother to dress and go down to the damn Crown Room tonight, if that is all right with you. Let's just relax—order something up. Champagne for two? Eh? Just you and me, right here? Listen to the static on the radio? Look out at the ocean? Pitch a little woo?"

"Why, Marcus, Lovie, what a nice idea!"

And they passed a pleasant evening together in their room under the radish-domed roof of the dear old Del.

13

They returned to Willowstone, their dingy pile in Greenwich, and spent a melancholy fall there as workmen labored at necessary repairs to the roof and chimneys, and Ida speculated on new carpeting and drapes.

One evening in late fall Marcus sat in his study staring at his radio, listening to it, as if it were another person in the room, as it told him of the results of the election. Harding had defeated Cox and was President. Marcus bowed his head and prayed.

He prayed to the Spirit Father, the Informing Intelligence of the universe, to forgive and to help him—to help him if he could in any way be of aid or assistance to bumbling Warren Harding, our leader now, restorer of the Party. Perhaps Marcus could help to allay Harding's inner devils (Warren burped and rumbled his way through life with what he labeled "indigestion" but was simple frustration at having to live with his dreadful wife, called "the Duchess") and to forestall by all means non-violent the demons that would try to prey on him from without, taking the form of men, those demons that Marcus feared did now dance upon Warren's very walls. He prayed that the great Power help him do whatever he could in this direction, just as a true physician strives ever to defeat the Enemy, the ever-lurking itch, Disease . . .

Ah! Warren had taken, he learned, the evil one-eyed Harry Daugherty with him to Washington, and was giving the fool high office, while the Heepish Smith shuttled back and forth between the

Capital and Ohio, keeping the lid on things. God only knew what they were up to . . .

Marcus prescribed himself whiskey, doses-large.

Young Marcus was in his first year at Yale. It seemed difficult for him. He was having tutors in mathematics and in Greek and Latin, though he reported he was doing well in History. He truly did not seem to possess a medical mind, which must be mathematical, analytical and linguistic, as was the Homeopath's. And Mark confessed, even still, that the idea of the Law seemed the dullest possible to him.

Well, Marcus thought, what to do? It would not really do to force the lad into something he did not wish or could not handle. We do not need to create another dentist who suffers every time he has to behold Teeth in a Mouth. Ha ha. Something would emerge, the proper course would reveal itself there at Yale with such fine instruction, in time. Maybe Mark would fall in with the son of someone prominent, a scion or an heir. Such often was the road to achievement in such hallowed halls as those of Yale.

Meanwhile Mark was well set up there, and they had moved back here to Greenwich to be near to him, and he had come to visit them one weekend. Marcus had pulled strings to have him placed in even better quarters, in Wright Hall, for the spring term. They would go and make sure of his room and furnishings, having let him wander in there by himself at first, to make sure of his comfort and happiness.

True to his word, Mark's father Tom Northway had moved his family this fall out of the old rambling wreck of August Krause on Euclid Avenue and into a solid house, redbrick with white trim like all those other Shaker Heights houses, on Carleton Road. It was in fact the nicest part of that dull city of Cleveland. Tom had taken a great loan from the bank to do this. Marcus planned to visit him soon and to present his younger cousin with a nice sheaf of Standard Oil stock which he could convert to cash. (They would let it be unbeknownst to Mattie.) Thus he could, if nothing else in his life, own his own damn house!

Then, Marcus vowed, Tom Northway would be forever after on his own . . .

How tangled life got, and in what patterns. Now he was trying to help the son realize whatever potential he had. (Much, much greater than that of his foolish father!) He mused, the memory coming to him, enjoying it, relishing recalling the details of it, as an artist might remember painting a certain picture, or a potter remember taking up the rough clay to make a pot.

When he had first come to the aid of his cousin Tom, son of his own father's younger (and except for non-notable Civil War service and imprisonment, shiftless) brother Elijah "Lige" Northway, Tom was a year younger than was the boy now whom he had subsequently named Marcus Northway II. The year Tom Northway came to him was 1895. Tom was nineteen years of age. Already Marcus had engaged the suite at the Waldorf.

Yes. He had met Edison in 1885 and gone in venture with him on the California deal a few years later. For he was not poor then and was successful and respected in his practice. Now Al's son Charles kept also in the Waldorf; in his digs he had many large stuffed owls. This was a quirk he must have taken from Al, who likewise had the bad habit of stuffing birds and of sticking them around in various rooms of his Winter Home. However that may be.

He did not remember how Tom made his way from Ashtabula to New York that time in 1895. He supposed he must have sent him train fare. The lad walked and gawked around Manhattan for a while before he found his way up to him, quite late for his appointment. His eyes were brightest blue, a little popped due to his persisting thyroid tendency, his hair blond, his cheeks ruddy and his suit cheap blue serge. He was the epitome of the Country Come to Town.

Marcus produced cigars and his silver cutter, which seemed to fascinate Tom, and poured out glasses of whiskey. Tom declined the cigar. Marcus asked him if he'd had whiskey before. "No," he said.

"Ah, but you did not grow up in Whiskeyville, did you?"

"No, sir. I have always wanted to see that place. Is it like our Ohio country? Ohio's all I've ever known."

"Some like. That northern Ohio soil is better for a greater variety of crops, more of the common crops, though it can't beat that Rome Valley country in my state for growing spuds. But hops, there, mostly is the crop. From which they make—this! No—Wines and gin were mostly what they made, as I recall. You really have not taken whiskey before?"

"Really no."

"Well, that's all right. Drink it. I am surprised you were not given it medicinally even as a boy. This is the best Kentucky bourbon whiskey. I drink it for pleasure as well as for its medicinal value. Smooth, isn't it? Eh? Now, Tom, you want to be able to afford a glass of good whiskey when you'd like, and to afford a place of your own that is respected and respectable and not full of cow and chicken shit to drink it in without asking any other jack-fool's leave. Most of all, boy, you want to do something with whatever's in you that's worth a damn, make something of yourself, do something useful that will win you the regard and reward of others. Do you hear?"

"Yes, sir."

"Do you have ambition, Tom? Do you plan to be on the side of those—chiefly myself—who wish to make something of the Northway name?"

"I sure do aim to do my best, Uncle Marcus."

"I am not your uncle, Tom. I am your elder cousin. But call me 'Uncle Marcus.' That's all right. I like it. What are your intentions, Tom?"

"Well, sir, I have me a fairly good job now and I figure that . . ."

"My God, boy! You don't say, 'I have me.' Faulty grammar is a mark of ignorance. It will hold you back from the trust of those who matter. A good job, you say? Jehoshaphat, boy, do you call assisting a veterinarian there in Ashtabula a good job? What kind of future is there in it? Can you even replace the man you work for? Have you studied Veterinary Medicine? Have you forgotten the wisdom of Epictetus the Stoic, who said if you want to be able to wrestle, learn to wrestle? No! By all that's holy . . ."

"I never heard of Epic-whosis, Uncle . . ."

"Eh? Ah? Of course you haven't! You suffer from a stupid lack of education. That must be rectified, like this whiskey! And a field chosen! I am going to have another whiskey. I see you still have some. A glass of whiskey isn't meant to have its rim licked, Tom. It's not mouthwash. That's right! Good lad! Now I'll pour another, and we'll figure on this together.

"Do you realize, young Tom Northway, that I am the only man in this Northway family to my knowledge in America ever to get out of the fields and gain a professional education, not counting the plague of ministers, and become a doctor or the equivalent, say a judge?"

The boy looked at him as if maybe he was both. Marcus did not consider that Tom had patience, aptitude or talent for becoming a physician. He did not believe that he ever really would be ambitious. They decided on dentistry. It was a branch of the profession; the training was less rigorous. To be a dentist would be practical and professional as well.

"I," he said, "will help you to your goal."

"Thank you, Uncle Marcus, very m-much."

Marcus told Tom he would have to work; he could not use him for carte blanche. He told him he was lucky, for he, Marcus Northway, had had no Dutch uncle. He told him he had found the iron in the Northway blood. He told him he had to aim to surpass his father. Every man does. "Much as I love your father, Lige Northway, Tom— and who would not love such a jolly, gregarious soul—I know he is not cut out to be able to help you much."

As he recalled it now, the lad had then said something sharp to him as if he had put down his father, poor old Lige, something about how he was sure he would never surpass his father in regard to the love and affection that all felt for him. Tom Northway stammered as he spoke. A later examination revealed that he had no physical problem; he did not stutter, he stammered. Marcus had told him that as part of his progress he must take steps—breathing and diction exercises—to conquer this nervous stammer.

So Tom went to Case Institute, in Cleveland, in Dental Study and did all right as a student, although in subsequent practice he had been somewhat lazy. In the picture of him as that boy which Marcus retained from that fateful interview Tom seemed to have straw in his hair, and peach fuzz on his ruddy face. His son Mark, now, was tons smoother than was Tom and no doubt would become a gentleman. By God, Marcus thought, suddenly seeing himself at that age, I was the rough one of us!

He got up and went and retrieved a box of old photographs he kept of the family. Here was one of a bunch of boys on a wagon load of hay—he supposed he must have been one of them. Ah, here was one: marked "May 1864, Marcus A. Northway": what a lean young Rough of sixteen years! Why, Sally Ann must have cut his hair with pruning shears!

He had no real memory of that Self at all.

Yes—It had been a long road from that rough boy to, say, when he had met the great T. A. Edison in the City then in 1885.

Edison was at the height of his fame already, and playing businessman with an office on Fifth Avenue when Marcus strolled over to pay his respects to him.

They got on famously from the start. The Homeopath took the liberty at once of examining Edison's ears. Marcus could attest, contrary to what you hear from those who only speculate, that Edison did not pretend to deafness as a shield to his work. It may have been an asset to him, letting him cut out noise and work with the single company of his thoughts, but he did not cherish the deafness. Nor could his hearing have ever been restored by any means or methods medicinal, operative or manipulative. The poor fellow had his ears torn forward in his youth and had developed through the years a mastoidal problem that kept making his hearing worse and worse. He genuinely could not hear. He chose to make a virtue of it, taking God's curse or gift to him as beneficence in his genius mind. Always in his deafness he presented a kindly mien to the world. Yet even today, Marcus knew, and knew medically, T. A. Edison grew more deaf and there was no cure for it and it was no pose or sham of the Gentle Giant.

"Call me Al," he said right then and there in his office on Fifth Avenue. "All my pals do. And what do folks call you?"

"Doctor Northway, generally. But my given name is Marcus."

"Ho!" the Wag laughed, beaming at another farm boy who had done all right. "'Doctor,' is it? Ha! Ho ho! Well, you've been around, I reckon. I'll call you Marco. Okay? Marco Polo! And if 'Al' don't come easy to your lips you can call me Kubla Khan! Say, do you chew? No, you wouldn't—Here, here's some fine cigars a fella sent me, or he says they're fine, he does. This fella Dick I've been negotiating with. Last name of 'Dick.' Ha! Ho—"

They were at that time thirty-six and thirty-seven years of age, Edison one year older than Marcus Northway, and were exactly of a height together, as the many poses of them together in photographs in various years of friendship testified.

They smoked the cigars from the fellow, indifferent at best, and talked for several hours that first meeting. Talked of California. Al needed a Big Light to turn on for his rejuvenation somewhere significant other than New Jersey or New York.

They spoke of other subjects, some medical. Edison was immensely interested, as Marcus long had been, in the subject of potency. Marco Polo was able to enchant him with knowledge of the subject from ancient China to the present. The subject provided for them a basis of lasting interest, and Marcus had been able to be of service to him in its regard through the years. In 1889 Al married Mina Miller, a socialite years younger than himself.

Thinking of all this, he thought he must write to Mark. He must inspire him. Strange he had not thought to do so before. Ida had written Mark a chatty note or two and he had set down procedures for the lad to follow in avoiding germs in dormitory life . . . Surely the boy would benefit from knowing the story of his own study, his arduous quest for learning . . . He uncapped his pen and pulled sheets to him and, in a moment, began to write:

Dear Mark,

I took up my studies at your age at the Cleveland Homeopathic Hospital College, the first and oldest Homeopathic college in the nation. My course was perhaps easier than that you are following now, for I had my goal clearly set and my purpose narrowed to Physician from the start. I was always interested in healing, and in the various remedies in the family, my first memory being of drinking some bitter tea, which I now believe to have been Throatwart, and feeling the effect of its tonic power.

Even as I began my studies, the dreadful era of Heroic Medicine was well on the wane, and Homeopathy dominant, having more colleges and advocates than the Regular or Allopath school.

As noted, I was from a boy cognizant of and subject to folk remedies—Catnip tea, Honey flour, peppermint, all kinds of herbs—but Homeopathy is not that. It was founded by a German, Hahnemann, in Vienna, 100 years ago, under the principle: Similia, similibus curanter. (Let likes be cured by likes.) (Opposed, as you can see, to Allopatheia, or the application of external influences to symptoms.) Hahnemann thought that disease could be cured by giving very small doses of drugs which in a healthy person would lead to the incurring of symptoms like those of the disease, thus creating a small case of the disease, or Enemy, which the body could fight. Homeopaths believe in the Spirit, in the power in and of Nature, and in the Rightness of the System of the Body and its relation parallel to all systems. The small doses H. called Infinitesimals.

He was of course ridiculed.

By my own time my Crowd had much changed its tune. The need for pragmatism and cooperation in the entire profession was always apparent to me, and I have done my part pragmatically and had for the most part the respect of both sides. I twice consulted with Sir William Osler on cases (Ida McKinley, Edith Roosevelt) and counted him as friend. It was clearly stated 50 years ago in America that Homeopathy must be redefined to include only the Law of Similars and to abandon the insufficient doses. I and others have done so in our time, and I myself have experimented with several practices, surgical to mystical, across the board, and with many medicines.

Ever I have been guided, like the wise Edison and genius Burbank whom you now know, by common sense and Test of Application.

My point, Mark, is that with proper initial study life provides later many opportunities for the exercise of one's own distinctive thought and contributions in one's field. I pray that you find that field, that it be duly professional and worthwhile and worthy of your talent and our name, and that its crops be abundant.

I remain your loving Sponsor, glad always that as we have said, our Hearts beat as One.

> Ever yours,
> Uncle Marcus

After re-reading the letter and addressing it to New Haven and sealing and stamping it, when she came in he said to Ida: "Do you think I might— mean actually, by law—adopt the boy?"

"No," she said.

He put on his hat and coat against the chill wind and went to mail it.

14

In February, cold but clear, they motored over to New Haven to visit Mark in his new digs at Yale College.

Ida was dressed fit to kill for the occasion. Upon arrival Marcus took a photograph of Mark and her standing in front of the dormitory, Wright Hall, by a Rampant Lion. She wore a padded-silk brocade coat with a fur collar and sleeves of fur and with a fringe as on a large rug along the bottom. She must, he thought, have had the coat made to order. When developed, the photograph could be inscribed "Boy, Lion and Bear."

Ida also wore a great curved hat like that of Napoleon and strings and bands of pearls and a dozen of her rings. Mark was well turned out, as he greeted them, in a homburg which seemed too old for him but which he must have purchased himself and managed to wear rakishly, and the cashmere overcoat and scarf Marcus had bought for him. Marcus himself was bundled up and with some salve in his nose against a slight abstract feeling of coldishness.

Albert had polished the silver Rolls Royce so it gleamed, and they made a good show as they pulled up. Mark's room was on the third floor of the ivy-covered dorm. Looking down at them from there, at first, he looked a bit sad, or lonely, displaced, Chinese. Maybe it was the narrowness of the windows in the bleak old building.

Ida, Dowager Empress of China, as she appeared to be, did not come up into the dormitory, not seemly for a lady. Marcus went up with Mark to see his room and thought it quite appropriate. Albert hauled up the things they had brought. The lad had mentioned a slight interest in taking up the sport of polo, a rather expensive avocation, but Marcus wanted to be indulgent of his happiness now. He had gotten for him a supple polo mallet made in England similar to the one used by the Prince of Wales. With it came jodhpurs, helmet and boots of the finest leather, also made in England.

"Gosh," Mark said, "I'm not even sure that—"

"Give it a go, sport," Marcus said, attempting to use the vernacular of the time and place. "There is nothing like good equipment to encourage performance."

He went down the hallway to the bathroom to relieve himself as Albert went back down to help Dennis bring up the walnut study desk they had strapped to the side rack of the car. In her own concern to create pleasant surroundings for the lad Ida had brought in the trunk a pair of silver and ivory lamps bought on her trip to Rome, Florence and Venice a year ago. Marcus had suggested they were too ornate for the boy, but she insisted. Bless her good heart, she wanted him to have them because they were favorite objects of hers among her possessions. Also she had brought him a rather unbelievable silk-brocade Chinese bedspread which might be taken for a cousin to her coat.

As a final indulgence Marcus had brought the boy an onyx and ivory-necked banjo for his recreation hours when not studying, a step up from the ukelele.

As he made water, Marcus hummed a tune, remembering his own brief ukelele days: "If you like-a me like I like-a you and we like-a both the same, I'd like to say this very day—do do da dee dee dee—"

Coming back along the hall he heard a voice, a somewhat snide young voice, from within Mark's room. "'Sport' is right," it said. "We'll have to call you Marco Polo!"

Entering, he peered at this slim young snob.

"I am General Northway," he greeted him. "Often myself called, as a matter of fact, 'Marco Polo' by the great Edison."

"Hey, wow!" the young fellow said and came right around him

without offering a name or a hand and departed the room, having to make his way down the hall crab-like as Albert and Dennis approached with the desk.

Marcus shook his head and went to look down out the window. Ida, below in her finery, was engaging two young men in coquettish conversation. God, what havoc La Pajarita would wreak if ever she caught on to the existence of Yale College and other such havens of young, rich youth.

"Who was that rude fellow? A Morgan or a Rockefeller?"

"No, Uncle Marcus. He's just a Taft from Cincinnati."

"I could have told him I visited Germany for his grandfather, whom we called, that is, Theodore and I called, 'Fat Boy.'"

"Well, I sure am glad you didn't."

"Nor did I thrash him with my cane. I will leave that to you, to deal with his rudeness and lack of respect."

"He's not a bad guy. Really. Okay? We're both Ohio boys. Gosh, he's about the only friend I have around here."

"Oh? And what is the situation with the Clubs?"

"I don't really know. They don't exist, as far as I'm concerned. Or I don't, to them, I guess."

"Well. But your studies are improving? Eh? And your study habits. Your education is the main thing! Though we hope you will be—are—happy here. It is a pleasant room, isn't it? A bit larger than most, I believe. You are happy here, or happy enough, aren't you?"

"Sure. I'm fine. And I do appreciate—"

He looked around the room, at the lamps, the polo stick, the desk, the banjo.

"Of course. Now let's go down and rejoin your Aunt Ida. Did I tell you we are dining with the Dean? Taking him to dinner? Yes—"

They walked down the stairs arm in arm. "*Perseverant dabitur*," Marcus said to him, voicing the Latin motto he had come up with to go on the Northway Coat of Arms which Ida had had created. 'Twas a masterpiece, too, with more than the usual parts and elements, including, Marcus thought, at least one lion or rose too many.

"You bet," Mark says. "*Hic haec hoc.*"

Be a Northway, boy! Marcus says, in his heart.

Dear God, was he the only Northway with some iron in his pizzle?

The next day they drove down to Washington and arrived with enough light left to visit the monuments and the cemetery at Arlington.

Albert took a picture of them at the Lincoln Memorial. Marcus turned away a moment, controlling his sentimentality, feeling tears well up, before Mr. Lincoln. His sad, strange, good face. The Preservation of the Union, so that the Destiny of the Nation could be realized. Surely the greatest nation in history, and surely ever greater—!

"After law school, you might consider politics," he said to Mark. "Ohio has furnished many leaders to the nation, many presidents."

"Hey, okay!" Mark laughed, and winked at Ida, who also laughed. They mistook it for a joke.

At Arlington Ida noticed that he was wearing spats. "Why," she said, "you haven't worn spats in years!"

"Against the cold," he explained.

As they walked, now Ida and young Marcus arm in arm, Marcus retreated to the car and produced three tumblers of whiskey. Albert and Dennis sipped theirs up front. Albert had told him he was retiring this year, back to a small spread he had bought in Colorado. Marcus had said that he would visit him there but would not climb onto a horse. Dennis would remain with him. Albert was a bit younger than himself; it was hard to think of him as retiring, leaving his service. Of course he would be hard at it, ranching there, the tough old black Rough Rider.

"I shall miss you, Albert," he said, sitting in the silver Rolls, two old pals drinking tumblers of whiskey, Albert next to his loyal son.

"And I you, General," Albert said.

Walking back towards them, Ida's eyes were sparkling, her cheeks rosier than ever, and Mark Northway seemed the most vital, precious boy alive.

They stayed overnight in the District of Columbia.

In late afternoon, as Ida rested and the boy went to his appointment with the senior senator from Ohio, Marcus slipped away, with Albert driving and Dennis riding shotgun.

Old Ike greeted him at the door of the White House.

"He was here, but he has slipped out, General."

"Does he slip out often?"

"Yes, sir, and she slips in some, too, truth be told." Ike shook his head, like an old sad dog. "But she's not in town now."

"Where is he likely to be?"

"Maybe with the Boys. He likes to go over there, afternoons, evenings, to take a hand."

He shook hands with Ike and left, giving instruction to Albert to drive to H Street.

The house was small. He got out to go up the walk, taking his cane along. It seemed to him to have gotten colder, on the edge of bitter.

"Watch the hood ornament. Hell, watch the wheels," he instructed his troops. "This bunch will steal anything if you look away for a minute."

"Can't I come in, General?" Albert said.

"No." He did not want it to seem as if he needed an army. "I will give the Yell if you are needed."

A Negro butler greeted him at the door.

"No," he said. "The Chief's not here right now."

Marcus pushed by the pretentious little fellow and went on in. Harry Daugherty was at the table with a few others. Jess Smith was not there. The so-called head of the so-called Bureau of Investigation, Means, a big moron in a derby, lounged lugubriously against a wall, giving him the eye.

Daugherty was spading with another gent at the table.

"Take a seat, General," he said. "You are welcome. Take a card."

Marcus stood and beheld him. Daugherty had a peculiar look, the effect of having the one blue eye and the one brown eye. Actually the eye was opaque, a wall-eye. (*Leukoma.*) Marcus sat and took a card. He bet them both, spading. The next round he would not bet as he divined Daugherty had an ace. He laughed and put his cards down.

"What's the joke?" Daugherty said. They did not like each other, little tinpot Harry Daugherty and Dr. Marcus Northway. Marcus handed him back the bill he'd won.

"I never play cards," he said, "because I have the ability to see, that is, to sense, what is in any hand."

"You could make a fortune in this town," Daugherty said, wall-eyeing at him. He, and all the others, were drinking whiskey, illegal of course. Harry Daugherty did not worry about the law since he was Attorney General of the United States. And ran the Gang.

"I have made a fortune otherwise."

"Yeah. Terrific. So you're on the Chief's trail?" he said, continuing to spade with the other fellow, spading simply being seeing who had the highest spade. Even Ohio boys could play it. "He's out shopping this afternoon, I believe. Out shopping with the Duchess. He's a family man, Doc. We are restoring the virtues of the Family, restoring family values to the country. Why'd you come by here? Ike tell you he was here?"

Marcus rose. "I wanted to see you, Daugherty."

"Yeah?"

"Yes."

"So?"

"You're nothing, Daugherty. Warren Harding made you. Oh, I know you think you made him. Now it is your responsibility—your deep responsibility and damn it, your privilege—to help him. I want you to know I hold you responsible for what happens—"

"What the hell you think I'm doing, Northway, with every ounce of my soul and body? Hell, I love the guy!"

"The *guy* is the President of the United States. You are spading. Drinking whiskey, breaking the nefarious law that you should be working to repeal! God knows what else that you—all of you Ohio skunks—are doing, in regard to that! Sitting there getting paid off—"

"By God! You'll take that back!"

The large man, Means, moved towards him. Marcus raised his cane.

"He's got men in the car outside, niggers in uniform," someone said.

Daugherty sat at the table, flushed and angry. "Take it easy, Northway," he said. "There's always more than meets the eye, you know."

"Yes. Of that I am sure. You may take my warning, as coming from good Americans, those with regard for Warren Harding, Daugherty. And, speaking of meeting the eye, have you ever sought medical advice about that eye? It would seem to me, upon casual observation, to be susceptible of treatment, not surgical but perhaps medicinal. I know a fine ophthalmic clinic. How much sight do you have in it, if any?"

"I see good, Doc, good as I need to. Warren's dad—ain't he one like you? Hell, he offered to operate on it! My God! I like it fine the way it is. It excites the ladies, eh, Means?"

He winked the good blue one, creating an even odder effect.

"Gentlemen. Daugherty," Marcus Northway said, and left, to their general laughter, aimed at himself, he had no doubt. Scoundrels!

"Did the President receive you?" Ida inquired.

"No. He was out shopping with Mrs. Harding."

"I thought he wanted to see you about Brazil. Oh, I am so looking forward to going there!"

"Yes. We will make a formal appointment later, I am sure. This was not about that."

"Well, what was it about, then?"

"I wanted to warn him."

"Of what, for Gracious sakes?"

He looked at her.

"I don't exactly know, Ida. A deep feeling I have—as if the Itch were going to erupt within me. Somehow I feel that Warren Harding is in danger."

"He is always in danger, that big handsome sloppy fellow, of playing the fool. It's not your worry, your concern, is it? Do not get some obsession on me, Marcus, in your older age. Are your bowels right?"

He stared at her, then had to smile. Not a bad diagnosis. Turned to go into his study.

"Don't go off in there and spend all evening drinking whiskey."

"I'm going to write."

"Yes. Write a bit, and drink a bit. I know. I know. I know."

Oh yes, Ida, my dear sweet Lutie's nurse, you know. You remember, and you know now. Here's to you, Ida, he thought, lifting the glass to his lips for a swallow. Here's to you, you bear!

Sitting at his desk, he took sheets and wrote:

To the Editor of the *World*:

The laws depriving the people of this country of freedom through Prohibition brought about by men and women who have been mysteriously financed—and who, therefore, have had a great incentive to push obnoxious legislation against a great and real Majority of the people by devious methods—were at last carried through from state to state, resulting in the Eighteenth Amendment.

After a trial of two years the values of alcohol in its various combinations, prepared from the vineyards of the country, from the hops fields and farms of barley, wheat and rice, have been supplanted by Poisonous materials of all sorts . . .

From whence and from whom came the money to ordain such an imposition upon the people? Who are they? I venture to prophesy that its Congressional advocates at least will have a long vacation at the end of their present terms . . .

Let each citizen seek his physician and obtain from him his professional opinion as to the value of the various preparations of alcohol in sickness! Beer and wine only are now discussed! Nonsense! Beer is scarcely used in sickness, and but little wine. The brittle thread of life is held in various crises by stronger stuff! Whiskey is what is required . . .

He awoke later that night to Ida's shaking him as he sat in the chair at the desk. He had fallen asleep writing and was embarrassed.

15

The next month the naturalist Burroughs died, at the age of 84. Everyone thought, as Burroughs did, that he would live forever. Marcus had heard that Burroughs knew Emerson. Recently Burroughs had gone on a Tramp, as they called it—the Vagabonds, they called themselves—with Ford and Edison and Firestone, going through towns with banners flying from the Ford cars advertising Firestone tires. Warren Harding was along with them, camping in the woods, being photographed, bloviating around the camp fire while Al dozed off. It was truly hard to believe that he was President when he did things like that. Of course, our nation of morons loved it!

Marcus had met Burroughs only once, that was in Fort Myers there with Edison in 1914. He was a lively bearded gnome. Marcus had read some of his stuff. Burroughs could and would write whole essays on Fish or Birds or Apples. Yes, apples. Marcus believed that apples were the fellow's favorite. He would call 'em noble, man's best friend, putting Apple over Dog! Oh yes—

In December he went into the City to view an opera with La Pajarita.

"So she is back?"

"Yes. Back from Europe, with much, she says, to tell about. I have not seen her now for a year."

Ida pouted badly. He would have to bring her a purse or hat, or both. "You do not enjoy the opera," he said to her.

"Maybe I would now. Hell, I like music, Marcus!"

"Well, do you wish to come, and meet her, and go with us to the opera? It is a good one, with lots of action—'The Masked Ball.'"

"No. Go on. I will let you have your fantasy."

He thrilled to the sense of her, her passion for the story of Gustave, Verdi's strange story, the illicit love, the guilt, set in a time when true love could only be attained at terrible sacrifice. He touched her shoulder, and she shivered, and looked and smiled at him, and went back to raptly watching the characters on stage, soaking in the music and the dramatic rhythm of the whole. He was glad that he lived in such a civilized time. Never had things, for him, seemed in such perfect balance.

At the end of the Yale Spring term, he and Mark had dinner together at Marcus' Club in New York City. They had agreed to visit, just the two of them, at the end of each term and to assess it. Marcus told Mark of his anti-Prohibition activities, in speeches, appearances and writings, attacking it from the medical viewpoint, as they dined on roast beef and trimmings and shared an aged bottle of Bordeaux. The lad seemed stiff, or tired, hardly laughed or smiled. At brandy time Marcus said to him, "How did your grades in your courses come out? Have you received them yet?"

"Passably. I passed everything, me and the tutors, even Greek. I am not returning there, Uncle Marcus. I hate it. I have no friends. I'm not a polo but a tennis player, and I have no time for that. I am incompetent in science and I hate the idea of the Law, I know it's not the field for me, and—Oh hell. I'm really terribly sorry."

Mark Northway looked as if he was going to cry.

"Well. I am glad that you feel you can . . . Ah . . . Oh my. That you can tell me man to man. You are sure? I mean, such tiredness of spirit after hard mental work is not unusual. I myself was called to a case in which . . . "

"No! I'm sure. I am positive. Certain. And . . . so . . . damn . . . sorry . . . to be . . . letting you down . . . "

"I am sorry too. Indeed. You are making a great mistake. A great mistake. Not only in the studies—Why, young Taft, and so many others of important families, so many contacts in the nation, so much future possibility of preferment—"

"But they're not my friends. I'm not one of them."

"By God, has anyone slandered us, insulted you, or our good name? Jehoshaphat—"

"Oh, it's not like that. They just mostly give me a royal pain in the ass, Uncle Marcus. The thing is, I want to go home. I really do. And that is what I'm going to do."

"Where? Back to Ohio State? Sweet Jesus, boy!"

"No, sir. Not State. I mean, I'm not sure. Back to Ohio though. I want to go to college, just somewhere else, somewhere that's my own choice. Dad sent me off to State, and then you and Aunt Ida sent me off to Yale, as Prince Marcus Northway II, in some role I just can't play. I don't know. I have another summer job in the advertising agency, at home, in Cleveland. I guess I'll just take it from there, and roll with it."

Marcus Northway looked at him, the handsome replica, as he had thought, of himself. He tried to control both the sentimentality and the anger welling up in him.

"I hope that you do, find the right place. On your own. I truly do. Yes. You know that you will ever have the love and the support of myself and your Great-aunt Ida."

Ida would be furious.

"Yes. Sure. I appreciate . . . All you've—But I'm so damn sick of saying 'I appreciate'—"

"Here. We Northways are sentimental sometimes, I fear, but we don't do that. Waiter! Here—Do you have another bottle of this Bordeaux?"

"None for me, Uncle Marcus. I've reached my limit."

"Oh, you have, have you? Well, I have not. We did not have such as this fine Red from our grapes there in Whiskeyville. You had better have another glass, my boy—Mark. For . . ."

For he would in all probability, now, by his own young, foolish and selfish choice, never taste such a rare vintage in his life again.

The next fall Mark went to another college, a small college in mid-Ohio. He wrote Marcus that he was on the tennis team and taking a "general course" of study. He would graduate from there in just a year and planned to go on into the field of advertising or sales.

"Well, it just shows you can't make a spoon out of a horn, a purse from a sow's ear—"

"The boy had potential, remarkable qualities—"

"Can't make someone what he can't be," Ida went on. She was remarkably more understanding of the lad than he thought she would be. Well, their hearts had not beat as one. How foolish, to think they really had. He was too old for such romantic conceits! He made a sour face, with the thought that if ever their hearts had beaten in unison they had damn well ceased to do so . . . .

"Do not be resentful, Marcus," Ida said. "That is not Christian. And it is not like you. Of course there is nothing harder than to try to help someone and have a back turned on you. It makes any of us mad. But the boy tried. It wasn't in him. Maybe a little later on, when he grows a bit more along his own line—"

"Pish, and posh. And flap, and doodle too."

As young Mark Northway had walked away from him that evening, beautiful boy whose almond-eyed, roman-nosed visage so emulated his own, walked away from him under the street lamps of the city, going in another direction away from him, something— some hope he'd had—dwindled down and died in him.

It was 1923. In two months he would be seventy-five years of age.

It was strange, yes, wondrous strange, to reflect that by all odds only another quarter century of this life remained to him.

For a moment he let himself feel lonely and alone. For a moment he was swiped at—a glancing blow to the head and heart—by funk and fear.

Well, his heart was strong, and beat in unison with itself. There was much to do. If much was taken, much remained! Prohibition must be repealed, or at least the physician's right upheld to use whiskey freely in medical cases! His reputation was to be regained, given the polish and luster it deserved! California was to be conquered, the Bailey-Northway stamp put upon it!

What else? Eh? Eh?

That'll do, by God, for openers, he replied to himself, and after that we'll see what else turns up—

This assertion caused him to smile, and then he laughed out loud and gave himself a wink. (If others had been there to see him laughing and winking to himself they would have thought him for the moment possessed, or a half-wit, a dervish or a maniac.)

But no one was there, and he kept on smiling and chuckling and nodding his head with its now-wild locks of white, and bent over and began to massage his calves and thighs to make sure the blood was flowing right.

THREE

16

At Warren Harding's request, and to Ida's immense pleasure, they voyaged to Rio de Janeiro to represent the United States at the Brazilian Exposition. They had ambassador status and had an open touring car and servants at their beck. Their duties were but ceremonial, and Marcus had opportunity to investigate the drinking habits of those aboard ship and later in Brazil, concluding that the United States would soon be at a loss commercially in the world by denying access to alcohol aboard its vessels on the high seas. In Rio, Ida bought mostly wall hangings, jewelry and vases.

Marcus wrote articles for the newspapers in America demanding the right of physicians to prescribe the unlimited use of whiskey for the bridging of disease; and when the District Court in New York City became the first court in the nation so to decree, he took it as a personal victory.

He spent much of June in California, warming more and more to San Diego as a locus for resettling, and looked at several properties in that town and across the bay in Coronado. He leaned towards the peninsula as more unsettled and susceptible to shaping, as he and Lutie years before had helped in significant ways to shape the fledgling community of Fort Myers in Florida after Krause's death and their union. She had shown him how one's money might make a difference and allow one to leave a lasting impression, as the long palm-lined street named for her and the statue of her at the crossroads there yet attested.

Roaming in San Diego on his own, as Ida stayed East to consult with various genealogical experts on the grandeur and nobility of Northways past, Marcus chanced to notice in the press that a prominent Bullfiddle, as he called them, one of those damn "Christian" propagandists for Prohibition, was speaking outdoors in Balboa Park. He made his way there that evening and, not believing that the Bullfiddles should have their way in the duping of the public, rose and took on the fellow as he spoke. The fellow was some startled at his forcefulness, his logic and his volume.

"Prohibition," Marcus proclaimed to the large crowd gathered around the gazebo there, "in these years of its tyranny has had deadly—I say, deadly—effect in its withdrawing of whiskey, the stimulant above all others in the crises of diseases."

"Who says so?"

"I, Dr. Northway, former Surgeon General of New York, say so! At least half the doctors in the country say whiskey is necessary to their practice. The others are either inexperienced or culpable in neglecting their cases!"

Boos and applause. "It is larger than a medical question," the Bullfrog on the platform bellowed, catering to the Christian vote.

"Yes! Quite right! Americans will not much longer stand to be treated as schoolboys by a slight majority, if that, of the people and by servile Congressmen! We were not drunkards before this damnable Prohibition law but the strongest people in the world!"

"It is not a medical or a political issue but a Christian issue!" roared the Bryan toady.

"Jesus," roared back Marcus Northway, "as my faith understands Him, was Himself Physician, and would gladly heal and by means of any agency—be it water, wine or whiskey—if they'd had the stuff—whichever might be handiest. He would use whiskey medicinally, if He were to return to our age now . . . "

"Oh sinful! Sacrilege! Heathen . . . "

"Oh hypocrisy! I tell you, sir . . . "

At this point Dr. Northway's voice gave out, and he could not continue shouting but had to repair to his car for a libation of whiskey mixed with honey for his throat. Many congratulated him and shook his hand, and one fellow in politics and business in the city there invited him to speak on this same subject in San Diego in October, pleasing him greatly.

Upon his return, Ida, somewhat discouraged by finding Tories in the Revolutionary War in the family line, sat and drank a sherry with him as he sipped his whiskey. She hardly ever drank but did like champagne and sometimes sherry or the Bailey's Irish Cream, all nice and soothing and fattening. She had become recently even heavier.

"If we should go to live in San Diego," she said, sipping at her Bristol Cream, "I would want a bit of money—" By Bit of Money she meant a large amount—"for causes."

"What causes?"

"Whatever they have that need money so that you be President of the Cause and have your name—our name—put on the front of the Program. Don't they have a zoo?"

"It's pretty well established. I believe they need a new monkey cage. 'Ida B. Northway is the charming and wealthy new president of the Monkey Section of the San Diego Zoo.'"

"Hah."

"Well, they also have a Symphony Orchestra, I think, not as well established. What kinds of programs would you have them play, Rag or Jazz? 'This evening's program is due to the kind generosity of Dame Ida B. Northway, who studied Asian music while leading the Japanese in Tokyo in singing the *Star-Spangled Banner*.'"

"I'm proud of that, all right!"

"'The first program of its kind devoted to the jazz compositions of the American composer Scott Joplin . . .'"

"Good idea, Marcus! Throw a few Americans in with your Mozarts and your Rooshians! They'd do it, too, in California! There's a progressive spirit there! Well, are you writing your talk for them there in October? Read it to me, Lovie. I think you are doing important work, and I know you want it to be good, so that you can get a leg up on being a Leader there."

"Yes." Marcus brightened. "Actually I will first give the talk here, at a meeting here in the Waldorf, then in San Diego, or actually in Coronado. They have arranged for the auditorium of the Del Coronado."

"Where she danced!"

"Yes. Ahem. First, you see, I take a crack at that scoundrel Harry Daugherty . . . "

"What is the title of it, Marcus?"

"'Prohibition Enforcement Viewed as Interference With Medical Freedom.'"

"Is that as snappy as you can get it?"

"Yes. It is."

He went and got the speech and returned and sat, adjusting his pince-nez.

"'Ladies and Gentlemen, Members of the Press: The report published September 13 in the papers of the country, stated to have come from Attorney General Daugherty . . . '"

"Dirty little man!"

"'. . . is a matter for serious consideration. If we look back to the time when our Government was first formed it might be entertaining, at least, to know just how many Presidents have been teetotalers . . .'"

"Hah. That's good, Marcus! Didn't you say McKinley took about a gallon a day, of the whiskey?"

"'If it should please Mr. Daugherty to place on the witness stand, were it possible, our Congressmen, Senators and the various executives of our respective States, just to answer one question—Do they absolutely refuse, socially, alcoholic beverages of various forms offered to them on various occasions?—the answer would be . . .'"

"Himself, you said, sitting there at cards with his glass of whiskey!"

"'. . . interesting and valuable. On a recent tour through South America . . .'"

"What a good idea, to use that, Marcus . . . "

"'. . . during the Brazilian Exposition there, we had a fine opportunity to test out *liberty of opinion and action*. Leaving New York on an English steamer with an open bar, I was astounded to note that it actually looked lonesome for the lack of patronage. Of course, wine was used at the table.'"

"Used quite a bit by you!"

"'During our stay in South America, of two months, only one case of inordinate drinking was noted. The man was American. The bars at the hotels in Rio de Janeiro, Buenos Aires and other cities were patronized, however, they were not used inordinately but as social centers where gentlemen might exchange the pleasantries of the day . . . '"

"And, oh, they met us in Rio in an open, chauffeured car festooned with flowers on the fenders . . . "

"'The cafes, somewhat similar to Paris, extending out into the streets, were occupied, with the little tables arranged here and there, but always quiet during the sippings of the various beverages carried along with cigarette smoking. As one wanders down the streets in any of these cities one is impressed with the number of places where alcoholic beverages are for sale . . . '"

"Yes. True. It's dreadful."

"Ida . . . To continue: 'In the drug stores and the best grocery stores a supply can always be obtained without restraint.' My point, Ida. 'The physicians and surgeons there are not hampered by red tape enforcement brought about by fanatics and those trying to restrain and limit the pleasures of others . . . '"

He saw that she was becoming restless. It was a pretty long speech. Maybe he should cut it.

"I also point out, a new reference, the danger of the spreading power of enforcement over pleasure, the nefarious so-called Sunday Blue Laws."

"Ah yes. Blue indeed."

But she was gone, out the door to shop, to Altman's, the only store she felt worthy of her patronage, to assemble new wardrobes for California.

Well, it was fairly interesting, lashing out at Prohibition, though he knew in his heart it would be a giant putrid leech upon the neck

of America for years to come. But if they could win the victory of
alcohol for physicians throughout the nation . . .

Their life, his and Ida's, was settling down. He would buy the
land and the grand house upon it and they would move to California
and that would be the adventure of their later life, he expected. He
unfolded the *World* to see the news. He himself did less and read
about what others did more by now . . .

Dear Christ—

Dear God, Warren had been sick, in San Francisco, in a hotel
there, from food poisoning it said. Came in from the boat trip to
Alaska and—What? Ate tainted crabs? How could that be? Who—
in the holy hell—else ate them?

He stood and paced, thoughts whirling. Who was attending
Warren, attending the President? Was it only that fool Warren had
dressed up in a general's uniform, poor Doc Sawyer? How long
would it take to get to California? Damn, he had just been there—It
would take days either by train or car—

As Marcus Northway paced there in his suite in the Waldorf-
Astoria Hotel, President Harding, having had a magazine story about
himself read to him and saying he felt better, went to sleep in his
hotel room in San Francisco never to awake.

17

Jehoshaphat!

Coolidge was president. Marcus Northway had never met him, or even seen him up close, or given him much regard. So far the dour Calvin had given the nation scarcely a word. He was a stick.

What a strange and terrible string of events.

Jake Northway was one of a horde of morons who put silver dollars on the rails as the dead leader's remains passed over and flattened the coins to be kept as souvenirs. Jake did it as President Harding's funeral train passed through Newton Falls, Ohio, on August 7. Poor Warren, they kept him, made up like a harlequin, in the window of the train as they rolled across the continent from California, taking forever to get to Washington.

He had been depressed and sad and searching for a new handle on things, surrounded by fools and mountebanks, going there to Alaska, and had made too many speeches on the way getting there. Then ate the crabs! But no one else, it seemed, got sick from them!

Oh foul—most foul!

Marcus and Ida stood among the crowd of mourners in Marion with Al and Mina Edison. Edison shed a tear. He had loved Warren Harding as a kind, friendly Ohio fellow with roots like his own. It had been much publicized that Al once said of Warren, "Any man who chews tobacco is all right." That was the level of Al's wisdom in public affairs. But they shared each other's immense popularity, Al taking Warren on the celebrated Tramp a year or two before with Ford and Harvey Firestone.

Marcus clasped Edison's soft old hand and they had a few words, which Al pretended that he heard, and he rasped that Marcus and Ida must come to see them in the winter in Florida. Marcus nodded that they might, the idea of doing so stirring many memories in his heart and mind and adding to the poignancy of the laying away of sweet stupid Warren Harding.

Too many people were crowded in the funeral space. The Chief Justice, the Fat Boy, nearly overturned his carriage getting in and out of it, he and the new President, the stick the nation was stuck with, looking ludicrous together, like the Drum and the Drumstick.

Warren's wife, the "Duchess," held up well, he must say. He had brought along some salts thinking of her and her grief but did not need them. N— was not there. Of course she was not. What had they done with her?

The newspaper accounts read later claimed that Harry Daugherty seemed crushed and lost, but Marcus did not think so. He looked sly as a fox to him.

It was Warren's father, old Dr. Harding, who broke down. Marcus saw that Amos Kling, the Duchess' father, had the nerve to come and stood off looking at the pageant—they took Warren into and sealed him up in a monstrous gray crypt, like a Pharoah. Kling was a main one of those who had called Warren a "nigger." As Marcus observed to Ida driving away from the funeral, if Warren Harding was a Black it did the race honor, for he truly was the handsomest man in America. Dennis, in front, driving them, shook his head, Marcus could not tell whether or not in agreement.

He investigated the death of Warren G. Harding, medically, using utmost discretion, as best he could into September and concluded that he was murdered, assassinated by his own people, by the Ohio Gang led by Daugherty, a corrupt pack of wolves, for what reasons not now clear but which doubtless history would reveal. Murdered him like a Caesar. What such perfidy—killing one's own leader—would lead to in the future course of our nation, of the United States of America, was inconceivable.

He managed to find and talk with Harding's physician, also a

Homeopath, the incompetent "General" Sawyer, who obviously himself was not well, and also talked with Dr. Boone, and read all the medical reports and articles that appeared.

It was six days between Harding's "indigestion" in Seattle— diagnosed by Sawyer as food poisoning from bad crab meat—and his death from multiple causes amounting to lack of breathing capacity and stoppage of heart function in the bedroom in the Palace Hotel in San Francisco. Nothing particularly was done or prescribed by these doctors but rest.

Marcus came to the firm belief that the President was poisoned— a variety of slow-acting poisons might have done it—and let die. All, in his opinion, were implicated.

Warren, finally, slow as he was, had wind of the corruption surrounding him, that those charged with bringing solutions were as corrupt as anyone else. He had wind of all the evil and corruption his laxness and ignorance had allowed, and was terribly upset. He went off to Alaska on his so-called "Voyage of Understanding" trying to think it out, get a new handle on it, and met his mortality, his death by the hands of traitors who feared a new, forceful, moral Harding.

Nothing had been wrong with the crab meat. No one else suffered from the self-same crab. Harding in fact ate his out of the same plate as Reddy Baldinger, his friend who had been a reporter on his Marion newspaper in his pre-political days. His "indigestion" was no more than usual, for with Warren "indigestion" was a constant nervous condition. Marcus himself had given Harding peptic remedies for years. The nervousness came from the frustration of his marriage to his wife and his foolish but real love of his young "girlie" N—. His death was a Set Up.

Dr. Northway was itching to exhume the remains and look for traces of the poison. But, for the sake of the nation, for the sake of the Party, for the sake of order and sanity, we must not do that. Indeed he would fight anyone else on this trail who tried to do so. The Major and Theodore would agree. Such, at the deepest and highest levels, were the demand and necessity of Polity.

They must now look to Coolidge for what he claimed, for Rectitude.

He sat down and wrote the new leader, offering his services in any way that might be helpful, national or international, medical or political, foreign or domestic.

"Warren," he had said to him as they left Sagamore Hill now those five years ago, "or, as I should say, my dear Senator Harding . . ."

"Yes, Marcus, dear Doctor Northway, you saved my father's practice, his very life and reputation, on that one case . . . "

"Yes. Well. He was incompetent for that level of practice. He had no readiness for complications. But that is not the point . . . " Now Marcus realized that for the Hardings that was just the point. "The President . . . " (Meaning then Theodore, T. R.) " . . . truly hopes that you can unite the Party, help its recovery. Otherwise he would never . . . "

"Shoot, Northway. Say it. He would never have given me the time of day. Eh? I'll go beyond that. If you hadn't led me here by the hand, the Colonel would probably not even deracinate that he would deem or deign to divulge his doubts to me, or maybe even in so circuitous a circumstance see me . . . "

Harding went on to say, in his peculiar way, that he held the honor of the Republican Party dearest to his heart. Never would he besmirch it. As for the Presidency, he said back then, he was really damned if he knew what he felt about that, himself. He wished to help the Party as a senator. He loved being a senator. Marcus believed him. Warren loved the Senate racket. Senators got up on their hind legs and bloviated.

Marcus believed that in his heart Warren Harding wanted it like crazy—but then was not educated enough to know what to do with it or how to handle it. For one thing he had not even the most rudimentary sense of economic systems.

But he was trying. When Marcus formally called on him last year—Marcus' sixth visit to the White House to be received by a President—Harding did not offer him whiskey or engage in down home humor but was formal and serious in putting in his hands the commission to represent the United States at the Brazilian Exposition. Marcus' impression was that he had a deep wish to be a good president, to rise above the problems and himself. Now he believed they killed him because he was trying to be upright.

They said Warren was depressed on the Voyage of Understanding. That must mean that he was thinking. Trying to think things through. Thinking always did depress him.

The story of Warren Gamaliel Harding was a sad and tragic story, as was the story of those who trusted and believed in him. It grew sadder when one thought his was also the story of America. Theodore Roosevelt had been to Marcus Northway Sir Valiant-for-Truth. All the nation was saddened by his death, as now by the death of Warren Harding. Both died so young, Theodore at sixty, Warren, dear God, at just fifty-eight years of age. When Theodore died the trumpets sounded for him in Heaven, and in his friend's heart. But now no stirring bugle blew in his heart for Warren. What a contrast between the two! And . . . come so quickly—it was hard to grasp—what sad contrast between their ages, their Americas.

Back then, in 1920, as he began, in the speech much quoted and often ridiculed, Marcus thought that Warren really was trying to be, after the terrible war, a healer. "America's need," he had intoned in that peculiar alliterating style of his, "is not heroics but healing, not nostrums but normalcy, not revolution but restoration, not agitation but adjustment, not surgery but serenity . . . "

Harding was using Marcus' own metaphors, though Ida asked him at the time, "What in the world is the man saying?"

Well, he would have to let it go, leave it to the Daughter of Time.

But right now, if he had Harry Daugherty by the throat he would gladly forsake serenity and try a little surgery!

18

In January Marcus, distracted and at loose ends, took Edison up on his invitation to visit him, staying in what the Wizard called his "Guest House" next to his own house on his estate called Seminole in Fort Myers, Florida, the town that Marcus had a small hand in making in years past— that was through Lutie, of course.

It was warm and pleasant there, though there was the promise of cold winds blowing in from Michigan, meaning that the moron Henry Ford and his entourage were on their way. For some years now Henry had been wintering in Fort Myers with Al Edison. Henry had the house next over from the Guest House, built it seven, eight years ago. It was a small gray house with a low porch, with a shack behind it holding, you have guessed it, cars. It had a well and a pump and a pipe across the fireplace so Ford got hot water. But compared with Edison's two houses, and his ingenuity, and even with the technology available now in 1924, Henry's house and plot compared to Al's two houses and large beautiful spread with all its exotic trees and plants as a flivver to a Rolls.

As Al was here with his wife Mina, Marcus had brought Ida, even though she was not eager to come. Al had married his young wife in 1885. She was still a year or so away from fifty, still looking young and fresh, while Al himself was now seventy-seven, a year beyond Marcus but seeming to the physician's eye quite more than that year older.

Ida was loathe to leave California where, at long last, they had

134

bought their house on a large lot in the residential center of Coronado and were in the midst of plans to renovate it and make it into their dream mansion. Ida had dubbed it "Northway Lodge" and hung the back yard and garden of the two-story English lodge with dozens of Japanese lanterns. She was staying only several days in Florida before returning to tyrannize the renovator.

Marcus was staying at Seminole Lodge a week, then repairing to a cottage he had used for years on the lovely island strip of sand nearby called Sanibel. His doctor (M.A. Northway) had ordered him to relax.

"Ah, Marco boy, you're looking natty there," Al said as they took a walk together, Al with his eternal cigar coddled in his yellowed left hand. "Where'd you get those white shoes? You're the dude all right, aint you?"

They were in fact two handsome devils, Al quite a bit more casual and rumpled than Marcus, who wore white vest and trousers and white shoes and dark coat and necktie and pince-nez to Al's rumpled summer suit, down at heel scuffed brogans, old planter's hat and collar all undone. Two keen sets of eyes, two shocks of white hair, the two men just of a height though Edison quite heavier than the trim Dr. Northway.

Al was jovial today. Upon arrival yesterday Marcus had hardly a word of greeting from him, such had his moods become. At best he was an unpredictable companion. Sometimes you thought you were in the presence of God, of complete Vacuum, silence. Sometimes you were with Thomas Alva Edison the great inventor, Benefactor of mankind (so very true), and you must just listen as he would tell, again, about himself. Often though still he could be Al, the famous fellow who could not quite believe it all himself and was really yet just a kid, who would call his friend "Marco" to joke and be a wag.

Edison's place, called "Seminole" for reasons obvious to those cognizant of Florida history, was on the Caloosahatchie River. It ran to the Gulf and back to the Everglades, the only river that ran across the state. Just here the river was a mile wide, and Al had his houses pre-built in Maine and erected here along the Caloosahatchie.

His pier ran half a mile out into the river, and he used to have his electric boat docked there, showing off his Batteries. This Fort Myers was indeed an old fort, abandoned twice. It had been a town of any sort for only twenty years when Al arrived. He would tell you the story any time: "I said, after I got here, there's only one Fort Myers, and ninety million people are going to find it out." So far, thank God, only about five thousand had, though a lot of Sports had always come through.

Old August T. Krause of Cleveland and his wife Lutie Morrison Krause were among those attracted by the fishing, after some fellow caught a great tarpon on a rod here instead of with the usual harpoon. Krause and Lutie both were drawn here by some strange fate from Cleveland—if you could imagine two more different places—and suffered for it, that is to say, died. And it must be added that Marcus Northway profited mightily in the bargain.

On his grounds Al had thousands of plants, hundreds Marcus would bet that Luther himself had never seen, all imported for some purpose or other connected with his schemes and inventions, nothing just for its looks, strange and unusual plants from all over the world.

After their walk Marcus sat by himself in the living room of the so-called Guest House and lit a cigar and took out a notebook thinking about having a go at writing something. Being with Edison had made him think he should get back to the Memoir. Ida was off in town with Mina.

It was damn funny, to be sitting again in this living room, now with these damn stuffed birds sitting all around in it—turned out they were Mina's and not Al's—in this brown wicker chair at this same little round table before the fireplace with, now, never a fire in it. Sitting here he looked up thinking he'd see Lutie, dear God, hear the rustle of her dress . . .

Well. Now, let's see. Al bought this place the year Marcus met him in New York, 1884 or 1885. He gave just $3000 for the grounds along the river here and had the two houses designed and pre-fabricated and shipped here by rail and assembled on the grounds. For he was quite famous already then, in '84. He had succeeded already in the incandescent bulb, figured out how to distribute electric power, improved the telephone, done the phonograph. This morning he'd asked Marcus why he carried a notebook. Why wasn't he talking his thoughts into a machine, putting them on a record? He showed Marcus the Bee Hives that he'd brought from Holland, for the wax for the phonograph cylinder and record. He had done all this incredible work in just five years there in his "Tabernacle" at Menlo Park.

But he was terribly tired when Marcus met him and was suffering from Brain Fag, and the doctors had sent him south, down here to the warmer climes for his rejuvenation.

"It was cold as Old Billy that January in St. Augustine," he would tell, "so I thought it was just about perfect when I hit here."

He had been famous, yes, but Marcus remembered reading articles back then, in the early and mid Eighties, that considered Edison not much a wizard anymore. He was looking for his health then, and for his old potency, and for another woman to replace his deceased wife and for something—for some hot other place—to electrify.

So he did the Hotel Del Coronado, then electrified his own house here in 1885. Fort Myers got excited and thought he was going to do the town. But then Edison got busy again back East, and into a terrible bunch of problems. He had married Mina, a young socialite, and honeymooned here but then nearly forgot he had this place, so that five years or so went by before he got back to Fort Myers.

Now it was, Marcus felt, his main place. Al loved it here. He roamed around it, as this morning, like some old Symbol. He had created some sort of exotic island and domicile here, so far from the simple Ohio of his youth and from mechanical West Orange, his lab all burned down there to his great grief anyway. Here in this place he could truly become T. A. Edison the Genius, Seer, Inventor, wandering through all the exotica, now contemplating, for the sake of Ford and Firestone, for their industrial needs, the production of rubber from plants. Contemplating much and doing little, as Marcus saw it, sad to say.

They had walked among the considerable variety of stuff. Brilliant orchids on a mango tree. A Dynamite tree whose pods explode. A Buttercup tree and purple bougainvillea. Along the river bank giant green bamboos. Then Napoleon cacti, a Cinnamon and an Allspice tree, and Coconuts, the farthest north they'd grow. Ficus elastica, the subject of his study now, the Indian Rubber tree. They went down the stone path to the pier, the river calm as glass. Mina had had birdhouses built out in the shallow river, for Al loved cats, she birds. An Hibiscus tree was to their left as they regarded the river, a Tulip tree just beyond, and Cabbage palms and many other kinds of palms along the path.

Walking back towards the main house Al said, "I am going over to the lab, Marco, old Polo. You can find your way to the Guest House all right?" Said it looking at him blank as Buddha. Could he have forgotten in the moment that Marcus—that Lutie—owned the house and lived in it for the period when he was not coming here?

Lutie's husband Krause bought it from Al when he got tied up back East, and Krause and Lutie lived here several years, then Marcus and Lutie did so just briefly. Marcus had no interest in it, though it was half the Seminole estate, half the grounds, when Lutie died, and sold it back.

Al moved his kitchen to this now Guest House then. He was incredibly sensitive to smells and could not stand the smell of food cooking. So now upstairs were the servants, on the second floor the guests, on the ground floor living room, dining room, sitting room, porch and kitchen. Al put all the distractions, guests, servants and bad smells in a separate house. Ha. Ha ha.

Marcus looked at the elegant sets of china put around on shelves and tables in the dining room. On the high shelf along the wall was a set that Lutie left for Mina. This living room was gloomier since Lutie had it. How bright she was! In it now one was made to feel drab, subordinate, a guest. He looked at a trophy platter, one of Edison's many trophies. It sat where an engraved silver urn presented to Marcus by Major McKinley for service in the Spanish War used to be.

The wicker chair creaked as he sat in it. Ah, he did not wish to think of all that, of McKinley killed with a ball infecting his vast belly, or in any way of old Señor Time always waiting to introduce you to his kid brother the Digger; nor did he feel like writing anything.

Going back outside he saw a lizard dart across the patio in his path, its red throat pulsing out.

He should not worry about the writing and begin to paint again.

There was a giant elm he had not seen, the only tree that reminded him of home. My God, he realized that he meant, by "home," for that instant, Whiskeyville! He wondered how Cora Bartlett was. He always got a birthday note from her and had been unforgivably lax in replying.

He walked across the street from the houses and exotic grounds, the street lined with palms that Al and then Lutie and himself and others had imported, and walked towards Al's lab.

He went in the entryway to the lab where Al had a desk and a schoolboy's chair. There was a row of old cabinets and rows of stoppered little bottles, enough small bottles and vials to suit an early Homeopath. No one was working in the lab. Al was sleeping in the chair, with a green glass bottle on the desk before him.

19

The next day Ford and Firestone arrived, sans wives. Henry, lean and dapper, came through the gate of the little fence between his house and the Guest House. They called it the "Friendship Gate." It was never locked between Edison and himself. And so on and blah blah blah.

Henry and his sycophant Harvey Fireplug were full of ideas. They were truly, in the opinion of Marcus Northway, full of it. They were hot after domestic rubber. They were going to form a company with Al and go full speed after it, he being already on its trail. Al was trying Florida Goldenrod among other plants and had begun to sneeze quite a bit. That was another reason Ida mentioned for going back to California, the goldenrod dust all around. She was full of real and supposed allergies. Mina Edison wanted to build a small new laboratory for this research for the inventor, with a bed in it, so he would not get stiff now that he was older from sleeping in his chair or on the desk. They always said he would doze a few minutes here and there, during the day, and work all night; but his present habits seemed to Marcus closer to narcolepsy. His great, yea incredible, fame seemed by now to be for him a form of Narcosis.

Ford was by now sixty years of age, or a year more. He thought he owned Thomas A. Edison, and in a way he did. (He was trying now to buy Luther too, moving much of Burbank's old stuff up there to Greenfield, the circus-land he had created at Dearborn.) Henry "owned" people by claiming them, as if they were mines, producing mines that you could claim and appropriate, men whose legends you could buy and attach to yourself. Through the years Ford had become a foil for both Edison and Burbank, as a ring of smaller stones serves as foil for the larger diamond.

Ford was a maniac about preserving their past, and his. Marcus once asked him if he had any toenails or nose hairs from Al, but Henry, the prig, just looked at him sourly. Marcus believed him to be perennially constipated. Al Edison was like Jesus to Ford, who proclaimed everywhere that he and Al, whom he had never called anything but "Mr. Edison," were best friends. He was having his hack write a book about Edison, glorifying him even further, turning even Al's failures into successes. Henry, who started in with the Edison Electric Company, knew that Edison had made him look good, just as Edison made the dwarf Steinmetz look good. And both men—Steinmetz now dead—helped defeat Edison. They were the ones who whipped him. Al was bitter about the little German but seemed not to realize the truth in regard to himself about Henry Ford.

Al could not believe Steinmetz would take over his electrical company and take his name off it. It made him feel so low then, in the Nineties, he said he never did know anything about electricity! Felt so low he turned to ore grinding, like a child with monstrous toys, until Mesabi came. But Henry also whipped him then, early in the century, on Al's cherished project of big electric batteries to power cars, Henry with his early Model N, his snorting, polluting machine, beating out the genius and his bid for smooth clean power that would have been so much better for the world.

Then Al had his operation for Mastoiditis, which took most of the hearing he had left. Then his friend Batchelor died. Then his lab burned. Then the Great War made him into another legend, the savior busily inventing weapons to annihilate the Hun, a Faust if you will, though actually it was all baloney for Al was inventing nothing then—or since.

And now they all sat in his lab across the street, Ford, Firestone, a couple of lab technicians, Edison and Northway, with Mina and Ida resembling an impressionist painting in their colored dresses and hats standing against the dingy wall.

"Ah, yes, dear God!" Al says. "Oh my, yes! Why, we'd sing 'Good Night, Ladies.' We'd sing 'We Won't Go Home Until Morning,' and we didn't neither. It didn't matter to me, how the singing was, I couldn't hear but the line of it. We'd eat pie and drink hot coffee and smoke cigars. And work! And never any damn'd whiskey, neither! No one got sick enough for that, Marco Polo! Ho . . . ho ho! I hear you're stumping the country anti-Prohibition . . . Well, I'll tell you and Ford here will tell you, Prohibition is okay. It should and will be eternal, by God! Ah, don't shake your mandarin head at me, old Marco! I know you've brought your nip in your Bag, in there, that's the only reason you've brought your Medical Bag here, aint it?"

Yes, he replied, to himself. I believe in whiskey as you believe in current. You are not transcendent in belief, as a Homeopath must be. To you all is Force, mechanical force. Luther and I know that all is bound, your electricity, the genius of your mind, the forces that form the pattern and control the plan of Nature, in connected Spirit.

"Ah," Al says, puffing out a cloud of cigar smoke, "glorious days, now gone forever . . . "

"Not if we can make rubber out of plants," chirps Henry. Then says: "You must all come this evening to my house, for supper and a dance!"

Ida smiles. She likes Henry Ford. Both are Irish. Marcus knows that she wishes, for she has said so, that she might sit with them around the desk and have a cigar. Why not? As a young woman Ida Burke Bailey probably smoked cigars with her father when Bailey would come home after a hard day's laying of track out there in California.

They said—Marcus did not know, was not close enough to him to know, and did not wish to be—that Ford had a young mistress, and that Clara Ford knew it, for the girl was always with them.

After serving them a meager supper, Henry, who was penurious and liked to joke about having no money, sat Ida at the parlor organ in his little house and had them all Square Dance. He of course called the dance. Then Mina played and Ida danced. Marcus did one round.

Ida danced around with Henry then with Harvey until Marcus feared they might break through the creaking floor boards.

"I had fun," Ida said, as she and Mina left the men. "Mr. Ford is fun," she said in Marcus' ear. "He likes the jolly old things, and so do I!"

Edison, who never exercised, the body being simply a conveyance for the brain, left for the lab when dancing was announced but returned to sit with the men afterwards on Ford's back porch, passing out cigars.

They looked through trees and shadows of trees and spinning fireflies to the Caloosahatchie, feeling its calm aboriginal spell. Henry and Harvey spoke again of rubber. They believed that America would fight the Germans again before long and that we would be desperate for domestic rubber. They spoke of how much rubber various Indian and Asian trees produced. Harvey spoke of bringing Al here a Moreton Fig tree, a foolish thing to do in Marcus' opinion. He did not voice his own opinion that they could get a good deal of sap by reducing Firestone to his essence. He thought that Edison was asleep, with the cigar smoke curling from him in the darkness, until he spoke.

"Speaking of Fort Myers," he said. No one was. Now he was back with them and was going to tell them Story #3.

"They called it 'Myers' when I got here. Wasn't even incorporated. Bought a house in Myers, first, then this land. Fourteen acres, paid three thousand dollars. Not bad, eh? Married Mina and brought her here, built a honeymoon cottage, first off. Then . . . Was an old doc here, Marco, just one. A Regular. They tore down the old courthouse and built a brick one and used the wood from the old one for a hospital. Now, let's see—1887. Ada Hancock was the first white baby born in the town. Winfield Scott Hancock her father. Ran for president, don't you know, barely beat by Garfield."

"If you Ohio boys hadn't rigged it, he would've defeated Garfield," Marcus said.

"Oh," Al laughed, "maybe so. I did everything, you know— telegraphs was my main ticket—but rig elections."

And went into Story #2. Growing Up: the boy selling papers and editing a newspaper with a lab in the boxcar of the train, there in Michigan. Then drifted back to the early days of Myers.

"Had a boat named for me, the 'Thomas A. Edison.' How would that make you feel, Marco Polo, to look out on the river and see a boat, loaded with crates of oranges, puffing by with your name on it?"

"Dead?"

"Exactly! Makes you think you're dead, to have your name on a damn boat! Burned up, at its dock, a few years ago, the 'Thomas A. Edison' did." He laughed.

"They say they are going to name a bridge for you, over the river here," Ford said.

"Eh?"

He repeated it, in the better ear.

"Oh. That. They're not even warmed up good, on that. Maybe by the time I'm dead they'll have it, an Edison bridge over the Caloosahatchie."

"They are starting on Highway 41, the Tamiami Trail," Firestone said. "From Miami to Tampa! We really do need to support that, Henry: Ford cars and Firestone tires along the Tamiami Trail!"

But Henry went back to what Al said. "You think they won't get that bridge constructed in another twenty-five years, is that it, Mr. Edison?" Flattering him, for that would be when Edison would be over one hundred years old.

Again Al did not, or did not choose to, hear.

"Jesus, Ford," Marcus Northway said.

Edison rose and tossed his cigar butt towards the river. He sure as hell smoked them more than halfway down. He said good night. Firestone obediently stood up. Ford motioned him off, and he said good night. Marcus found himself becoming stiff. As he made to rise Ford stood and faced him, his back against the railing and to the Caloosahatchie. "I'd like a word with you," he said.

Marcus sat back down and nodded at him.

"Is it true, Northway, that you are a medical expert on male potency?"

"Yes. True. Got a problem?"

"Not presently. I would be interested in looking to the future is all. Be interested, you know—"

"Sure. No guarantees. Except high fees. You may reach me through my suite and office at the Waldorf-Astoria. That is in New York City, Henry. Ha, ha. Even though I am now taking up primary residence in Coronado, California, I will keep operating in New York. Coronado is by San Diego there."

"California is a crazy place, bunch of loonies there. You wouldn't catch me there in California. Say, another thing . . ."

"Yes?"

This seemed to be about more than potency. Maybe immortality? Marcus believed that Henry thought of himself as pretty near immortal.

"I'd like—well, intend to—move all this lab's stuff, whole setup, up to the Village now, up to Greenfield, with the other stuff 'n' help Mr. Edison set up his smaller lab here for the rubber research."

"Yes?"

"Al's draggin' his feet a little, some reason. Likes all the old stuff here. Need to move though, need to move. Thought since you're here you might put in a word, eh, tell him what a good idea it is. Not that he don't enjoy all the Greenfield setup there already."

"Well, Henry, I would not presume . . ."

"Been thinking, Northway. You're an inventor too, aren't you? Eh? Northway Stretcher. Northway Field Case. Don't you have some new folk medicine procedures on this and that? Mr. Edison said so. Well, write 'em up, have my man help do it, in some pamphlets 'er something, put 'em there, put it all there at Greenfield, with Mr. Edison and your pal Burbank, give you a little 'Northway Corner' there in Greenfield Village, a little Medical Corner, eh? Put you in the pantheon of America. How does that sound, Northway? In exchange for helping me give a nudge from time to time to the Wizards? Eh?"

Looking at Ford's snake-like head and obsidian eyes, the Adam's apple moving in his throat as he talked back-lit by the moon and front-lit by the lampglow through the window of his house made Marcus think of the red-throated lizard that had darted across his path on the patio this morning.

He stood and tossed his cigar out over the railing and Henry's shoulder towards the river. A "Northway Corner," eh? From Thomas and Benjamin on to his father Samuel Cincinnatus, the Northways had never been much else than farmers, until himself, but they had, by God, never been anybody's dog on a leash either.

"That is kind of you, Ford, I am sure," he spoke formally, who had presented himself to the Emperor's Court for McKinley, "but I would not in any way be interested in such a proposition, at either end of it."

"Your wife, Ida, finds out you turned it down, Northway, with her ambition, you'll be up shit's creek, I expect."

Marcus laughed. "You say anything discrediting about me to Mrs. Northway at your peril," he said. "I mean, peril from her! I bid you goodnight, you little Michigan shithead."

He left Ford standing at the railing.

"He is by now a certifiable maniac," he said to Ida. "Wants to control everything."

"Well, the nerve of him!" Ida said. "But you don't need him, Marcus! See if I dance with him again! This bed is too small!" she said, heaving in it, in a voice loud enough for even Edison to hear next door. "That would be nice to be in that Greenfield Museum, Marcus, but we can build our own if we want to, can't we, right in Coronado?"

"Certainly, my dear. About the size of an outhouse would be about right. Stand the stretcher against the wall and put the field case on a shelf. Ha ha."

In his heart he knew that Ford never would have kept the deal anyway. Folk medicine indeed!

Ida departed the next morning by train from the new depot right in Fort Myers. At noon Marcus packed up and summoned Dennis, prepared to depart the Guest House at Seminole Lodge, leaving Al to Ford and Firestone and their schemes, which did seem to keep Al's spirits up.

He paid respects to the gracious Mina Edison, thanking her for her hospitality, and walked with his old friend to the front gate of the estate. They said goodbye by the Gingerbread Palm, Edison giving him his warm soft hand and generous kid's grin, eyes alive and sparkling, smile real. Ford said that Edison and he were best friends. Marcus believed that, as a disciple may be in some sense a friend to a master, they were friends. But now, grasping his hand, looking into his boy's eyes, he felt, and knew, that he and Al were Friends.

After visiting the old hotel at Punta Rassa he took the ferry over to Sanibel.

20

The small cottage on the beach was called, the letters faded on a wooden sign, Siren of the Sea. It was more run down than would be his usual taste, but he liked its comfort and easiness. It had the whitest beach he had ever seen, whiter than the duller sand color of Coronado's, looking to the other ocean, or certainly that of his other strip of sedge and grainy sand at Amagansett.

Billy, his brother William, had settled into a calm, peaceful life there at Amagansett running the little inn, and seemed content. But just now he had taken off, of all things driving in his touring car west. Or so he had written his brother on a card. The inn was closed for winter so that was no problem. Whether by "west" Billy meant New Jersey or Pennsylvania or the veritable Far West Marcus did not know, but then he did remember that Billy always had a fascination with the American West through such fiction as Ned Buntline's and the classic *The Virginian* of Owen Wister, who was friend and companion to Theodore. Marcus believed that Wister was still around and even consorted with the current writers such as this young Hemingway whose first novel La Pajarita had so much admired. She had read it in English and he was proud of her.

He hoped Billy was all right and would not get lost out west.

The sun was a vivid orange here at Sanibel over the beach, on which lay incredible shells of all shapes and whorls of color, shells of great variety and beauty, from the various currents which came together here from gulf and ocean.

And nymphs—Ah, yes! Nymphs could be seen playing on the beach!

The sun was blazing, and he would wait for it to abate before he went out to play with them. He sat in the coolness of the weathered cottage and lit a cigar and poured a tumbler of whiskey and let his thoughts roam back to his first wife Lutie and to being here before. His encounter with Ford also made him recall with relish the visit he and Ida made here in 1914. They were all younger and even crazier then, ten years ago.

That was the time Ford came, of course dragging Firestone along, and also bringing the naturalist John Burroughs with him to visit Edison. Ida and Marcus had been married just a year or so and were visiting in order to show her this important place in his life experience. Ford, for the sake of publicity, got up a Tramp, this an early one on a modest scale. But, aha, the praise and glory that day went to Dr. Marcus Northway, who acted as attending physician to this folly.

There existed from 1914 a photograph of Edison, Burroughs and Ford that Al had hanging in the living room of his main house and which hung it seemed in every public place in Fort Myers. Edison looks a bit taller and quite thicker than the others— Burroughs looking like an elf, Ford like a sharp-faced bird with an expression on his face like he is seeing once again, recalling, four eggs in a song sparrow's nest. All wear dark suits and vests, Henry natty as ever, Burroughs with his white bushy beard a bit rumpled, Al quite rumpled and stained, as if he had been doing chemicals in his lab. This was supposed to be the photographic proof of their great friendship.

The odd thing about it—and both Ida and Pajarita agreed—was that each gent is looking in a different direction: Henry off somewhere to the past or to the river; Burroughs at the ground, as if he had perhaps eaten a blissful apple and broken wind and is shyly saying "Excuse me"; and Edison straight ahead with his strange non-look, one of his greatest inventions, his famous Cherub look—I am wise and kind but am not really here standing beside these fools with a

large-boled palm behind me with its branches like swords over all
our heads.

Ford organized the Tramp, and they got in cars, the men in suits
and ties as was their wont when roughing it, the ladies dressed in
sensible light dresses except for Ida who mis-dressed in black
Western hat and a heavy black dress but who was eager and happy
to be along. They drove with fanfare to a spot of jungly woods along
the Caloosahatchie and ventured into them, with camp stools and a
tent and boxes and chests of refreshments and with Ford's standard
prop, a crosscut saw.

Henry spotted a young smooth-barked tree of whose genus
Marcus was not certain and declared that they would cut it down.
"Why?" Ida said, but they got busy at it, Marcus retreating from the
action to his camera, taking shots as Firestone and Captain Evans, a
friend of Al's, took a turn, then as Burroughs and Ford took a turn.
Edison, true to his dictum about the body and the brain, looked on,
leaning against the very tree that they were sawing at, something
that Sam Northway would have told him not to do.

The elderly elfin naturalist said something as he sawed away on
his end across from Ford. It looked as though he and Henry were
fighting each other for possession of the saw. Their stroke was too
easy on Burroughs' part and too heavy on Ford's.

"What?" Ford replied to Burroughs.

"Let the saw do the work," hissed Burroughs, at the time a
vigorous man of seventy-seven—now Al's own age—or seeming
vigorous when just walking, hopping along a trail like a chipmunk,
but pretty pooped at the sawing.

"What?" Henry said, not seeming to understand the principle
of what Burroughs suggested, letting the saw do the work, by which
as any farm boy should know he meant getting into a natural, smooth
rhythm at the work and using skill and not unnecessary force; but
Ford took it wrong and began to pull even harder on his end.

Burroughs stumbled forward towards the tree; the saw whanged
and nearly got Al, and did get Ford, in the leg, ripping through natty
trousers to the flesh of his thin but wiry leg.

"Oh no. No, no!" said Burroughs, letting go.

"Jehoshaphat!" cried Al.

Ford looked in surprise down at his ripped pants and bleeding leg. Clara Ford exclaimed and ran to him. Ida, a trained nurse, pushed her away and had Firestone set out a stool for Ford to sit on, motioning to Marcus who was taking one more picture.

"Here, Northway," Edison said, pointing to Ford as if he was some odd phenomenon just observed. Marcus put down his camera and went to the car and got his Medical Bag.

"It's not too bad," Ida said. She had peeled the trouser back. She looked like a Rough Rider in her Western hat and dark get-up. The scene reminded Marcus vaguely of the hospital camp in Porto Rico. Now the photographer from the Miami newspaper was taking pictures.

"What in the world," Ford said, looking dreamily at his leg. "Can't feel a thing."

Burroughs scampered off into the woods.

The wound appeared to be a shallow tear along the calf.

"Did you bring bromine, Marcus?" Ida said. She knew of his reputation over a quarter century for its strategic use.

"Yes," he said, bringing it out.

Bromine was a dark red liquid of an exceedingly pungent odor, not unlike chlorine and analogous to it and iodine in many respects, a non-metallic element obtained from sea water, boiling at 145 degrees and evaporating readily, a single drop being sufficient to fill a large flask with its vapor, dissolving in water readily by the aid of bromide of potash.

He treated Ford's leg with the strongest preparation, having cleansed the wound, 1-64 drachm viii, or 1-1000 oz. ii, after which the part was kept moistened with a solution the strength of which was measured by a solution of the color of light amber. Moistened then unremittingly, the Anger of the wound subsided quickly with no septic inflammation. Thus he treated Ford on the spot and later with a skill and care that won the admiration of all, including the press.

He had not considered tetanus in regard to Ford's wound, the saw being new and clean, a toy that should have stayed up on the shelf. The bromine would have allayed it anyway, he reflected; or maybe Ford would have gotten lockjaw and died from lack of prunes, ha ha.

"They—we—were all real lucky," Ida said, when the episode was over.

"Yes," he said, thinking she meant lucky he was there.

"Did you see the snakes?" she said.

"What?"

"I saw about six snakes. Two were patterned on the back and so harmless, but the others were the bad kind, moccasins. One slithered away from Mr. Burroughs when he started sawing. And there was one by Mina's foot as she stood there. Did you see that ridiculous bunch of flowers on her hat? As she stood there fanning herself while you were treating Mr. Ford?"

"Well, I had iodine as well."

"Of course you did."

"For snake bites I give ten drops of iodine in half a glass of water—Good God, did you really see all those snakes?"

She smiled at him triumphantly as if it were she, Ida, who had saved the day. Jerusalem, sometimes he thought she saw snakes all the time. Too often he beheld them on her wrists and around her neck.

On that same visit he also treated Edison, first to avoid abscesses from his Mastoid disease with alboline and oil of eucalyptus inhaled up the nose and with petroleum oil, aconite and belladonna directly in the ear, and for his recurrent Brain Fag with "Northway's Rejuvenator" composed of calves' brains, glycerine, spirits frumenti and sodium chloride.

Ford never thanked him. (Nor did he at all figure that he was belatedly thanking him with his nefarious proposal on his porch last night.) Never sent him a car. That was the same time, ten years ago, when he gave the Model T to Al, and another to Burroughs, had three sent here to Myers, keeping one for himself which he still kept in the shed behind his house, liking to say, "Replace it? Why, a Ford never wears out." And flap, and doodle.

Taking another small measure of the whiskey as stimulant to the mental process, he let his thoughts go on to Lutie. Sweet, beautiful, frail but oddly forceful in a man-like way—Lutie.

Lutie Morrison was born in Cleveland in 1863. By all accounts and the photographs he'd seen she was a charming girl, a gay and good spirit as a lass and young woman. Her father was a banker, and the Morrisons were in the Cleveland Blue Book. She was a belle of local society and finished at Miss Finch's School in Manhattan. Either in New York or in his native Cleveland, for he roamed both cities, Lutie met August T. Krause, a prime associate of John D. Rockefeller. Krause was said to be worth about twenty million and to be one of the ten or fifteen richest men in America. Old August, who also had his hands on railroads with some other eminent pirates, took a shine to Lutie, who gave him her hand when she was but twenty-two, in 1884, the same year Marcus met Edison on Fifth Avenue, just before he married Mina Miller.

What, he suddenly thought, of all these older men and younger wives? Ida was eighteen years younger than himself, as Lutie had been fifteen years his junior. La Pajarita was just forty-six by now. Mina was—is—eighteen years Al's junior. But Luther . . . By God, Luther! He had them beaten to holy hell, his lassie Elizabeth Jane, who'd been his secretary, was forty years younger than himself, he marrying her when he was sixty-seven and she twenty-seven—and he is seventy-five and she just thirty-five by now! To the Horticulturalist, of course, goes the Palm!

Lutie and August Krause produced a sickly son called Bernard, and it was for the health of this frail boy that they were advised to move here to Florida.

This Marcus considered crazy. California, not Florida, was a salubrious clime. There were a lot of crazy doctors in this country. To send people for their health down to this potentially pestilential place was crazy.

But Krause adored to fish, as did Lutie. Marcus wished he had indulged her in it more though he had indulged her in enough. Because of this love of fishing the Cleveland couple—he was called Oil Baron by the locals—went down to old Schulz's Tarpon House at Punta Rassa, the only hotel around, in 1891. In February then they sailed up to Fort Myers and looked it over. It suited Krause well enough, and Lutie decided Fort Myers was a project she could get teeth into and make go. It was well past the time when you could take hold of a town and shape it, in Ohio.

They were shown the second house on the Seminole estate and bought the one house and about half the land for $4000. Next year they moved in, and Krause began spending a barrel of money in Fort Myers. He bought some large citrus groves, orange and grapefruit, and tried his luck at rice and coffee. He had been lucky with Rockefeller and the other Fellers, but he was never lucky in Florida, what with drought and one thing and another, and he lost a pile of dough. Then he began spending more time back up in Cleveland and New York, and he up and died in Cleveland in 1900 with a huge sheaf of shares in Standard Oil stock and a bunch of other assets clutched to his bosom, which dear Lutie quickly took to hers.

Meanwhile Lutie herself had bought a small hotel and named it for Bernard and got involved with a developer in Myers in a fancy downtown hotel called The Palms.

Marcus examined young Bernard several times. He had a form of the dread phthisis, a weakening of the lungs and general system. Little could be done for him. He died in 1902 to Lutie's deep dismay and grief.

Marcus had first met Lutie Krause in Cleveland when she was married and he a bachelor there and met her again after he had gained fame by his service in investigating typhoid fever in Porto Rico and was a still-young major general after the Spanish War. They fell into conversation about her frail son. He visited them down here as they lived in Seminole-2, staying in another house along the river or in this cottage here on Sanibel. She solicited him to contribute to the palms placed along the thoroughfare of Myers, after many of

Al's first imported palms from Cuba died.

Together they tried to get the town Marshal to keep the pigs and cattle from being driven up the main street along to Punta Rassa though they had always been driven along that way, but the fight was useless in those days. It was hard to imagine grace and greatness for the town then with the cattle in the streets and the Crackers cracking their great whips at them and the pigs rooting through yards and under houses. Al built his famous swimming pool, reinforced by bamboo and fed by an artesian well, in 1900 and never swam in it. Krause died the same year, and Lutie planted herself firmly in Myers, and Marcus found himself often drifting down her way.

"You are even more handsome," she said, "out of uniform."

Krause had been a substantial man but unfortunately of the visage of a Toad.

Marcus first spoke of his affection for her in Fort Myers and first embraced her on a visit to her house at Mamaroneck, the place that inspired his desire to want his own place on Long Island. They had kindred interests—her son's health, everyone's health, Civitas, and, let us face it, sexual attraction. Though frail, Lutie had been passionate.

They married in 1905 in a church in Cleveland and kept for a while in Krause's pile there on Euclid Avenue, later let to the Tom Northway family, and then here, soon giving up Seminole-2 as Edison decided again to winter back here with Mina, and living in another house on the road along the river.

Marcus gave up active medical practice and dutifully attended Lutie, her needs and her considerable estate and fortune. They had a brisk six years together. Lutie helped pave the streets and floated The Palms Hotel and did everything civic and cultural she could as he himself took up the cause of paved roads as the key to civilization and progress. He had felt like saying to Firestone and Ford that without what Lutie and he had done years ago there would be no construction of a Tamiami Trail—but, as Sam Northway liked to say, "What fools don't know they don't miss none."

She died untimely here in 1912 at the age of forty-nine, he being then in his sixty-third year. She had no children surviving and no close family not ahead of her in years, and he came into her entire fortune, that of Krause before, which Marcus must say had grown considerably since through an array of investments balanced so as not to depend too much on any one thing, the land, import-export, Stock Market, gold or the lovely oil. In his heart Marcus was as conservative as all the Northways had ever been, with crops in the field, cash in the bank and a sack full of gold coins under the mattress.

He had loved Lutie and considered her one of the Graces in this world. She was attended in her final frailty by a nurse well recommended, Ida B. Bailey, whom he hired in New York to be Lutie's nurse-companion. He and Ida Bailey worked well together in medical terms. Feeling within himself, then, Ida's strength and his own need for order, stability—hell, just being married and not a damn bachelor at that point in life—he soon married Ida.

So it was.

Now the beach—la playa—called. He rose and looked out and saw the Nymph, nymph of nymphs, out there playing on la playa, down the way Dennis reading his Socialist magazine in a beach chair as she searched for shells. He must put on his bathing costume and go out. Out to her, to Youth and Beauty, and to the ocean, the great Salt Womb to which we all return.

The sea gulls were in a frenzy of feeding along the water's edge while awkward beaky pelicans dove after their meals on a slant, flapping large ridged wings. The sun lay at eye level now in the later afternoon and bands of gold and emerald lay across the sky like strips of his mother Sally Ann's sewing across her sewing table.

He was glad to have thought of his mother, Sally Ann. Now he had brought together in the progression of his thoughts all the women he had loved, and did now love.

21

The next several years were spent in endless renovation of the house they had bought on their pleasant avenue in Coronado.

Ida loved the place. It was her dream come true. But unfortunately every detail weighed on her and nothing, it seemed, could be done once or, often, just twice done. Marcus had decided to commit a sizable fortune to the house and gardens, and it was a damn good thing he had. They would move in the house and then out again, back and forth from a suite in the Hotel Del Coronado or staying in a small house on the lot next door to "Northway Lodge," a house which Marcus in his wisdom had acquired as a buffer zone, somewhat after Edison's example.

Coronado was a placid, serene town, with some wealth. The Lodge being well within the town and off the water shielded the Northways from any storms and also from the noise of airplanes, for Coronado was also a busy and historic naval base, at beach's end, with many air and sea ships and amphibious planes. Many notable aviators had gamboled here, developing the sea-plane and such. An admiral lived on the other side of them and a naval captain from Texas, young Nimitz, a splendid fellow, kept the Symphony box next to theirs. Marcus bought the San Diego Symphony box immediately as they came to Coronado and made significant contributions in the cultural fields, so that Ida might become involved with some authority. Every prospect of local society excited and worried her. She fretted and seemed uncertain, happy as she was, and was terribly demanding in her confusion. Several times he had had to prepare a nostrum for her nerves. It was enough to drive a fellow to strong drink, to rectification. Ha.

Meanwhile Marcus boarded up Willowstone, the mansion in Greenwich; double state taxes tempted him to sell it. As a charitable act he turned old Krause's pile in Cleveland, now that the Tom Northways were firmly set in their house in Shaker Heights, into a boarding house for the elderly, Miss Maguire's Home.

He had a study at the side of Northway Lodge here in Coronado, with private access. Through the window he could hear Ida giving the contractor hell. "You and I exist to please Madame Northway," the poor fellow would say, and wink. Marcus let him get away with this impertinence for it was true. They were just now finishing adding a third story to the house! "What in God's name for?" he had said to her. "For the servants!" the daughter of the foreman of the railroad gang had replied.

"I dislike distraction, Ida. I do not want servants lurking in the house!"

"You won't hear them. You'll get used to them. Mr. Edison has servants in his house."

"A separate house, Ida, for God's sake!"

"Well, they will be up there and we will be down here, except for when they are working down here, of course."

"Why can't we just let 'em ride on over here on the trolley?"

"Because there isn't any, Marcus, pay attention! And we will need a steady bunch. They will be Mexicans, you know. And where will Dennis stay?"

"Not in this house; he can have the little house next door."

"Fine. You need not worry about being bothered by the servants on the third floor. There will be an elevator, just like we have at the Waldorf!"

He'd known, of course, that that was coming.

They installed the elevator, a very fine Otis, first to third floors. Ida did not think it quiet enough, and it bumped slightly on landing. After her first ride up and down in it, Ida emerged and said, "It will not do. It must be absolutely smooth. Take it out and do it over."

The contractor looked at General Northway in despair.

Marcus nodded. "Do it," he said. They did it over. It was a damn smooth elevator.

Marcus had his study all paneled in mahogany. He thought it magnificent.

"It looks like a bar! I won't have it!" Ida screamed upon beholding it. "Rip it all out and re-do it," she ordered.

He nodded at the contractor, who on Ida's say-so redid the study all in black walnut. It looked fine, he thought, if a bit dark. For someone so thoroughly Irish Ida was becoming Germanic on him, like a German general.

They were also redoing the grounds. She was leaving that up to him. He had consulted Burbank on plants and Edison on electrical systems for watering and for an alarm inside the house. He liked the idea of getting such high-powered advice for free.

Once or twice he came upon Ida in her Morning Room, in which she sat regally and issued orders to the servants, weeping. She had sheets and envelopes of the stationery she'd printed and embossed with the Northway Coat of Arms spread out before her. "I don't know, Marcus," she cried. "Oh help me, I don't know!" She was trying to invite, accept, respond, carry on a correspondence like some character out of Henry James, not sure of which stationery fit which occasion. "Oh, I need a social secretary!" she said.

"Not quite," he said, a bit sternly. "I will help you. Here . . . "

He was sitting, then, one late night of that year, 1926, when he felt that he was receiving, so he came to inner attention and received a Thought message from Burbank. Luther called on his wave-length to him signifying that he was deeply troubled. He asked Marcus to come and help him. Marcus felt this message strongly but thought he could do nothing until morning and so retired to a troubled sleep.

He rose before dawn and summoned Dennis and told Ida he must go to Luther.

The water in the usually calm bay was choppy and gray as seen from the car window on the ferry. Dennis drove him up the highway from San Diego towards Santa Rosa.

He had been worried anyway. In some strange and un-characteristic way Luther had become embroiled in a controversy, having issued some statement about God and religion and having to go preach in a church about what he had really meant when he was severely criticized for it. Marcus was sure Luther was shocked to be so criticized. Thousands of letters had poured in to Luther, and, just like the gentle fellow, he was reportedly trying to answer every one of them.

He had been excoriated for saying, "I am an Infidel. So was Jesus Christ."

Never—Jesus!—was there a more religious and humane person than Luther Burbank on this Earth, whose beauty, practicality and dietary he had aided through his fruits, trees and flowers. His critics made Marcus rage, and weep. He wished that he could take a whip to them!

By God, he thought, aren't all of us who think, who engage in constructive thought and work, in some sense Infidels?

Was not Jesus Himself an Infidel, who did not believe in and changed established religious thought and order? Did he not confound the Pharisees, chase the money changers from the temple, love Mary Magdalene, add Love to the Commandments?

What Luther said was: "I believe in a divine Ruler of the Universe, no matter what anyone calls it, be it God, Force, Allah or any other word for it." Quite right. Quite true, and right.

He pulled his gold-cased watch and clicked it open. Nine o'clock.

Marcus had sent a Thought message but received none back.

If Luther were—

Ah. No. Now he sensed it, understood.

Ah, Burbank, dear man, too soon, too soon—

Marcus tapped the glass separating front and back in the Rolls. "Albert," he said, "stop. Turn the car around."

The driver turned his head a moment to look at him. "Dennis," he said.

"Oh. Yes. I was thinking . . . of . . . "

"My father."

"Yes." Of Albert, and of Edison, of Luther, of himself, of men his age . . .

Back home he found the photograph he cherished, of Burbank and Northway standing arm in arm, friends, in front of the Grafting Apple Tree at Santa Rosa. The small picture was framed in gold, and he gently hung it on the dark wood wall of his study.

Burbank was born in 1849, just a year later than Marcus Northway, and was but seventy-seven when he died of a heart attack, or so they said it was. As the week and month went on his critics were silent, only one truculent old canon of the Episcopal Church intoning that he had engaged in sacrilegious work with his "new creations," that the only New Creation ever in this world was the faith and church as proclaimed by Jesus Christ. Marcus got up and walked out when he said it, leaving Ida sitting in their pew. Burbank was widely mourned over the nation and the world. He, like Edison in his field, was called Wizard: "the wizard of the flowers."

A year ago Edison had written Luther, having heard some rumor that Burbank might retire, telling him to go on, never to stop working, that he himself, Edison, was coming on to eighty years of age, his mind, he claimed, more active than ever. Marcus had thought the letter, which was published, to be unnecessary, hortatory and assertive of a fact not so. But Luther loved the letter. "Oh, dear great wonderful Edison," he replied, saying he had no thought at all of not going on with his work forever.

Marcus sat in his garden, to which Burbank had contributed horticulturally and Edison had contributed mechanically, contemplating. He felt no sense at all of any further message, no intimation at all of Luther's spirit from Beyond. What he felt was that he was dead and if ought remained of him it was the daisy, the cactus without spines, the plum and the potato.

Deep within himself he was frightened by this thought.

A week later he received a letter from Utica from Miss Alice Northway, retired librarian, saying that Cora Bartlett had died, at just his own age, there in Whiskeyville. Cora, of all vigorous people, he had expected to live to a far older age. Miss Alice wrote that nothing apparently was wrong, that Cora seemed to have passed on simply from loneliness and time's neglect.

The funeral had already been. He would have gone if he'd had time. Perhaps one day he would return and visit her grave. But probably not. He did not wish to stand again, and without her, or with her below him beneath the earth, among all those graves of Bartletts and of Northways. Nor would he be buried there himself, by God! He would order himself burned, cremated, his ashes flung— where?

Ah! Dear girl, I see you clearly. We ran together through the fields there when young, so young. We stood then, when I, so proud and such a fool, deigned finally to visit, to return, stood together by the trail where—

He got up and turned Al's sprinkler system on and watched it whizz its water, as his thoughts also whirled then steadied on his friend: Cora Bartlett gone, last of an American family.

They continued working on the house and a year and then another passed. In the fall of '27 Marcus sojourned for a while in the Waldorf suite, leaving Ida in Coronado to unpack the crates and boxes from their foreign trips that she was cramming into the Lodge. He was pleasantly surprised to find Edison visiting his son in the son's Waldorf office, which was filled with stuffed owls. Al sat in a chair, his belly spread before him, and motioned for Marcus to come close. When Marcus bent down to him, the old clown took the diamond stickpin from his necktie and pretended to pocket it. Then he whispered to him, "Lindbergh."

"Yes, Al?"

"What'd he do, Marco? What'd he do?"

"Flew," he said. "Just took off and flew."

Al sat and shook his head. Marcus straightened, his knee popping, but Al did not hear it. The old genius was right: there had been a hell of a big change in heroes in America.

As he turned eighty, Marcus was honored by being named Honorary President of the American Institute of Homeopathy. He wrote then with bravura of the pleasure he felt, ending his letter by saying, "I am invigorated, my colleagues, at this honor you have done me. Hold steady, for there is yet great truth in our Faith and Practice!"

His bravado was a sham, hiding disappointment. For the third edition of Dr. Wellknecht's tome on medical practices and cures had come out, once again overlooking Rotary Dilatation and Marcus

Northway's other claims to fame, even though Marcus had barraged the Allopathic Prig for ten years with statements and evidence of these claims.

His last statement was on his use of orificial surgery, practiced in strategic cases since 1880, to good results but of course ridiculed and reviled as a practice by know-nothings like Wellknecht for two hundred years. But he had cured chronic eczema and skin ulceration on a young woman by loosening the head of the clitoris and the dilating and clipping of irritated points at the various outlets of the body and had cured a fellow who had cracks and squamous eruptions with swelled joints of the hands by simply stretching the rectum and cured a woman of phthisis by the operation of trachelorrhaphy through the years. Yet now he resigned himself to lack of the recognition he deserved and decided to do so in good spirit and not get cranky in his older age. And except for some doodling and notations on diet and proper elimination he pretty much stopped, with great relief, writing the damn'd Memoir.

In the nation the sap Coolidge did his time and now Hoover was coming on the stage. As they came to the last year of the decade, the country was in a mess, largely brought on, Marcus would assure you, by Prohibition. Morals were corrupted as a senseless law was naturally thwarted by a free people. Hoodlums controlled the manufacture and sale of spirits. Immense profits were made from the sale of the perfidious and hardly healthful beer. The nation wallowed in a Hogarthian bath of gin. You had to make your own damn whiskey to be sure it was pure! Whole cities were run by gangsters, with killing rampant on the streets. Marcus would not enter Chicago now if backed by Theodore and the full body of Rough Riders. The growth and use of sugar was astronomical. Volstead had not figured how easy it was to make booze!

His campaign for the medical use of whiskey in necessary cases was largely won in the various states, but Marcus despaired for the nation as a whole. Americans all hated being in the Prohibition vise but did not know how to get out of it. The national mood swung to disillusion. Cynicism ruled. We got drunk on Heroes. And Runyon, the Colorado Kid, got famous writing his smart, flip stuff. Ah, 'twas a wondrous age!

Ford had brought out, after all these years, a new model, the Model A. (That was a good example of Henry's logic, A comes after T.) It actually had colors other than black and was making a hit, or would if people could get one. Marcus believed that Ford's hold-up on production of the car was helping to cause this senseless so-called Bull Market, ever new highs in stock prices. A big money crowd had gotten behind the firm of General Motors and bought it heavily and so helped to start the present roller-coaster upwards.

Marcus, on the other hand, had divested himself of everything but the oil stocks and was all in cash and oil, mostly in Mexico backing some Texas boys down there, and gold and some Western land. Through Albert, dear good soul, Marcus had bought a goodly part of the state of Colorado. He owned grain fields there and grain fields in Nebraska but had no particular desire to go there and behold them. He believed he owned a mountain but realized he was beyond his mountain phase; he would stay at sea level, breathing easily.

One good thing about all this damn'd so-called Prosperity was that young Marcus Northway—Mark—was doing well in Cleveland. He was partners with another young buck, had their own advertising agency, just four years out of college, and was making money, he'd reported in his regular quarterly letters, so maybe the lad had had a point. His last letter reported he was contemplating marriage and would like for Marcus and Ida to meet the young woman. Well, Mark was twenty-five by now. Marcus supposed that was not too young to marry considering if he had no greater ambition. No need to wait 'til he was fifty-three! Ho ha.

"And what will we get him for a present when he marries?" Ida said. "A nice bit of money, to set by for the future? A down payment on a house? That would be generous, and kind, and like you, Marcus."

"No, my dear. Nothing like that. No great beneficence. I will leave the choice of wedding gift to you. Something significant in a merely symbolic way, I should think, like silver."

"Ah . . . You can give 'em that great huge useless urn that McKinley inscribed eight hundred words on to you . . . Well, don't make a face. If it's so dear to you, why don't you polish it? Let's see. How about the lamp? The big one from China? I believe that Mark admired it—or maybe it was Mattie who did so. Yes, I think I'll give them that. You know, in the Morning Room—the big gold and green lamp we brought from China with the vines patterned all over it like snakes."

"Yes. Splendid."

He knew that Ida thought the lamp would dominate any room they put it in and so keep them always reminded of them. But, he thought, the Chinese lamp would do. There remained a certain coldness in his heart.

As he so quickly then in June turned eighty-one, he had additional letters from his kin in Ohio, one from Tom Northway and one from his son Mark.

Tom's ill-typed letter began breezily. He hoped Marcus and Ida would come to the wedding they were planning for August. Then immediately and jocularly he asked if his elder cousin could spare him the brief loan of five to seven thousand dollars? He had, he confessed, gone out on a limb. Who wouldn't, right now, with all the profits being taken? He'd bought some Common Stocks that were sure comers, sure things. He would be glad to pay Marcus interest on the loan.

Marcus was amazed, then furious. He set the letter aside without answering it. In his mind he replied, not on your life, Tom! Get out of it. Don't be a moron for once in your life! Why, you are over fifty years old! Good God! There were a million fools and idiots out there, but Northways did not need to be among them!

Mark's note was manly and sincere. It came with the formal printed invitation to the wedding.

It would mean so much to him if they could come. He knew they would love his bride-to-be, Louise, and that she would love them. He enclosed a photograph. She had been a college beauty though had not graduated, having been captured by Mark. She was several years younger than he was. She was lovely in the picture.

Her eyes were rare, clear and knowing, her smile sweet, her figure graceful. He was pleased, and moved, for Mark. Certainly the boy had had a stroke of luck in this department. And her father, Luke Whitlock, was a professional man, a prominent lawyer in Cleveland. He had been a judge and run for Congress, as a LaFollette candidate! But still, he'd run. Her mother was a Hathaway, Mark reported, related to Anne Hathaway. Her name was Remember.

He showed the letter and photograph to Ida, or returned it to her, for she had been kind enough to open it for him.

She regarded the picture sternly, as she always regarded beauty, then murmured something sweet, and said, "Are you sure, Lovie, you don't want to go?"

He took pen in hand and wrote Mark Northway that his fiancee was lovely and he was pleased for him and looked forward to meeting her but regretted that he and Ida were not able to attend the wedding.

In October Ida came reeling into his study, violating his sanctum, distraught, looking as if she might be drunk. She had to come in sideways through the door; she had grown so much stouter still.

"Ma-mar-cus . . . " she wailed, or moaned.

He looked at her, then down at the newspaper, realizing, and rose and went and held her, hugging her gently back and forth, soothing her in a croon: "We're fine, my dear, we're fine, Ida, dear, it's all right, it's quite all right, we have not lost a penny . . . "

"Oh Marcus! Oh Marcus!"

Oh black and dreadful day, *October 29 of 1929*!

She seized and squeezed him so tightly he thought she'd maybe broken his back and ribs. She was shaking from the emotion of thinking they had lost their money.

He took her downtown to the Soda Shoppe by his bank, and

they had double dips of strawberry ice cream, though it was raw and cloudy along the California coast. They went across by ferry to San Diego and up to Sunset Cliffs and looked out over the water there, Ida holding tight to him. He thought of standing there with Mark and then thought of Tom Northway, thinking the fellow had probably lost his money, and felt sorry for him, and thought that he would like to go to Amagansett and paint a while when spring came.

He read that Ford and others had "honored" Al Edison up at the Greenfield museum and circus there in Michigan by re-enacting the Incandescent Bulb on its fiftieth anniversary. He read that Al was so tired that he could not sit at the banquet and did not speak to anyone but sat outside and, the report said, wept.

It made Marcus want to weep for him.

23

As the new decade came, there in Coronado, Ida Bailey Northway became, at least to her own satisfaction, finally a Great Lady.

This had its ups and downs, as the Kid used to say, for she could be imperious in her Great Ladyness, and Marcus knew no cure for it.

She was on the Board of the San Diego Symphony and in a few years would be president. On his side, General Northway was honorary commander of the San Diego American Legion Chapter. He had contributed heavily to the War Memorial in Balboa Park which now bore his name.

Though active and seeming happy, Ida had increasing bouts of illness. She had taken to going to a Regular, a Dr. Southard, in town, and had abandoned all sense of Similia. This damn Regular was giving her pills, narcotic agents, to make her sleep at night. Marcus was flabbergasted that she would thus turn to the Allopathic school.

They discovered that Tom Northway was indeed in deep trouble. He had not asked for help but in checking with Tom's lawyer Dan Funk, distant kin to them, Marcus found that Tom Northway had suffered heavy losses of money he did not have. He had had to mortgage his house and now stood to lose it. Tom was one of a million Americans who held stock on margin through the last summer and lost it in the first hour of the first great Drop on the fateful morning of October 24.

Well, what could you say? Tom Northway deserved his fate. He and those other fools had caused the Drop!

"Do not help him. Don't bail him out. You have helped him enough, all through his life! He would just . . ."

"No. I won't."

He was sorry to admit it to himself, but there was an utter coldness at this point in his heart toward Tom Northway and his family and his fate.

The daughter Lellie, saucy girl, had refused a year or so ago to come to New York to interview with Miss Finch for possible Finishing. Now she was planning to marry in the fall a fellow named Morris Lanier whom Ida feared might be Jewish. "Let us pray he is," Marcus said, "and is financially astute." Actually, as Marcus' check revealed, the fellow was of French extraction.

The news also came that Mark Northway and his partner had suddenly lost their fledgling advertising agency, lost it to the lack of clients in the bad economy. Marcus trusted that he would rebound. Ida was also firm that they had done enough for him. The lad's wife's—Louise's—father Judge Whitlock, it seemed, had his money in bonds in a bank that failed in Cleveland and lost all he had.

Dan Funk reported that Tom Northway claimed to him that he had considered jumping from the top of the Rose Building when his loss came. Marcus doubted the story. He thought it was just Tom's high sense of drama coming forth. Marcus had never heard of a Northway ever seriously contemplating ending his own life. Northways cherished life, deplored its brevity, desired to keep on going . . .

But the Ohio Northways were in a leaky boat all right.

The Great Lady had taken to inviting the upper crust of Coronado and of San Diego, such as it was, to lavish parties—entertainments— at Northway Lodge.

She would serve formally in the dining room, ringing a silver bell for the serving people, who were hired professionals from the Hotel Del Coronado and not just their daily retainers. They dined by candlelight at the long gleaming table and drank French wine. Marcus had stopped taking wine, for it brought on indigestion and the Farts, the only cure for which was whiskey, which you should stick to in the first place. The military from around there especially enjoyed these shindigs, as Marcus enjoyed their company and their respect.

On this particular evening old Admiral Shute and his goitered wife came to General and Mrs. Northway's gleaming table. "The Japs, the Japs," the Admiral bellowed, deep in his Bordeaux. "The Japs are on the march, building their bloody navy . . . "

The Admiral often confused himself with Lord Nelson and affected an English accent and vocabulary. "Beware, sir, the bloody Rising Sun . . . "

Rising at the head of table, Marcus vividly recounted for them the story of Ida's remaining standing after the Japanese played their anthem that time in Tokyo, and declaring, "Now we shall have the national anthem of the United States of America!"

"I did, I did!" Ida declared. "And they played it, too!"

There were chests stacked along the walls in the dining room full of clothes and other things brought back from over the world. It was Ida's favorite after-dinner sport to rummage through the chests and boxes, laughing and telling all her stories going through the Japanned lacquered chests of stuff, herself a large ruddy heap sitting by them on the floor, and have her guests all dress up in some costume or other, and do plays, and speak memorable pieces, and dance and sing.

Tonight they did the *Mikado*. They did it all in Japanese costumes, in honor of the Japs' foolish bloody ridiculous striving to build their navy and conquer China and Manchuria. No one had ever before seen such acting and singing, even at the Savoy! Titipu had never seen anything like Ida in her gown of crimson silk! But the exquisite Madame Esmeralda, who happened to be playing in Tijuana and invited to be among them this evening, stole the show, with her costume fashioned simply from the silk drapes, a fan of ostrich feathers and a head dress of bananas taken from the fruit bowl.

"She's the Rising Sun itself," old Admiral Shute declared, himself in mustaches stained from the corks of the Bordeaux, "and ain't she bloody beautiful!"

The evening turned formal at the end, with post-frolic coffee, brandy and tobacco.

Then Dennis escorted the Admiral and his wife, who in her Japanese silken finery had seemed to feel herself young and attractive again and had taken a minor role not calling for singing, home. Marcus and Ida bade farewell to the dozen guests. He walked Madame Esmeralda to the door and out to the driveway to her Italian roadster and watched her roar away. She declared before leaving that it was a lovely house, and a lovely time, and she and Madame Northway shook each other's hand. Ida stood at the doorway watching the guests depart. Then arm in arm they walked back into the house.

"She was nice," Ida said. "I'm glad you asked her; she was lively. Is she Mexican? She was right, wasn't she? It was a lovely evening, and fun, wasn't it?"

She glowed. She allowed herself wine on these occasions, and took a large part in the fun, so deeply did she want these evenings to be memorable, smashing successes, and talked of in the towns.

"You had fun too, didn't you? You have to admit it. You even put a costume on, tonight."

"Yes."

He said he would turn out the lights and turn on the Safety System.

He checked the safe concealed in the paneling of the Morning Room. He straightened the costumes back into the chests in the dining room whose wallpaper, hand-made in Paris, reflected the pattern of the flowers and shrubs in the garden outside the French windows. The servants had left the kitchen spick-and-span, all the brass-fitted, wood-doored food safes latched. He turned off the annunciator, then turned off the ballroom lights.

He had never said to Ida how much, though a much larger house, this house reminded him of the house where he grew up in Whiskeyville, the layout of it, even to a small ballroom, so much the same.

Out back he had built a redbrick wall around the yard, and within it had his farm boy's compost heap and vegetable garden. Under the big-boled palms, nearer the house, the planting, he thought, was striking. The lemon trees and the Chilean jasmine smelled so sweet that Ida wanted to try to make a perfume of it. Ah, well, this was her place, after all, the culmination of her dreams, finally at last her California home, and soon she would be president of the Symphony across the bay. His heart was glad for her.

Al had drawn up the Safety System and electrified the house, drew the alarm and system so a switch could be hit to light up these grounds and the hallways inside and a signal sent to the police. This pleased Ida, who, having once had nothing, deep within her feared that it all would be taken from her. Standing at the latticed dining area and table in the yard, he smelled the trees and flowers and fern garden over which Al had installed the electrically motorized sprinkler pipe system, so that with every use of water and light he thought of Al, as all Americans should.

A woman seemed to come across the garden to him as he turned out all the lights. It was not Ida—or the Nymph come back, now readying to head back out of this country and sail the ocean once again. It was not Cora. For a moment he thought it must be his mystic mother, come to see this grand house across the continent from where she'd lived, spent her life and never got away from —

Then he became angry with himself. This was not his kind of mysticism. This was silly, senile! What was wrong with him?

God, how rare she'd been tonight!

24

When Edison died, in that sad year of 1931, Marcus traveled east for the funeral.

He grieved, though could not be irrationally sad. The bumbling body had, for the genius, become a burden to the brain.

They laid him to rest under an oak tree on a hill. It was a pleasing prospect, as they say, looking out over the scene of his success in the period of his true activity. What more can we ask?

Now he had become immortal, in the only possible sense. Like Burbank.

Now he was forever young again, forever tapping on the telegraph key, finding the filament for the incandescent bulb, speaking "Mary had a little lamb" into the phonograph.

Now he was forever, to all Americans and to prosperity, the real and truest Hero, young Genius, forever young, no need to play the silent smiling Buddha anymore.

Now he was Thomas Alva Edison.

Henry Ford was at the funeral. He was in deep melancholy because Al had died, as if Al had let him down. Marcus went over to him. They did not shake hands but nodded to each other. Ford looked at him as if he were Hamlet's father's ghost, not that he would know that allusion.

"I didn't think he'd go so soon," Ford said, looking off into the sky.

"Mortality is a thin dime, Henry," Marcus said.

But the damn fool wasn't listening.

He went to New York and sojourned, then on to Washington. The Fleece of Washington was white as snow on this December day. Everything sparkled in the sun. He took his cane and walked out from the Cosmos Club into the sparkling day.

He walked quite a way, slipping through snow and ice beneath his sturdy shoes, in his greatcoat with hat pulled down on his head, old Leo the sharp-pointed hickory and brass (and Spanish steel inside) partner picking their way along, heading towards the Capitol.

At full noon, after a good trudge, he walked down New Jersey and crossed Louisiana and in that strange way of our nation came to sudden splendor of sun on snow and vistas and dear old grounds and structures he had half-forgotten.

Going in, the carillon chimed, it clanged and banged, a little off but proud, asserting, sending its tones into the air. As he walked in, gray squirrels frisked in the sun from upside down on a tree to him, why, they actually came running after him until he thought, I will have to kick you, little bastards—but then took off after birds.

He looked down the vistas of snow and avenues and buildings to the pointed monument. By God, he thought, it was finer than Paris. Why, come to think of it, it was finer than anything! "Land of hope and glory . . ."

The great stairs up to the speckled pillared domed building were behind him. Mr. Justice Marshall sat there beside him green with cold and age and let us hope wisdom looking down the vista.

And the exhilarating thought came to Marcus Northway, I am a free man. I am a free American. And he walked on down and over to Pennsylvania to the White House.

When he started up the driveway, a sergeant of the guard with two soldiers, rifles slung, came to greet him.

"Sorry, sir," he said. "You can't come any farther. White House is closed today. No tours today."

Marcus cocked his head and looked at the sergeant, who could not see through his coat to the ribbon in the buttonhole of his suit but seemed to regard him with respect. He was a tough old Master Sergeant. Marcus would wager that he divined that the lion's head was attached to a sword sheathed in the cane. On the other hand, he must have figured that Marcus was neither an assassin nor a Bolshevik, though it was getting hard to tell.

"Thank you, Sergeant," he said. "I am just beholding it. I have no business there. I did not wish a tour. I'm just an American passing by."

"Yes, sir."

Marcus batoned his cane and saluted him. He came to attention and saluted. Marcus turned and walked away. He was going to be stiff as holy hell and had better find a taxi to take him to the Club and its stock of good whiskey. Were he here to meet the President—now Hoover—on some business as of yore, it would be the seventh time he had been received by a President in his office in the White House.

FOUR

25

There came some rumor or report—or actually more than that, an intelligence, in the press—that the liner carrying among other notables Madame Esmeralda, the internationally known fan dancer and singer, on her return from Spain and Portugal had met disaster in mid-ocean, with some passengers saved but many lost. There was a report that she was lost but that was not true. It could not be so. Surely she was saved. They must wait for word and trust that that was so.

Of course she was all right. She had been in danger, for he had felt it, the spirit waves had come to him, but she had transcended it—was in the chill water but was saved—oh dear God, had transmuted perhaps, become a bird, a fierce strong bird of Spirit, yes, and flew up away from it, the deep chill stormy water, from danger and death, and was La Pajarita, and on her way to him—and he would wait to hear.

He locked himself in his study. He had a new writing project, a manual for health in America. Finally he would make his mark and market his cures to the nation and the world. "A Healthy America." He would call it that. He scrawled it across the first sheet in heavy black ink. What to begin with, of all he knew? Ah, yes . . . of course . . . the bowels . . . proper eating and evacuation . . .

"Marcus! Open this door, Marcus! Answer me. What is the matter? Are you all right?"

"Go away, Ida. For God's sake just go away and leave me alone!"

What is the matter with today's doctors and surgeons? Gallstone operations as well as unnecessary appendicitis seem to be common, some with fatal results. These unnecessary operations can be prevented by avoiding food which develops putrefaction in the intestinal tract, as shown by the awful odor in the stools, which is from the ingestion of beef, ham, veal, sweetbreads, and mutton or lamb in conjunction with the feature of stagnation of suspended peristalsis due to the irregular attention given the bowels.

Let the doctor determine upon the hour for the physiological and systematic demands of the bowels—then keep the hour regardless of duties!

Even if you should be waiting to see the President of the United States and this demand occurs, you must meet it. Yet such an embarrassment can be avoided by steadily determining the hour. The best time for most to select is between six and eight in the morning, as other dates cannot well be arranged during the day.

Oh . . . Oh . . . Mi Pajarita . . .

Now you must be a moron not to realize that fruit is an antiseptic and meat is a putrefactive. Fruit is a blessing, a laxative and emollient, while meat constipates and engorges tissues. Fruit dissipates odor, while meat engenders stench in intestines. With regulated bowels, excluding meat, no appendicitis.

The food value of the grape is greater than most fruits. But others containing fine content of acid, sugar, solids and protein are pineapples, oranges, grapefruit, limes and the tamarinds. The banana is the principal such food used in Cuba and in Porto Rico . . .

Ah Jesus, no! Please, God . . .

Ah dear God constipation is a fearful Enemy as it blockades the physiological processes . . .

Fruit must always be on the table . . .

Grapefruit for breakfast without meat is a good beginning . . .

Remember siempre that . . .

Ida was awfully good when she understood. She let him be, to stay in his study and scribble, or pretend to, to smoke and swivel. She only exhorted him not to take too much from his stock of whiskey. Actually he took none.

One day when she did knock at the private door of his retreat there was a visitor. Rubbing his eyes, Marcus rose, wobbling a bit, smoothing his vest and adjusting pince-nez, to greet him.

But the large grizzled black man did not shake hands but came right to him and embraced him, *un embrazo fuerte*, and they stood there for a long moment hugging one another.

"Oh Albert," Marcus said.

"Yes, sir, General. I thought that I would come to see you. I knew you would be sad. Oh, the lovely, beautiful girl you saved . . . "

"I am not sad, Albert. Here, have a chair."

"Sir?"

"She is all right. She survived, you see. We are in touch by Thought, or soon will be. I know her spirit lives. She is alive, somewhere. She is not . . . dead."

Albert looked at him, best shot and horseman of the Rough Riders, craggy-faced, his eyes sunk deep in his head, Marcus Northway's age.

"Yes, sir," he said. "Her spirit is alive. Well, General, I have come to take you on a trip. Dennis will drive. The car is ready. You must pack your field kit. We are going to Colorado, going on that Western trip we were always going to take. If we don't do it now, General, why, hell, I don't know when we are likely to."

"Oh, my friend . . . "

Albert stood. "Tomorrow morning," he said.

"Yes, Sergeant," Marcus said.

He packed his field kit and Ida packed his boots and clothes. When he rose, she was already up and out, going in to town, and a new contractor was pulling in the driveway to add more storage space upstairs.

Later, in the evening, when Ida had dealt with all problems in town and had set the contractor on his proper course in the upper story, dealt with it all as a hammer strikes a spike, she invaded Marcus' darkly paneled study and rummaged around a bit in there.

She found the newest pages of "A Healthy America," the "book" he now claimed to be spending his time on. Actually she found he had completed nearly fifty pages of it, all about healthful diet and exercise and proper elimination and so on. The latest little chapter was titled, in his now wavery penmanship, "Give Up Meat Products And Eat The Laxative Fruits." "I believe that in the future in intelligent societies cereals and nuts will take the place of meats," it began. When he died, she would find several dozen more pages, but she would put it all in a folder and put it deep in a chest of other stuff and would thank God the long trial of his damn'd scribbling was over, for him and for herself. If she'd had it typed up and printed and made into a little book, it might have brought Marcus Northway the recognition he was seeking, for it was miles ahead of its time and almost contemporary in the truth of its assertions about the equation of energy and health and food and exercise. But, now, in the study, she set it aside on the desk and reached for his glass and the damn whiskey from the drawer and poured herself a glass of the rich amber stuff and sat and smelled it and took some sips, and contemplated her husband and all his ideas and demons, leafing through another something there that he'd been writing out.

He seemed to be arguing against those who had criticized that crazy Luther Burbank for his so-called "new creations." Someone had said there was only one New Creation in this world, the work and church of Jesus Christ. She didn't know about that, particularly, but remembered when the fellow had said it—that creaking old Canon Watson, in their own church here, the church they had practically bought and paid for—that Marcus had huffed out of the church leaving her in the pew embarrassed.

"Burbank was doing God's work, for the benefit of mankind," she read. "As Edison said, 'What is God, if not Intelligence, which may and should be used for the reforming of God's creation through man's ingenuity on this earth?'"

Ah! She swept the sheets aside, nearly threw them in the wastebasket. These men! Marcus and all of them! Dear God in Heaven. They were "new creations" themselves, weren't they, and weren't they creating all of us who followed along in their own image? Life was rich and rare, most wonderful and strange, it seemed to Ida, the way men were allowed to live it!

Now a trio of them, an old black man and his son, Albert and Dennis LeMaistre, and Marcus Northway, slowly coming out of his trance, drove to Colorado and visited the land Marcus owned and then Albert's own small ranch. They drove to New Mexico and visited Taos where the mountain men had come and Santa Fe where the French bishop had built his beautiful church. Being from as far west as you could live on this grand continent, he seemed to be going somehow to the real "west" to its east. Wasn't that odd? They went on up to Montana, to the Glacier Park, and to Wyoming, where Owen Wister set his book *The Virginian*. Marcus did not wish to go to the Dakotas. He had always half believed that Theodore had manufactured the Badlands.

It brought a sense of reality, if also of myth, seeing all this land, this country, the mountains and rivers and meadows and tablelands of the West. They used to say, as euphemism, if you died you had "gone West," so he reckoned the trip was appropriate, as metaphor, and reality.

Going on in to Texas, they stopped at the Pass of the North, El Paso, because he wished to see Albert Fall, who had done Warren Harding in with Teapot Dome. The old rogue lived in a little house in El Paso looking to the mountains. He shambled out to greet them, chewed on his mustache, said he had some new deals working. Jehoshaphat! Marcus would have liked to kick him. But it confirmed a central notion he'd always had: most men were more stupid than evil. Old Albert Fall did not seem to understand at all the magnitude of what he'd done.

(He'd throw out his spade—qualify his notion—on Harry Daugherty, though: Daugherty was evil.)

As that blowhard Mencken said, America had produced many Boobs, about half off the damn frontier and half from the corrupt cities and sleepy villages, he supposed.

"Are you feeling better, old man?" Dennis said, rolling on back true west towards California.

"Yes, you insubordinate pup."

They had left Albert LeMaistre, dear fellow, kind friend, back in Colorado. They had not climbed any mountains together, but they had stood and looked at them.

26

In that same year Mark Northway's wife Louise gave birth to a son, but almost two months prematurely. The young couple was in dire straits and so could not leave the baby in the hospital in Shaker Heights but took him home to their apartment and incubated him in an overheated room. Though blind in one eye, the boy survived and in his first year became healthy and vigorous, for which they all thanked God. Marcus and Ida went by Cleveland on their way to New York, for they had business there and at Willowstone, and paid their respects. Meeting Louise Hathaway Whitlock Northway, Marcus thought her lovely. She said that her mother, Remember, whom they also met, was mystic. Marcus' old Romantic heart stirred with love and affection for the girl, so frail but strong, with her young son.

They had named the boy Marcus. Now there was another Marcus Northway: puny, cock-eyed and half-blind, but with a devilish grin and gurgle to him, real.

"Named for his father," Ida said, "not for you."

"Doubtless, Ida, doubtless. But there he is: Marcus Northway Third."

"Don't be a fool. He's not Marcus Aurelius, any more than his father was. He is a Junior, not a Third!"

"Jehoshaphat, woman! His name is Marcus Northway!"

"Ah! Yes. Well, my love, they are calling him, you noticed, this little one-eyed wonder, 'Bo.'"

"Well, let them call him that, then. I got used to 'Mark.'"

"And why not? You are the Marcus, the one and only Marcus."

"Actually, I really have never quite gotten used to it, to 'Mark.' I believe that is because it makes me think of that curmudgeonly fool Clemons, tried to get into society over in Hartford there."

"Mark Twain was our greatest writer, though I never read him. Everyone used to say so. Greatest writer for men, I mean."

"Hah! A pessimist and a Softheart. Excoriated Theodore, don't you remember, Ida? Twain said Theodore was clearly insane because of his love for war and his campaign for activity and virility. That was not true. Theodore abhorred war. All of us, all the leaders and the generals, military and medical, abhor war. What Theodore Roosevelt loved, you see, was the threat of war. And the power and ability behind the threat. We have grown so pitifully weak now, I fear, in the Navy and the Air Corps . . . "

"Yes, yes," said Ida.

They sent the young Northway heir a set of silver plates and cups all chased with squirrels holding nuts in paws made by Tiffany and engraved "MN III." Mark Northway replied rather formally, it being the depth of the Depression, that he was sure the child would grow to appreciate the gift.

Marcus knew from Dan Funk that it was whispered, including by Tom Northway to Harry Northway and others in the family, that he and Ida were oblivious to the so-called Depression and its devastating effect on so many in this fractured country. That was not true. He was not suffering from it but was not oblivious to it, and was content that America would come out of it in this very decade. The inevitable war would do it, and bring the nation back to individual and national discipline and achievement. In that way, like Theodore, he valued war.

In the family the situation was that Louise's mother and father, he a gentle man six and a half feet tall, had lost their house in Cleveland to his failed bank and unpaid taxes and were now living with other relatives in the old farmhouse of Remember's mother, a remarkable woman of more than one hundred years of age, on the far edge of Cleveland where it used to be all farm land. Soon Mark and Louise with the baby had to stop paying rent and also went to live there. The old house of Milo Hathaway had no plumbing or electricity but used well water and an outhouse.

Mark Northway was doing his best, Marcus understood, attempting to sell brass cooking ware door to door in the city. (So much for advertising!) Tom Northway had lost all he had and would have lost his house in Shaker Heights as well had not Dan Funk advanced him the money to save it. Funk said he felt obligated to do so since it was on his say-so that Tom put up more collateral to "save" his stock investment. Marcus murmured to Funk that he appreciated the kindness of his heart while deploring his judgment.

It was at this juncture, as Marcus Northway approached his eighty-fourth birthday and the young couple and the parent couples were on a terrible treadmill with no end or solution in sight, as the nation faced the cruel early spring of 1932, that Marcus decided once more to intervene.

He would try again to help, as they all so badly needed help. Specifically he would try to help Mark and the lovely girl, Louise. He would go the second mile, or was it the third mile by now? Whatever . . .

"No!" Ida said, or exploded. "No! Are you out of your mind? You fool! Let well enough alone . . . "

It was the only time she had allowed herself to call him that. It infuriated Marcus.

"It was you who begrudged them a proper wedding present! You who said you would not be helping Tom Northway out of his jam, when he was begging you for money for his losses . . . "

"He never begged," Marcus said with dignity. "And it was Dan Funk who bailed him out."

"You said . . . "

"I have changed my mind."

"Ah . . . " she said. "All right. All right, Marcus. You have a good heart, a damn good heart, as I of all do know. Just . . . do not overdo it. Make it something they can do . . . not a gift. Then maybe they won't resent you—us—for it. Make them a fair and reasonable proposition. I insist on being in on it! Something we two decide on together. Do not in any way let it be charity, but let there be a place for their own real effort in it, and then, why, for God's sake, leave it up to them!"

He did not fight her. Where was this energy coming from? He knew part of his anger came from how difficult it was for him to summon up this impulse, this Christian part, and act on it—let alone face Ida's ire over it.

"I will ask them to come here," he said icily, sweeping his cigar around the Waldorf suite.

"No! Why? Oh God . . . We need to go home, to our real home, Marcus. You need to plant your garden. I am thinking of having the kitchen cabinets rebuilt. I have Symphony and I have bridge and I have Church. There is going to be a chamber music ensemble. I do not see why they can not come to Coronado, stay at the Del."

"No! I mean, my dear . . . " Still icily. "We . . . we have done that." "Marcus!"

"And we will not touch the damn kitchen! At the cost of half my fortune, the kitchen—the whole house—is now exactly, I think, as it should be. Jorge will plant the garden. The Symphony does not tune up until August. I did not know that you had come to love chamber music."

"I do! I adore it!"

"We will have it then. An ensemble of chamber music, for you and for them, here in the Waldorf."

"No! I mean . . . Well, that is nice of you, Marcus, and considerate of my feelings. I know you do not . . . "

"And we will host them here. They have never been here, except for Tom when he first came out covered with straw, a clodhopper from the country, so long ago. Here it will all be more . . . objective."

"All right. If that is your wish, if this is what we must do at all. But we will agree, you and I together, on our proposition to them?"

"Yes. It will be under terms we both agree to."

"All right, Lovie. Fine, then."

They looked at each other, bright blue eyes and eyes nearly black, hard-eyed. He would as soon have negotiated a treaty with the Germans or the Japanese as with Ida Bailey.

"I do not want the Whitlocks here," she said. "There is no need for them to come, even though I perceived you were quite taken with that tiny woman, Louise's mother, that Remember Whitlock. They are not really family."

"Well. Maybe there is not need for anyone but Mark and Louise to come."

"No. I do want Tom and Mattie here. I want them to come and to act right! With the children, Mark and Louise. And I do not think you should send them, any of 'em, the money to come, the train fare to New York. If they want to come, to accept the invitation, let 'em by God get here on their own!"

"Dan says Tom is back in harness, he and Mattie probably can swing it. But the young ones have no money at all. I was thinking that since I am asking them to come here . . . "

"No!"

Again he was surprised at her vehemence.

"Let them borrow it if they must," she said.

He sat down at his desk and wrote them letters inviting them to come in April, to stay as his guests in the Waldorf, to hear a proposition he and Ida had for them, for the family.

Ida heard years later the consternation the letters caused.

"I'll be G-God-damned if I will go!" exclaimed Tom Northway. "N-none of us will go!"

"Oh, it might be nice," Mattie said. "Why not let them pay for a stay in New York City? We need a vacation. It's been so grim here. Why not hear what they have to say?"

"This is not right. It's ridiculous, in fact," Mark Northway said, now a man halfway desperately on the edge of thirty, a boy no longer but a man out of work and out of prospects too. "First it's the little silk suits for Bo, and the silver plates and cups from Tiffany, in the middle of the worst depression in history . . . "

"They mean it well. They mean to help," his young wife said. "I truly think they do. Let's go. I think it will be—oh, maybe—fun. We'll have to take Bo, we can't leave him."

"I hate to be summoned," Mark said. "I've been through the whole thing before!"

"Oh come on," said Louise. "I think it sounds glamorous. New York. Staying at the Waldorf! Maybe it will be the most wonderful summons we'll ever have. You know you still love the old boy, deep down, even if he did try to rule your life."

So they agreed, and borrowed the money to come, and brought young Marcus Northway III, or "Bo," slightly more than a year old, their incubator baby but by now a healthy boy, and came in April from Cleveland on the Pennsylvania line in to New York's Grand Central Station.

Dennis and Marcus met them in the new Rolls Royce. It was a deep blue, that now having become Marcus' favorite color. Old General Pierce had his former silver Rolls and from time to time Marcus saw him rolling through the city in it as if it was original with him. The new car had a bar, which Marcus kept closed except on out of town trips, folded into the backs of the front seats, and had cutglass vases inside on each side filled daily with fresh flowers. It was a seven-passenger car, and when all had embarked for the trip from Grand Central to the Waldorf, Tom Northway sat like a giant frog on the jumpseat. It was terribly awkward. Mattie just smiled at Marcus as if he were Methuselah and did not say a word. Mark Northway gawked out the car's curtained window as if he'd never been in the city before. The baby burped and cried.

"He's wet," Mattie said.

"He'll be okay 'til we get there," said Louise.

"Well . . . I am pleased you came," said Marcus.

Tom Northway let out what could have been a snort or a loud sigh, and Mattie smiled at him again as if he damn well should be.

"And how was your trip? Did you enjoy it?"

"Oh yes!" said Louise, the only one seeming to be excited at being here. A blue-eyed, fresh-faced young mother, she was, Marcus judged, indeed lovely. "Mark and I ate in the diner! It was the first real 'date' we've had in months. On the table in the diner was a fresh red rose in a crystal vase, it kept trembling on the table as the train curved this way and that . . . "

Mark looked at her as if he might be embarrassed at her telling this to his old "uncle" who had summoned them.

"Then . . . At night, in the Pullman berth, Mark was up above, and I had Bo—he slept so soundly—next to the window. I pulled up the shade to look out, Uncle Marcus, and saw all the lights as we went by. I loved to watch and feel the rhythm of it."

She quoted from a poem of Emily Dickinson about lapping the miles and licking the valleys up, or some such thing, but the others sat like sticks.

"I w-wondered," said Tom Northway, "w-why you had us c-come here. I thought you were l-living there in C-Cor-a . . . in California . . . now."

"That is correct," Marcus said.

They were greeted at the ornate gold and white door to the suite, with the Northway family crest and "Perseverant" motto over it, by Ida, her white baby grand piano lit by a Tiffany lamp behind her in the living room.

"Tom! Mattie! And the children! Look at the little one. Dear God, is he wet already? Well, Tom, are you enjoying Rover?"

"Rover?" Marcus said, herding them through the doorway, and seeing Tom's wife Mattie stiffen in her tracks.

"R-Rover . . . " Tom began.

"The dog I sent him," Ida said, beaming at this secret she had kept from her husband, whose opinion of dogs as pets was that human beings who permitted themselves to be licked by the germ-ridden tongue of a diseased, flea-infested, dog were morons. "A perfectly gorgeous, trained Irish setter. I thought you would adore him."

"I . . . " Tom tried.

"Rover is happily with Ed and Viney, in Mesopotamia, on the old farm there, where I sent him," Mattie Northway said, giving Ida a chilled cocktail of a smile.

"Well, I never!" Ida exclaimed, looking imperiously at Tom.

"She was afraid that R-Rover would d-devour her b-bird," Tom said, making a comic face at Ida.

"Dennis," Ida said, "please be good enough to show them to their quarters. That's all right, Tom, Dennis will get your bags."

"I am able to carry my own—our—bags," Tom said, with a glare and no hint of stammer.

The suite had several bedrooms and baths, but on Ida's orders Marcus put each couple in a room on the floor above. Ida did not want them too close, "in our hair," "disrupting our schedules," for fear of tension or that the babe might bawl. Marcus was fascinated, beholding him, with the tiny boy, his eye crossed and lacking full sight because of his prematurity but otherwise looking extraordinarily like a "Marcus Northway," that is to say, like a little Chinese emperor. He was, Marcus believed, not only babbling words but already trying to speak in sentences.

"Sure," said Ida, "and by the time they leave he'll be helping you write 'A Healthy America'!"

27

The first morning Ida had a great breakfast brought into the suite and at 9:30 began to fuss and fume because they were not there.

"Why in the world can't anything go right? It will get cold."

Marcus, if the truth be known, had had his hot Vichy water and lemon and had himself quite forgotten about the breakfast. Oh Lord, he remembered that she had told him to tell them all to be here. Instead he had donned white flannels and blue blazer, thinking they might all go for a stroll up Fifth Avenue. Rather than 'fessing up, he stood at parade rest and let Ida do what she would do.

She rang Mark and Louise and said in her unmistakable, now shrill voice: "Where are you? Breakfast is already here!"

"Just changing the baby, Aunt Ida," Mark says. "We didn't realize ... We'll be down in a minute."

Calling Mattie and Tom, and reaching Tom, Ida barked: "Come down here and eat breakfast! You come this minute, Tom Northway!"

"What did he say?"

"I don't know, his dreadful stammering. You would think . . . Why, I . . . "

But she was gracious in a few minutes as the young ones arrived, flustered and looking thrown-together. She seated them at the gleaming dining room table, and when Mattie and Tom came in minutes later, Mattie wearing a housecoat and Tom red-faced and with his eyes popped out and in unpressed pants and an old flannel shirt, Ida pointed them to their chairs at table. Contemplating all the cooling stuff on the board, Marcus took his place at head of table and diddled with pot and cups.

"My God!" Ida, who stayed on the fly, screamed. "No! Germs! Oh . . . Marcus!"

Poor Louise had put little Bo down beside her on the immaculate white carpet. She looked at Marcus. He rose and moved around the table and bent and picked up the little emperor, who gurgled and grinned at him, making his heart sing, and sat with him in his lap in a chair near Louise. His knee had popped as he bent, but he did not mind that all had heard it. The baby seemed terribly small and light in his arms but the lad's heart beat strong. "I think it's clean," he said, "but Ida is correct in regard to the imminence of germs. No use tempting fate."

Mark and his mother and his father stared at the carpet, bright as any Greek shepherd's fleece, and at Ida and Marcus as if they were crazy; but the young mother looked sweetly at him as if he were a rescuer, which in point of fact he was.

Mark came to and pitched in. "He sure has taken a shine to you," he said.

"Yes," said Tom graciously. "He c-certainly has."

Ida sat. "Isn't anyone going to eat?" she demanded. "I had this all specially ordered and prepared!"

The Waldorf had furnished honeydew melon, of which Marcus partook, and thick lamb chops, hash browned potatoes, coffee cake, a rasher of bacon, scrambled and shirred eggs and much else in the spread. Mark picked at it, as Ida chided him. Louise just looked at it all. Marcus observed her put her lamb chop in her napkin, then go into the bathroom with it. He turned "Bo" over to Carmelita, whom Ida had engaged as nanny for the infant. He wondered why they called the little beggar "Bo." He would have to ask. Louise came out of the bathroom looking pale. He hoped the chop had cleared the pipes. Tom Northway had eaten just about the whole coffee cake and was about to destroy the rasher of bacon. Marcus thought that Ida would be pleased with him, eating like a horse, the only one really eating, but in a while she gave Tom a sharp look and said in that voice that could be somehow deep and shrill at the same time, "I have never been so insulted in my life, Tom . . . and in my own home, too!"

Mouth full of egg he sputtered. "W-what in the h-hell, Ida, are you talking about?"

Marcus chuckled. In another life, he thought, they would have been great lovers.

"I have never before eaten a meal with an unshaved man!"

"Except her father." He could not help it. Laughing, he whispered it into Louise's ear as she sat next to him. She snorted in reply.

Tom Northway stood and quivered and pointed his finger at Ida, who sat like the Queen Mother in her chair at the head of the room. His eyes were blazing, his face becoming red.

"You s-said to get down here th-that very minute. I almost came in my pa-pa-pajamas, God damn it anyway!"

And stalked out.

They all looked to Ida for her reaction.

She smiled merrily and even, dear God, winked at Mattie, sitting across from her. "One thing you can say about the Northways," she said, "is that they all have wonderful tempers!"

"Why so do you, Ida," Mattie replied. "And you are no more a Northway than Louise or I."

Ho ho. Ha.

"I believe I'll take a stroll," said Mark, looking at Louise.

"Fine, dear. Bo's asleep. Carmelita's with him. Go on and stretch your legs. I'll be fine."

Ida bustled to call up the caterers to clear away the mess of food and china, silver and napery.

"Would you like a smoke?" he said to Louise.

"Love it!"

He led her into the study, into his sanctum. She sat in the leather chair where the Colorado Kid and a few others had sat through the years, and he took his place in his leather chair at the desk he cherished and opened a drawer and brought out a pack of the smooth-tasting Turkish cigarettes he kept for Pajarita and, courtly, rose and offered her one, and lit it for her.

She turned it in her fingers, exhaling, offering a quizzical smile, studying the exotic cigarette.

"All this luxury," she said. "All these things . . . " Her hand holding the cigarette circled the room with its various trophies and appointments and acquisitions.

"All that you have . . . When the whole world is depressed and going broke. When half the nation doesn't have enough to eat."

"Ah," he said, swiveling to look around, clipping, lighting his cigar.

"Oh . . . ! I know you can't help it."

"Well." She was right. She was a wise young woman. He could not help it. Puffing at the Havana, Marcus felt strangely powerless and out of it, with all he had, all he had done, about as real and relevant as the Book of Nahum, or as his Sunday school teacher used to abbreviate it back there in Whiskeyville, Book of Nah. What . . . in the holy hell . . . difference did it make, really make? Well. Her almost fragile face; eyes light blue; cornflower-color hair. She was a find. Her mother, they said, was mystical. She brought grace and beauty to the family, as Mattie had before. Yes: grace. Lutie, she'd had it, too.

Suddenly she, this one, Louise, young Mark's girl, his find, began to giggle like she really was a girl, then guffawed, laughed out loud.

"Oh dear! Oh my, Uncle Marcus . . . You see, I must tell you, we were eating when she called. Oh dear! What a treat. Breakfast in bed. We had fresh figs, and scrambled eggs and bacon. And Mark had to jump up and shave, we had to dress and get the baby ready . . . Oh God, I've never moved so fast!"

She made a face. Marcus began to laugh. Pretty soon they were roaring, tears running down their cheeks.

They stayed a week. Ida kept a busy program for them. She had wanted Tom and Mattie to come, "to act right." Tension stayed thick in the air. Each day Mark, now a six foot man becoming heavier than Marcus would have imagined and wearing rimless glasses but yet with his bright eyes and Northway features and matchless smile went off on his own, obviously to escape the confines of the hotel and family. He said he went off to check prospects with advertising agencies and such. Marcus took it with a grain of salt, seeing no indication that Mark had any real intention of coming to New York even if he happened to meet Bruce Barton on the street and get the offer of a fabulous job. Mark and Louise seemed dedicated to the plebeian life in Ohio. Mark always returned in the afternoon from his excursions ruddy and refreshed; Marcus suspected he'd had a nip. Now Mark seemed a different person, a man coarsened from the naive, eager boy he'd been, going on stamina and often, it seemed to Marcus from a medical viewpoint, false energy, manufactured "enthusiasm," a man whom now he scarcely knew. It made him sad, and he made a try to go beyond it. He asked Mark if he would like to take lunch with him one day at his Club.

"Oh. No. I don't think so, Uncle Marcus. But thanks. I mean, thank you very much."

It was damn awkward. Marcus' club was somewhere his namesake did not wish to go back to.

For relief, leaving the "girls" to their own devices, Marcus went off to the club a few times on his own, just to sit and smoke and read the papers and write out checks for Ida's bills and a letter or two to Coronado, an instruction to the bank or to the Legion post, or a note to Billy about the affairs of the inn there at Amagansett. What the women did, bowing to Ida's control, was wait in the suite for vendor after vendor bringing to them silver, linens, handmade baby clothes, and make appointments for photographers to come and appointments to try on clothes at Altman's. "It is the only real, that is to say, elegant, store in New York," Ida said. "It's not Paris, of course. Now, Louise, you might as well have a few really nice things. God knows when you will be able to afford them for yourself! Mattie, you come along and help Louise choose. I know you won't get a penny out of Tom!"

Ida did stop short of offering to buy anything for Matilda Northway. Mattie would have struck her with the heavy Ohio umbrella she carried, not trusting for a moment the weather, streets, traffic or people of New York.

Louise was terribly good about it, aghast and embarrassed as she was. Ida bought for her, picking it all out herself, declaring she knew best in this line of endeavor. She bought five evening gowns, truly handsome they were, and should have been, costing three or four hundred dollars apiece in Depression days, as well as several matronly-looking ensembles that made Louise appear to be at least a decade older than she was or wished to look. "I don't know when or where I'll wear any of them," she said, "but, you know, they do make me feel like Cinderella."

Ida beamed. It made her happy to be buying for the girl. Mattie Northway just shook her head and helped to box the stuff to send back home. Tom Northway stayed glum, grim and silent, a fat fly in Ida's ointment.

Sitting in the club Marcus wrote his brother William to ask if he had paid the taxes yet? He feared for Billy still. Billy kept sloppy books and records. But he was happy. William Northway was for the first time in his life really happy. Fruitcake, shortcake happy. For he had found a woman out west on his trip and married her and brought her back to Amagansett. Marcus had promised Billy he would come and visit and meet her, and he would, when this was over.

He'd found the woman in Oklahoma. She was from the Indian Territory. She was an Indian. Billy said she was Osage, said she was Osage royalty, kin to Billy Bowlegs. Ida exclaimed, saying she had no desire to meet her, what had gotten into Billy, was he going beyond the stage of simple-minded and losing his mind! Marcus had sat down when he received the intelligence and roared a laugh, then cried tears of joy for his little brother and sent him a box of Havanas and sent a handsome benefaction to them both. Her name was Liz.

In the afternoon he managed to get Louise to himself for a stroll. He took her, her arm in his, along the row of boutiques of Peacock Alley off the hotel, by Cartier and Tiffany. No one was in the gilded shops.

"May I buy you a trifle, some pearls or a diamond or a ruby, a brooch to adorn your new evening gowns?" he said, only half in jest.

It almost made her angry. She gave his arm a shake. Why, Pajarita would have had the pearls around her neck in such a flashing instant!

Gliding along with her he said: "I believe you were a Flapper. Eh? Are you not a dancer?"

"Oh, yes! Of course. A famous dancer, Uncle Marcus. I do the Charleston and the Black Bottom, all of them. We must go out and dance them all, you and I! And you—you are an old roué."

No accusation had so delighted him in years.

He begged off that evening when Ida took Mark and Louise off, Dennis driving and guarding their bodies, to a Speakeasy, where she'd heard from some source or other they had delicious pompano. Ida did not drink there but was excited by the music, the jazz, in the place. The next night, on Marcus, Mark and Louise went out, just the two of them, their only time on the visit to be out alone together, to the Persian Room. They came back to the suite and had a brandy with him, Ida sitting by him.

"It was wonderful," said Louise, all flushed and delicately beautiful. "Thank you so much, Uncle Marcus. It was Eddie Duchin. Have you heard of him?"

"Why yes, my dear, I believe I have."

"Oh, I'm sorry."

"Oh no. Don't be. Why, it reminds me of a story. Years ago, you know, dear, in the early Twenties, the jazz musician Paul Whiteman took his orchestra over to Berlin. It was the first time they had heard jazz and they sat there like stumps, not reacting or seeming at all enthusiastic. Whiteman was disappointed. 'I thought they would warm up to it,' he said. 'Why?' said the master of the hall, this German fellow, 'What were we supposed to do? Should one,' he says, 'demolish seats or go mad? What is proper at jazz concerts?'"

Louise and Mark laughed.

"When did you hear that? Who told it to you?" Ida said.

"Someone who was there," he said. "I always liked that story."

"I know who it was told you that!" Ida hissed at him when the young couple had retired happily above.

28

"We must have it! You promised!"

Ida was referring to importing their own chamber music group and putting on a musicale right in the living room of their suite.

"Oh my. My dear, just for us? I know I said that we would do it, and I am willing, but in the light of everything else couldn't we wait, do some such back in Coronado?"

"No, Marcus! Not just for us! Be alert. We will of course invite an audience. Guests. Our friends. Dignitaries."

"What friends? Our friends are now in Coronado. We . . . "

"We will have it! Marcus? Don't you have a list?"

Of doctors, retired military Pooh-Bahs. "Ida, that is a list from years ago. As is your list from your Poetry Evenings years ago. Why, everyone on my list is as old as we. As I."

"I am sure they will then be very grateful, Marcus, for the invitation."

"Do you imagine that Mark and Louise, that Mattie and Tom, will—actually—enjoy it?"

"Enjoy it? They will adore it! It will be the highlight of their dull, dull, dull and ordinary lives!"

So he got out his list, and Ida hers, and dragooned as many of their old comrades and acquaintances as each could, having invitations hand-delivered in the city and Ida following up by phone, for the night before the finale, the Proposition Dinner as Marcus called it in his head, the musicale to be the penultimate event of the week-long visit, the Prop before the Proposition.

In the afternoon of his encounter with Ida, as she rode the phone finding suitable musicians, he smoked a cigar as Louise joined him, the young heir sleeping above them, to smoke a cigarette, this time of her own choice. Louise returned gratefully, for Mark did not smoke and Ida disapproved of it, and Mattie did not like it either, so that poor Tom had to go off on his own to smoke and dribble ashes on his vested belly. Louise loved to smoke. Her brand was Chesterfield.

"Goodness, my family, the Whitlocks, especially the men, have been great smokers of cigarettes, pipes, cigars, cornsilk, hemp, weeds or anything to hand. I envied those men sitting in their circle after dinner on the porch smoking and talking, and when I got to college— you know, being a wicked flapper anyway—I lit up."

"Here." He reached and got a box of the Havanas that he kept in good supply and handed it to her. "For the judge," he said, "your father."

The girl—why, dear Lord—got a tear in her eye.

"He'll be pleased. And Remember will make him go out on the porch to smoke them. He's six foot six, you see, and she's just five feet tall—but, boy, is she the boss!"

"'Remember,'" he said, trying to recall something. Then, by some miracle, his mind having become a labyrinth leading here and there, often aimlessly dead-ending or circling back to itself, he did.

"There was a seedy poet here. Vagabond fellow, came to read, set some poems to music, dance. Wandered the country. I believe he called that name, 'Remember.' Said she was the lost love of his life. Could that be?"

"Yes." Her eyes lit and she smiled. "Mother. That's one of the family stories, one of our legends, how she escaped being married to a poet. They were at Hiram College. Vachel Lindsay fell in love with her. She even brought him home, and he recited some of his early poems to her mother and father and sister and Aunt Sally there on the porch. Got carried away. Oh . . . " Louise giggled."They thought that he was crazy."

"Quite right, my dear. Quite right. I thought so too. He had a major aberration, in my eyes. Did not drink whiskey. Jehoshaphat!

Why, the fellow was offended when I offered him, out of the goodness of my heart, a snort."

"Anyway, she had her eye on this 'tall sycamore of the Wabash,' this Indiana boy. He was a famous basketball player. But Mother was too, you see, she was captain of the women's team at five feet tall. Oh, she was—is—fierce when she needs to be."

"And you live now, all of you, on the farm place of your mother's—Remember's—parents? And they have only well water and no electricity there where you are living?"

"Yes. It's kind of fun, Uncle Marcus. It's temporary, for now, of course. But we all love it there, we love the old place and are grateful to have it. My grandfather, my mother's father, Milo Hathaway, used to really farm the place. So, in a sense, for all of us, it's home."

He nodded to her, taking a puff. It was an odd, moving combination of defenseless wonder at the turn of things and family pride that she expressed. It was a feeling shared by many Americans just then.

"It's the Hathaway home, oh, going back almost a hundred years, to when they settled the Western Reserve, don't you see, Uncle Marcus?"

"I would say that they, that all of you, are most fortunate in present circumstances to have it now."

"Yes. It's truly . . . Well, so old-timey and real and even beautiful, with all the old trees and the fields, right on the edge of the city with a highway so close to it now. Dad and Mark grow stuff, which helps. Dad's practice is so small now, it's just that no one can pay him on time or at all anymore for legal services, though all seem to need them. It's the same for Mark's dad, for Tom. He's getting paid, he says, in truck and services now for dentistry, just like when he began. It's harder really being a professional than to be on a salary now. Why, Mark makes more actual cash money selling the copperware door to door than either of them."

"And shares it with them?"

For the first time he saw a darker glint, like a sandbar of strength, come into her blue eyes.

"What we've all had has gone many ways this last year or more, Uncle Marcus. That is why this trip here, being suddenly here with you and seeing all you have, your wealth—all that you just simply have—" She had got on that theme again, that one sour note on her lute, eh? " . . . makes us—well—uneasy."

"You didn't want to come?"

"Oh, goodness, yes. I was excited. I wanted to come. Mattie did too. We women needed a break, I'll tell you! Tom said at first he'd be damned if he would come running up here at your beck and call. Said you were . . . " Now her eyes twinkled as she dared to tell him. " . . . an old goat, up to your old tricks of making everybody jump to your command."

He nodded and half-smiled and put down his cigar. It was smoked halfway down and even in this Depression he would not depart from his rule not to smoke them down more than that. Oh no. He could buy a thousand more even of these rare-leaf fine ones if he wished. Oh yes. Ha. Ho ho. So, the Northways all sharing what they had in their hard times, like a family of Irish, Italian or Chinese immigrants, eh?

He winked at this honest girl, his namesake's wife, Louise.

"I am, indeed, an old goat," he said. "Your father-in-law is right about that, as he is about few things."

He prayed that they accept his and Ida's offer and set this situation right.

The photographer that Ida engaged, a man by the name of Foley, was a terribly white-faced fellow who seemed to live under his black photographer's cloth. He had hoodwinked Ida into thinking he made her slim and lovely in photographs and she adored him. He came to the suite and took dozens of pictures of them in various groupings and poses, setting up elaborately and forever. It tired Marcus. A month before this Foley had done the current "official" portrait of General M. A. Northway. It worried Marcus as he beheld it daily in the silver frame in the living room where Ida had placed it, as it resembled latter-day shots of poor old McKinley. He was seated formally with hands on knees, his diamond ring glinting, in dark suit, dark striped necktie, silk kerchief in breast pocket and rose in lapel, startled look in eye, fireplace and furniture visible behind, a Chinese urn and silver doodad and a large decanter of whiskey Ida brought in from the study on the table next to which he sat, and with vases of flowers all around. It seemed to be Ida's very serious intent, or perhaps her joke, to have the whiskey there. He looked Mandarin, and heavier than in his own mind he considered himself to be. When had he allowed himself to become so heavy, he who was all his life so trim? And his fleece was white as snow. He looked at the portrait of himself and saw, as Ida wished, some sort of Personage. He wished the Nymph were here, to see and laugh at it!

The photograph of the senior Northways that Ida chose as official Marcus thought rather touching, for they all looked amicable and serene and at peace with each other and themselves, which was not the case. Tom looked like the boy he'd been when he first bumbled in to this city to see his "uncle," all bucolic and sweet, his chin now double and coat buttoned wrong over his bulge of stomach. Ida also very nearly managed to look sweet, serene, and he saw that despite all she was actually happy, doing all this. Mattie looked the most sweet and serene, Matilda Elton Northway, with her kind smile, a real dark-haired beauty with her pearls given her years ago by Ida, a strand just a bit shorter than Ida's own. And here Marcus himself seemed an image of serenity, trimmer, thinner appearing standing in this picture but with a bit of a Buddha look, somewhat like all those photographs of Edison seeming to be staring blankly out at Nothing.

It was a touching picture, a false record, a flash of artifice. Marcus hoped Ida would not frame it in silver and exhibit it in the living room. He would make sure it got left here when they returned to Coronado.

On Easter they attended services at Riverside church, for Mattie and Louise wished to hear the highly touted minister, Harry Emerson Fosdick. Yet they all fidgeted through the long sermon. Marcus thought Fosdick, a fellow with Socialist tendencies, the greatest bloviator since Harding as he preached on the phenomenon of Resurrection. Marcus found himself gently napping, and dozed for forty days waking just in time for the Ascension. Afterwards as Marcus and Ida prepared for the evening, Dennis drove the other Northways up along the Hudson in the pretty near countryside of Marcus' native state.

In the evening they had the musicale.

Tom Northway, tired and grumpy, muttered to Mattie that he'd rather retire early than listen to some damn fools murdering some instruments. She replied that he should put on his best suit and manners and pay attention, it might raise his cultural level from Gallagher and who was the other one, up from vaudeville. He laughed at what a good sport she was and said, "Okay. I'm Cronkite."

She knew that one. "I'm Dubious," she said.

Then said, "Please, Tom. Let's just get through this. No more scenes. They are trying so awfully hard . . . "

His face stayed red, but he appeared on time with the rest of them.

Now the living room, all white with its gold-brocade drapes and white carpet and vases full of blooming scarlet and yellow flowers, was filled with tiny white chairs with gold on backs and legs. The performers arrived. A youth about twenty, short, with oily black hair and protruding dark eyes, a violin case under his arm, was already sweating in his too-tight suit. In came the pianist, oh my, a most unattractive, lanky young woman in a white chiffon evening dress, very low cut but not showing her bosom because she hadn't any. Following her came an apelike fellow of extreme hairiness and swarthiness, also perspiring profusely in his black suit, lugging a mellow-looking cello, hue of honeygold. When as the leader of the ensemble he smiled and bowed to Madame, his front teeth were gold as well.

Ida had bedecked herself in evening dress and resembled a Spanish castle with turrets lit with a blaze of Tiffany diamonds and pearls. General Northway was attired in white tie and tails to receive.

The rest of the Northways, little Bo lucky to escape only by his extreme youth, were made to form a receiving line at the door so that Marcus and Ida could introduce them to the motley stream of dignitaries who came hobbling and shuffling in: Colonel and Mrs. This, Commissioner and Mrs. That, Doctor and Mrs. So and So, Major Goat and Colonel Fox, Ambassador Frog and Admiral Toad, all roughly the same age of their respected host the Major-General, Ret.

Louise wore a gown and silver fox scarf Ida had bought for her and looked cool as the dawn and met them all, in line, smiling and murmuring like the Beauty Queen she'd been. Mark was extraordinarily stiff and rigid-faced in the rented tuxedo Ida had insisted he wear. Dr. Tom Northway, mere dentist, intent on being amiable and sociable, upset Mrs. Brigadier-General Potter in the line by complimenting her on the naturalness of the look and fit of her upper bridge when the old lady offered him her terrible smile. All were relieved when allowed to take their seats.

Dear Louise was seated, unfortunately, just a bow's length from the violinist. Mattie Northway was just opposite her, also unfortunately, for they could see each other's expressions, as Marcus noted from his perch by Louise. How lucky 'twas for them that Ida, resplendent in her finery, stout as a ship of the line, stationed herself at the other end of the room still near the door to welcome any late comers—that is, to chastise them!

The concert progressed interminably, going through the Bs— Bach, Beethoven and Brahms—into covert composers and sloshing, slippery, skewing sounds previously unknown to musical man or woman. Chairs creaked. Marcus' chair creaked, or it might have been himself. Coughs were politely smothered into large initialed handhemmed squares. Hems and haws were smuggled into hands, except by old Major Moose, who suffered a major attack of phlegm. Squirms. Twitchings. At the end of each selection a relieved clapping burst forth.

Then . . . Oh dear . . . The young violinist suddenly hypnotized himself into a trance-like orgiastic series of snorts and groans and movements of his body. Nostrils flaring, pores flowing, eyes

squeezed with ecstasy at his plucking and his sawing at the strings
. . . Fingers frenziedly plucking at one end while the bow extension
of his other arm reached faster and faster for whatever unseen stars
. . . Jehoshaphat! It was a performance to behold!

If Louise had not glanced across at the usually composed Mattie
all might have been well; but she did. Simultaneously their beauteous
faces crushed into mirth. Loud sounds came from each as they rolled
their eyes and tried to swallow sobs of laughter, whoops and giggles
that would not be downed. Happily the violinist was snorting so
loudly in the passion of his final crescendo that few noticed them.
But as Louise turned her tormented eyes and contorted face to
Marcus he himself had to let out a mighty snort of mirth and
sympathy, which he trusted those to his left and just behind would
interpret as a fart.

And then immediately as it was over Louise and Mattie made a
beeline together to the bathroom off the living room and locked
themselves in. As he passed by, he could hear the purge of half-
hysterical laughter coming from within.

Ida gathered the guests into the dining room on whose elegant
board lay among other treats a whole roasted pig and flagons of
champagne.

He paid off the performers, assuring them that it had been a
remarkable hour of music, and packed them back off to wherever
Ida'd found 'em. Then, despite the adequacy of the champagne,
Marcus motioned to Tom, who gladly followed him into the secluded
study where they decanted whiskey and had a spot together,
wordless but it seemed to Marcus feeling as close as they ever had
in this moment of mutual need.

29

At dinner, then, the last night, Marcus rose at the head of the table and ceremoniously presented a package to Louise. She untied it, saying, "My Goodness, this isn't my birthday . . . . "

The proposition was in the package.

Ida'd had painted a cameo portrait of Louise from when she was a Beauty in college. It was painted on ivory, and rather badly done, Marcus thought.

"Oh my," Louise said, having to behold, he believed, the portrait a moment or two before comprehending it was herself.

"How nice," Mark said, taking it from her to pass on to his parents. "We'll treasure it."

"What's this?" the dear girl said, holding up then a photograph and an envelope also in the velvet case, as Ida sat beaming at them, having staged the presentation.

In reply, standing at the head, brandy glass in hand, Marcus delivered himself formally of the deal.

"The photograph, Mark . . . Louise . . . is of a fine if not elaborate new house I have bought on our block in Coronado, where we live.

"Coronado is a good and pleasant town, removed from hubbub, a safe and charming place to reside, as we find it, and I am sure a good place to raise a child, with access of course to the larger San Diego across the bay, and all commercial and cultural amenities there. I know you like the water and hope some day to have a boat, and sail, and so on. You could have it now. Ida and I are offering you this house, if you will come live by us in Coronado. You would, we believe, have a great future in California! If we could, we would have you all—Northways, Whitlocks, all—in sunny California!"

He smiled around at them. Tom Northway, silly ass that he could be, stared at him as if he were gone suddenly daft. Mattie just slightly shook her head, and began to refold her napkin. Ida smiled hugely. She had instructed Marcus to put that California part in.

"What would I do there in Coronado, Uncle Marcus?" Mark said.

"Why, initially you could . . . would . . . work for me! I have a number of interests. There would be several possibilities. I own a small bank, and real estate, and overall need to pay attention to my estate and holdings. Beyond that stage, then, there would be myriad possibilities for a person with intelligence and enterprise."

"You would help us manage our resources, and add to them," Ida said.

"No, sir. I could not do that. I need to be doing something on my own, of my own. You understand what I mean? I mean, I am only temporarily, because of social and economic conditions right now, working out of my field."

Selling cooking pots from door to door. But the lad had spunk; always had; and spoke right up, soon as the horse was out of the barn, the lovely one beside him nodding at what he said vigorously.

"Yes. All right. In the envelope, then, Mark, is a deed. Yes. You see it? It is the deed to the I believe quite famous The Palms Hotel in Fort Myers, Florida. A hotel built and first owned by my first wife Lutie Morrison Krause, subsequently kept by me through the years until now and quite a tax burden, I must tell you. But a very valuable piece of property and the hotel of much future potential if renovated. It is out of season but in operation now, if somewhat in disrepair. You would need to check on the current management, I have not done so in a while. Also in the envelope . . . "

Mark took out the envelope within the envelope and opened it and fished out the check.

" . . . is a check for five thousand dollars. It is yours whatever you do . . . "

"Oh, now, listen, Uncle Marcus . . . "

"Oh, thank you, Uncle Marcus . . . "

"That is generous, Marcus . . . "

"W-where's mine, eh, Uncle M-Marcus . . . ?"

"Let nothing more be said of that. To help you onto your feet, so to speak, with my own and Ida's love, and to finance your trip to Fort Myers. You have a car, don't you, that you could drive down there?"

"Yes, sir, an Auburn. It's a great car . . . "

"Yes. Well. All we ask of you is that you go there and look the place over. See if you don't think you could make it go again. Take an inventory for me while you're at it. And then . . . "

"You mean, manage it for you?"

"More than that, my boy. In a few years, three to five years, say, if all is going well, this deed would go over to you. You would own the hotel and land completely. And we'd make you a loan initially, at fair interest, and of course invest in the renovation and provide capital to run it those first years. Eh? It would be a damn fine and fair deal, I assure you, Mark. All we ask is that you and Louise go and take a gander at it. What do you say, Mark?"

"You told me we'd end up in Florida, with a sailboat . . . "

Mark looked at his wife, all flushed from lobster, wine and emotion, and then at his parents, who were staring at him, and at Marcus and Ida.

Marcus gulped the brandy in the glass in his hand, which he had used for rhetorical balance, and sat down. He found himself quite tired, and felt almost as if he were drifting off some place, just as Mark Northway gave that wonderful lop-sided grin of his and declared, "Of course! We'll go and check it out. Thanks so much for your generosity, Uncle Marcus and Aunt Ida!"

Marcus nodded and did his best to smile back at him.

The old hotel was of course a White Elephant at present, sitting there on the bank of the Caloosahatchie. It used to be a hot and popular spot, but it had not made money in many years. Still, it was, if just for the location of the land, really very valuable, if they chose to work for it.

After dinner, as Ida regaled Tom and Mattie with tales of Brazil and China and Japan, he went into his study to rest for a minute. Mark and Louise were in the adjoining bedroom checking on the young one, "Bo" Northway, who was to him Marcus III. Idly he flipped on the annunciator, one of Al's inventions that let you talk and hear from room to room.

"God, I don't know. Maybe it would be fabulous! I bet that we could do it, Louise!"

"Sounds like a lot of work to me. And we'd be working—the more you think about it, just like the first deal—for them."

"Well . . . "

"And she is such a tyrant. And he is such . . . an old courtly dear, and an old devil, but you know better than anyone in the whole world that he's a tyrant too! He really is an egomaniac, Mark."

He turned it off and sat there, stung. Hurt. He had thought that she . . . That he and she were on the same wavelength. Egomaniac? She had called him . . . dared to call him . . . Turned on him after all his kindness!

He sat and shook with anger for a moment; but then did deep breathing and began to calm. Even smiled, slightly.

Egomaniac?

No, he did not believe he was that far along. ('Twas true, as the girl said, of course, that Ida was a tyrant.) He had always believed that he rather well balanced the egoism necessary for achievement with altruism in regard to what he attempted professionally. Maybe, he thought, Louise, dear—he could not, forgiving her already, not think of her as "dear"—I would be farther down the Ego Road if I were more recognized, truly successful in the eyes of the outside nation and the world. As it is, why, actually I am humble as pie. I remember Whiskeyville. I could have controlled them all more had I wanted to. "The time to help someone is when they need it," my father always said, and that is what I'm trying to do.

Of course, he thought, making that damn old Palms Hotel go was a tough task to set, but it was what he had in his quiver, what he had to offer.

Luther, he thought, Luther in his own sweet way was an egomaniac. And Al. And Henry. God knows, Henry. Hell, both Al and Henry were even beyond that, weren't they? Were certifiable Megalomaniacs. Yes. Because in some sense and on some scale I did not realize and attain, they—my true friends Luther and Al and the terrible Henry, who lives on and will live forever, I am sure, were all—are—Great.

Sad to say, in Ford's case, but true. Well. Should he turn the annunciator back on and explain this to Louise? Startle her and Mark—and little "Bo"—by technology as they huddle in the room just beyond and whisper to each other? She'd said he was an old devil, and the old devil nearly reached to do it. Ah, wouldn't they jump?

In a moment, feeling helpless and without Ego, he did reach and turned the annunciator back on. Mark was saying, "Well, whatever, Lou, I want to go and do it. I don't care what he's been or done—he's been always stern but kind and generous to me, even if I've fought him, as I've had to. But still, you know, I love him and will do this just to make him happy . . . And who knows . . . " With a lilt coming into his voice, the old Northway enthusiasm rising, . . . "it may turn into something marvelous!"

Marcus smiled slightly then, and sat up straighter; and in a moment walked over to the small window of his study and looked out upon the city.

That night Mark called down from their suite above. Louise was sick. Marcus dressed and got his Bag. Ida, huge in her robe, wanted to go up but he said no.

The poor girl was crouching by the toilet with nausea and stomach pains trying to rid herself of all the lobster and wine and rich food she was not accustomed to and all the emotions of the visit and the evening coiled among the food.

"Do you have some medicine?" Mark said.

Marcus shook his head. It pained him that Mark had never and would never know and understand him according to the premises of his life and his profession. That was what he had so badly wanted to try to teach him.

"Get me a glass," he said.

Gently he forced many glasses of lukewarm water down Louise's gullet as she crouched there by the toilet, and slowly flushed out all the rich foods until she felt better.

"Do not be embarrassed. It's a natural reaction."

She squeezed his hand.

He reached in his bag and got whiskey and put some in the glass. Louise sat on the bed and sipped it and soon was sleeping peacefully.

"Thanks," Mark said. "I've never really seen you be a doctor before. And you used no medicine, I mean, except the whiskey."

"I am a Homeopath," he said. "We treat the cause not the symptom and build a restorative bridge back to well-being."

"Well, thanks, really, Uncle Marcus," Mark said. "I was worried about my gal."

The next day before they left Ida tried to get Louise to eat a hearty breakfast. When she would not Ida said, "Oh, I know your secret, dear. I can tell. You're pregnant, aren't you?"

"My God, no!" Louise said, for the first time angry. "I'm having my period, Aunt Ida!"

"She is pregnant, too, whether she knows it or not," Ida said when they had gone. "What do you think they'll do? I will be terribly disappointed in them if they don't do it. I was not pleased at their rejecting Coronado out of hand."

"I told you they'd never do that. To be honest, Ida, it was a course I myself would never have chosen."

"Oh really, Marcus? Really? The great Marcus Northway? Why, you did it, managed Lutie Krause's affairs, for years! Didn't you?"

"Well . . . yes. I suppose that was what I did. And then nursed her too. And we nursed her together then, didn't we, Ida, dear?"

"Ah yes!" she said, brightening at the memory of their coming closer through the ordeal of nursing Lutie.

That night, still full of memories, she came to his bed.

"Oh no," he said. "I can't. Not tonight."

"What do you mean, you can't? Why, I just told Mattie and Louise that you could still satisfy me in every way! Are you going to make a liar out of me? Come on, Marcus!"

He turned away from her.

She left his room offended and upset.

Mark wrote, after their trip down to Fort Myers, at the end of April, that he had wanted to take over the old hotel and see if he could put it back on a paying basis until they got there and saw it. Then he decided it would be disastrous for all concerned. It might have been the finest hotel of its time catering to fishermen and yachtsmen on the Florida west coast, but its time was past. When was the last time he had seen it?

Several years it had been. Oh, maybe many years. He had not even driven by when they visited with Edison there.

The several story frame structure was in need of paint and repair. Only the palm trees and foliage were in good shape, and the grounds were ragged. The dock was in need of repair. The inside of the hotel was musty and un-aired, the furniture too old and massive and ugly for today, the carpets and curtains worn, all in terrible disrepair. Mark sent no estimate or even rough idea of what it would take in terms of time and money to restore it, so that Marcus surmised that he and Louise were put off by it from the first moment of beholding.

Ah well. That was the point, the test, of course: he knew it needed work like holy hell on wheels, did they want to dig in and do it? (His father Sam mumbles more country wisdom in his ear about looking the gift horse in the mouth . . .)

They did take a cursory inventory of furnishings, linens, dishes, etc. This was of some help to Marcus as he proceeded to move the White Elephant out of his zoo. Soon after they refused the offer, he sold it, hotel and the land it was on, and had no trouble getting three million dollars even at that year's depressed rates. When the recovery came, as it surely would, the location would be worth twice that, or more, for development. It was valuable.

On his last trip down there after he had sold it, Marcus stood at twilight looking at the old pile of a hotel along the river where he had sat out on the dock and fished with his friend Edison. He had ordered all the lights on in the Palms, and all around the lights in trees and from lampposts buzzed and blazed. He stood there and beheld the grotesque decaying structure, empty and forlorn, and for a moment wondered how he really could have thought to offer the monstrosity to them, to fresh, young Mark and Louise.

Then he had the lights turned off and watched as the hotel seemed to extinguish itself, to fade away along the dark Caloosahatchie, and turned and walked away with his fading memories to the now dingy train depot, once so new and promising, for the long ride home.

Subsequently Mark Northway obtained a job in sales with a rubber company in Akron. Akron was a burg that stank of burning rubber from all the rubber factories there. They had moved there with, sure enough, a second child on the way. If a boy, they planned to name it for Louise's father, the judge, Luke Whitlock.

The company, Marcus noted with what satisfaction he could take from it, that Mark went with was in direct competition to Harvey Firestone's. He bet that Mark would outsell Fireplug's boys like crazy! He bet . . .

And then . . .

Well, he would now keep in touch with the lad, and his growing family, from afar.

30

If you took away the water this Sea Point Inn would be much like the old Robinson House Hotel, in Ashtabula. A quiet clientele came and rocked and watched the water instead of the horse-drawn vehicles going down the street in the old days in Ashtabula. Marcus no longer smoked, but he had brought a box of the best Havanas and left them open on the desk of the lobby in the inn. Billy came in and out and picked up a couple a day and went off and smoked 'em somewhere. It was a boon to Marcus, by now, that he and Billy got on well. Hell, he thought they even liked each other, though neither pressed it. Now Billy owned the old inn, he had deeded it over to him, and Billy kept it up pretty well, now that he had his woman.

Marcus was on the narrow beach, a strip of sandy sedge. The woman, Liz, came and sat by him on one of the canvas chairs on the beach pointing to the ocean. She was dark and wore silver and turquoise and had a mole on her ruddy cheek. Marcus liked her.

"Why don't Mrs. Northway, Ida, your wife, come and stay with you when you come here?" she said.

"She likes California," he said. "She is happy in her home there."

"Don't she want to be with you on your birthday?"

"Mrs. Northway and I have been together for a long time now, many birthdays."

"Well, what are you doing out here? I see you have your writing board. I thought that you were painting."

"Oh yes. Both."

"You have two easels set up, and your paints. Why, you're doing two paintings at once."

"Yes."

"What are you writing?"

"A little book. A manual, you might say. On health. Yes, a little guidebook to benefit . . . ah . . . " Dear God, he was not about to say "mankind," was he?

He went inside, out of the noon sun, to work on it a little. He was working on a chapter called "Forestalling Old Age—Looking Young and Feeling Young."

He wrote:

In the morning take a hot bath lasting five to ten minutes, massaging the entire body by rolling muscles, elevating legs, and with open fingers pulling from feet to thighs, thus unloading the tissues of the structural changes incident to metamorphosis; also deeply knead the bowels by rolling motion from right to left following the line of the colon.

Half the work of the kidneys will be shifted by this procedure.

Calisthenics, adapted to your age and lasting ten to fifteen minutes following the rub, will be found efficacious and will prepare you for the day. A peristaltic twist motion is most excellent for the bowels.

As for the bowels: No lasting health can exist without daily evacuations, at a regular hour in the morning, and two are better than one. Keep your mind on desire, and do not read, as it switches off concentration. Nature will awaken you each morning, if you will only heed the internal monitor which awakens you by a pleasant or startling dream—as of a bird in flight. Rise at once. You will find the dial of the clock always the same. Wonderful is Nature to show you the way to physiological health!

Position in bed is of the greatest importance. On retiring turn to the right, and to the left during the morning hours. The changed positions much facilitate intestinal movements.

Later he went back out on the beach.

The old Sea Point stood on higher ground than the shore. It was a three-story double rectangle structure. A good span of ocean front could be seen from Marcus' spot on the beach—dunes with sea oats waving along the strip of beach and water. Across the road behind was a meadow, and beyond that someone seemed to be growing spuds, as if they were in Rome Valley there! It was a quaint and quiet place, this sea point.

Down the beach Albert . . . Dear Lord, Albert was dead these two years! No, it was Dennis, loyal Dennis, casting out for bluefish. Ah, 'twas true, "there are as good fish in the sea as ever were caught."

Now Theodore, who had recommended this place to him, came huffing and puffing down the beach, marching vigorously along in the sand. "Are you enjoying your place here, General?" he says.

"It is about all I am up to, Colonel," Marcus in his mind replies.

Liz appears at his side, as if by magic, but is real. He sees her smooth brown feet, toes planted in the sand. She has, he sees, some of the fish that Dennis is catching, has them in a net.

"These are for your dinner. Are you enjoying your birthday?"

"Oh my, yes."

"How old are you by now? Billy said he wasn't just sure. Hell, my Billy, he don't know how old he is, or won't admit it to me."

"If Billy doesn't know, how can I be expected to remember?"

Marcus smiled and winked at her. Her eyes flat and depthless. His Nymph's had not been obsidian, but liquid, brown and warm.

I must, he thought, go to the bathhouse soon and wash off this damn sand. Have a cold bath and exercise the limbs and then a glass of the Restorative.

It was another June day, here at Sea Point in his home state, and it was in fact his birthday. It was the year of Our Lord 1933. He was eighty-five years of age.

He trusted the next fifteen years would prove as interesting as the last.

Liz came back by, looking again at the two easels he had set up.

He took brush in hand, again, half-posing as the artist.

"Like your boat," she said. It was a single-masted sloop bobbing at the inn's dock that he was rendering. "What is the other?"

"Ah . . . "

"It's three boats, isn't it? I see it now. But that water don't look like this water here. It's not here, is it, Doctor?"

"No," he said. "Not here. Not now."

He dabbed at that easel, with the three boats, then turned a bit and looked at it.

On the canvas the water is deep blue-green, out from the sheer white cliffs. Out past a reddish-purple bar making a triangle are three small sailboats, the top one with red sail, the others with sails of white—and the water getting deeper green and blue, the deep blue and green of friendship and of love. They two—himself and young Mark—were not in the picture that he'd painted, but it is young Mark and Marcus together who look and see this scene.

He puts his arm around the lad's shoulder. Mark smiles at him. He is his namesake. Marcus feels the dear boy's systolic beating clear and true. Together they look out at the water and the little boats, in the embrace that will bind them always, two hearts that beat as . . .

31

Marcus Northway died the next year, in the month of October.

The American Legion Post in San Diego gave him a full official funeral at the War Memorial in Balboa Park which bore his name.

Memorial speakers praised him. The Chaplain invoked the Lord and the tribute: "Oh God, we call to remembrance Thy loving kindness and Thy tender mercies to Thy servant Marcus Aurelius Northway and give praise for all Thy goodness that withheld not his portion in the joys of this earthly life."

The solo "O, Rest in the Lord" was rendered by Madame Ernestine Schumann-Heink at the request of his beloved wife Ida Northway.

The Commander gave a tribute to him as benefactor, physician, inventor of the Field Kit and Stretcher, and patriot.

Canon Watson of his Church gave the benediction, and the Post Bugler played Taps.

His near neighbor Rear Admiral Alfred O'Malley, Ret., gave a tribute, saying, "He was a courteous gentleman, like Chevalier Bayard 'sans peur et sans reproche.' Who among us will forget his radiant smile as he came forward to greet his guests in his home? As he entered the room I felt it had been flooded with sunshine. Marcus Northway was my neighbor, and I regret I did not know him better as a friend."

Ida did not honor his request to be cremated, the idea of burning him being abhorrent to her. Instead she installed him in the cemetery at Whiskeyville where he had not wished to be in an impressive crypt adorned with his bust in marble and his name, dates and titles carved in granite, not far from his mother Sally Ann and his grandmother Clara Weatherwax and the girl Molly Leary who had been cut down from the hanging tree and married by old Philo.

Not wishing to live in their dream house without Marcus and tired of the endless effort of getting it just right, she put Northway Lodge in Coronado up for sale and moved back to Willowstone, the gray mansion in Connecticut.

Henry Ford heard of Marcus' passing and reflected Northway was the only one ever got away with calling him a shithead. Ford lived another thirteen years but pulled up actually two years shy of reaching Marcus' age at death. (Ha.)

Ida Northway lived another fourteen years but became chronically ill and had to be nursed through her last decade.

When she died, Mark Northway was surprised and upset but probably should not have been to find she had left him and others in the family only small amounts, leaving the body of the fortune acquired by Marcus Northway, as might have been predicted, to her nurse.